FARAH COOK

City of Assassins

Contents

About the Author

Farah Cook was born in Denmark and grew up in Copenhagen. She had a rich and highly imaginary childhood, spending most of her time outdoors. At the age of twelve, she began writing short stories to fuel her passion for storytelling.

Farah graduated with a BA in Social Science from Sweden, an MA in Arts from London, and an MA in Creative Writing from the University of Surrey. She has lived in many countries, including Germany and New Zealand, but settled in London where she worked as a Marketing Manager for large financial conglomerates.

Her passion for storytelling remained, and at night she started to write all the things she'd imagine. Her novel City of Skies is the first book in the Viking Assassin Series.

Farah lives in Surrey, with her husband, Christopher, and their two sons, Benjamin, and Noah. She speaks six languages fluently including Danish, Swedish, and German and writes full-time.

Farah is at the Faber Academy in London, writing her fourth novel, a Scandinavian psychological thriller under Johanna Briscoe.

Visit www.farahcook.com for more information.

I loved you; and perhaps I love you still,
The flame, perhaps, is not extinguished; yet
It burns so quietly within my soul,
No longer should you feel distressed by it.
Silently and hopelessly I loved you,
At times too jealous and at times too shy.
God grant you find another who will love you
As tenderly and truthfully as I.

By Alexander Pushkin

Dedicated to

Christopher: Because of you I am.

I

THE VIKINGS

1

The Arrival

THE PEACOCK BLUE sky hangs above me like sharp metal spears. *A sister?* The news is a murderous shadow slowly unfurling and crawling on my skin. *I have a sister?* My dad's words linger inside my head for a while, and I forget I am in the City of Vikings. I forget that I have brought my enemy, Frederick, here with me. The enemy I am in love with. Still, it is not Frederick's presence or even Mina's that occupies my mind. It is hers–Grethe, my sister.

I swallow hard while I try to get used to the idea of being told what Grethe is to me. It is not what I expected, and for some reason, the whole incident makes me angry because I was betrayed. In my head, I have the courage to roar and scream. My rage feels like a flock of hungry lions ready to pounce on its prey. Among a thousand questions I pull out one. *Why are you telling me this?* It doesn't stop there. Like a wheel of eternity, the question repeats itself over and over, and that's when I realize that my dad built a whole new life here. He has *his* daughter. He does not need me. Perhaps he never did, and coming here has caused an outrage among his people who think that I've come to raid their city.

For all those years, I longed to meet this man. I dreamed of uniting the broken bond between us—the one that has brought me here defying death. Was it all done so I could meet the sister I never knew I had? My yearning all those years for fatherly love seems a waste when he may never have felt the yearning for the daughter he'd left behind.

I keep the crispness of my words sealed behind my lips. I have found him. I don't want him to shut me out like he has everyone else. Why else would he have stayed in exile in the City of Vikings for all those years? My gaze shifts like a quiet desert wind trailing the Forbidden Areas. I peer at her, hiding my resentment. Grethe looks nothing like me. Her skin is butter yellow and glows beautifully. High cheekbones, peachy porcelain complexion, and her hair, a blend of hazelnut and warm honey. Small golden-brown eyes perfectly placed on Grethe's face devour me, searching for answers. With a graceful posture, she appears ladylike with traces of arrogance. She is not my sister. How I hate everything about her, because I am nothing like her. A delicate, but deadly looking flower.

"Sister?" I whisper, clearing the hot clump of air that blocks my throat. "I never knew I had one." I turn a wounded glance at my dad, but he offers me no consolation. Instead, he gazes back with stern emerald eyes. Eyes I feel I could get lost in, searching for all the answers he is keeping from me.

"Her mother passed away last fall just after Grethe's thirteenth birthday. It was the will of the gods," he says. My dad speaks softly, grief breaking into his deep voice.

What about Karen? I want to bellow. *What about your estranged wife?* But I keep silent. This is not the place to discuss the disability that pesters our family. I will have my time to corner him with questions. Until then, I try to make my surprise unknown. I avoid looking at any of the hundred murderous eyes gathered around us in the daunting assembly I find myself in.

"Earl Robert," says Balder, captain of the Viking army. He was the man that brought us into the city. He steps forward, regarding me flatly like a toad. "What are we to do with the captives, my lord?" He tilts his head enough to include Frederick and Mina who seem as outraged as I do. He clears his throat. He is about to suggest something. But the Earl speaks.

"Bring the boy and the little girl to the Ashes," he says. "Leave Nora with me." A cold wind billows his white shawl, softly cloaked around his shoulders.

"But—" Balder's voice trails away.

"They need to stay with Knud Forkbeard. Bring them away at once."

Frederick's pale blue eyes find me. He carries a noticeable worry in them. I wish he'd never come looking for me. I wish I'd never brought him here with me. This place is dangerous for him. He is not among his own clan members.

"Nora?" Frederick whispers. I gaze into his eyes. My name from his lips feels like a mysterious spell, enchanting and sweet. He stands tall, feet firmly rooted to the ground. He holds his breath.

Before I get to speak to him or to Mina, Balder saunters toward them. His big hands reach out, as if they were the claws of a wild animal. The strong, sturdy, metal of his helmet clinks, covering his head and hiding his severe face. The silver armor molds to his frame, emphasizing the hard muscles in his body. Frederick ducks. He avoids Balder's grip and stands to face me. He glances at the door that leads out of the assembly, as if estimating the time it will take to escape.

"You better come with me," Balder says and takes off his helmet, revealing every feature of his face from the saggy folds of skin under his eyes, to the square jaw and large pointed nose. A thick mop of golden hair flops against the lines in his forehead.

"Where are you taking them?" I keep my voice low.

"Nora," says my dad. "They must join members of their own clan, in the Ashes."

"The Ashes?" I say, lowering my brows. "What is there?" I try to hide the frantic emotions I carry. I bury them inside me like a rotting corpse. The place sounds like an execution ground. Are Frederick and Mina in danger because of me? Am I putting them at risk among their own clan to face punishment? They are not just my companions on this journey, they are my friends. I need them both to stay with me. How can I make them stay?

"Yes, it is Knud Forkbeard's realm. He will give them shelter while they are here."

The name still doesn't ring a bell. I realize I still have much to learn about the world of the Vikings—a world built according to the old traditions and customs they created hundreds of years ago.

"Knud is a respected Viking Veran lord. He is a member of my council. Knud rarely makes an appearance on these grounds—"

"Why?" I say. "Is he not allowed here because he's Veran?" My dad's eyes narrow. He is silent for a moment. He twitches. Beads of sweat trickle down his forehead.

"It would be better if the companions you brought with you

stayed with him."

I blow out a noisy breath. I try not to challenge what he said. He could be siding with the Verans. I cannot get the words to leave my mouth. The blood underneath my skin sails across my limp body, and I press my lips together in a slight grimace. I wish I wasn't so stubborn.

"But Mina is no Veran," I say. "Why can't she stay with me?" I lean forward to reach out for her hand. My eyes meet Frederick's. He looks beautiful in the crisp morning light.

"She is a rare being from the Veran clan," says Grethe. She tosses me a strange look. Her eyes are small and sallow and the irises golden amber. "Did you never care to notice? She has their clan tattoo on her collarbone." Grethe motions at Mina. One of the guards pulls down her shirt revealing the familiar symbol of twirling shielded knots Frederick carries on his wrist in black ink.

Mina, a Veran? Why did she never mention anything? She hid her tattoo. Mina has always been short on words. I never did ask her personal questions, but why would a Veran support the Goths? Magnus must have known about her. Unless Mina is a spy? I refuse to believe it. She has been a friend to me all this time. Someone I trust.

Mina may be a Veran, but that doesn't change her loyalty and devotion, which remain unquestionable. Frederick must have known about her. I believe he had his reasons for not telling me. Maybe he thought I knew. I don't act surprised when Grethe stares at me.

"It's the law, Nora," says my dad. "Verans must stay in the Ashes, or else we're taking a great risk."

"Against what?" I say and jerk my head around. "My friends?"

He doesn't answer. His breath falls heavy as if a stone was strapped to his chest. I can tell he senses a friction between us. I never imagined standing here speaking to him this way. I never imagined *any* of this. When I see five strong soldiers join Balder, I know they've come to take Frederick and Mina away.

Frederick cranes his neck. He wants to tell me something and looks at me, like death is a shadow in his company. But he doesn't. Silently, without showing resistance, Frederick and Mina follow Balder out of the assembly. The iron gate scrapes open and the soldiers' steps lay heavy imprints on the ground. Outside, the fury of the wind twists the branches and stirs the debris on the ground. Water drips from the pump, the force rod squeaks, and mold taints the stale air. Balder suddenly stops at the front gate with Frederick and Mina, as if he is waiting for an order before moving any farther.

The soft wind dances with my hair, playing hide and seek. The heaviness of the thick city walls covered in red dust remind me of the East, a place in the Triangle I vaguely remember. My senses explode, and I breathe in everything—the distinct scent of pine and wildflowers; the everlasting sound of creaking and groaning of tall swaying trees; the whining of bees; the pale sunless sky; and the fallen leaves bathing in muddy waters. I recall only fragments and the name of a faceless boy—someone I used to know in the East. Gustav. He used to be a friend of mine. Someone I once trusted.

The tattoo moves its branches across my back like the violent bashing of the sea. How can I forget that Yggdrasil is carved on my skin? Her black ink sprawls my body, tugging me toward the inevitable visions of the past. I shift my shoulders to ease the writhing pain she is causing me. Her time is near. She

8

wants to break free. Join her roots to the Nine Worlds.

"Nora?" says my dad firmly as if he is acknowledging my presence. "Come closer."

I pull out of my trance and let my eyes turn to him. I hold back my feelings from erupting like a volcano. He throws a veiled glance to the eyes prodding at us in the crowd. I take in my hostile and curious surroundings. The growing whispers and murmurs of people get louder. I notice glowing eyes flickering like burning candles in the dark. I taste their fear and hear their prying getting louder.

"She's brought with her the Verans. Why would she do that? They cannot be trusted," says one voice from the crowd. "They use the power of manipulation and dark spells. Do you think they will manipulate us? Two is enough to bring us all under their spell."

"Soon there will be more. Wait and see; they will want to bring down our city. She is guilty of letting them in. The Earl's daughter—a raider, an assassin. She must receive punishment. Will the Earl do it? Will he sentence his own daughter?" another voice says.

"He will not! One thing they are here for. You know of what I speak, don't you?"

"The weapons! Yes, yes, they want them."

"They all want them. Now they have tricked her into it. Fool of a girl. It will be the end of her."

"But she must do it— she must make her way to the world of Arres, and into the assassin city. But only if the young Duchess lets her pass through the gate."

"Don't be stupid! No one passes through that gate."

"She'd have to defeat her. Perhaps even kill her. Her own *sister*." The voice sounds like rusty metal scrap. It cackles

9

loudly.

My fear ensnares me as I listen to the whispers turning into murderous gossip. What do they mean? Have I been tricked? Is this all a game and am I some puppet playing along? The heartless whispers about Grethe. Yes, I can't stand the sight of her. I may have made that obvious by ignoring her. Giving her a cold reception. But why would I want to kill her? I barely know the girl. What in the name of the gods is going to happen now that I've gotten myself into the City of Vikings?

My dad peers at me; hope flickers at the edge of his vision. He walks to the deck at the end of the hall. He stands next to the grand seat in the assembly. Grethe follows and takes a firm stand beside him. I force myself to stand a little closer to my dad. My eyes dart up and down Grethe's petite figure. I crease my face as if I've bitten a lemon. *The answers are coming.* I snatch a deep breath of air, filling my lungs with the scent of wood smoke and fire, and breathe out a thick fume of anxiety.

The entire assembly eavesdrops eagerly. They are anticipating the purpose of the gathering. My stomach wrenches. All the words I want to shout I keep hostage behind my lips. I am afraid they'll spill out wrongly. Controlled by anger, by emotions and rage.

When I peer at him I notice my dad's gaze is somber. By the gods, I hope he is going to say something that releases the pain stabbing my chest. He opens his mouth. Soft-spoken words fill my ears like water fills a glass.

"May the great gods we worship grant to our city, and for the benefit of the Triangle in general, a great and glorious victory. May no felony in anyone tarnish it, and may the Vikings conquer and keep the land that belongs to them. For I, Earl Robert of this great City of Vikings, commit my life to the gods. May the strength the gods bestowed upon me lead me to defend these walls. In the gods, I lay my trust and obligation to the cause which was entrusted to me to defend." After he finishes his prayer he sits down. The grand chair makes a creaking sound. The long fibers of the white sheepskin look soft and lush. They unleash a heavy scent of blood. A scent of death.

A stammering voice from the crowd emerges. "Earl Robert, what m-matter do th-the foreigners have in our city?" Before my dad gets to answer, another voice raises concern.

"My lord, are they sent by the gods to punish us?"

"Punish us?" says the Earl angrily. "For what, my dear Ulrik?"

"Our s-ssins." The first voice stammers again. "For being the in- insurgent."

"There are no sinners or sins among the gods. We are warriors, Vikings, not labeled by any clan," he says. "Our battle is not against the outside world. This city was built to protect us from intruders, and anyone able to pass through the old wizard's spells to get here deserves a damned good reception, don't you agree? We should host a feast tonight to celebrate our own strength before the gods." He laughs a little. It feels strange to see my dad happy. I'd like him to stay this way. It takes away the sorrow, the anxiety, and the fear gripping my bones.

"The young girl," says Ulrik, taking a long breath. "Is she the daughter you left behind, my lord? The daughter who carries the curse to kill." Eyes in the crowd stare at me, maybe searching my face for evidence that I am the Earl's daughter.

"Nora is my daughter." says the Earl. "She has travelled far, crossing the Forbidden Areas to see me about matters that concern none of you. I shall resolve matters with her and you shall remain without worries."

Ulrik persists. "But I worry deeply my lord. She has endangered the city by bringing in the Verans. Soon, she will bring danger to all of us; soon, there will be more. And, soon they'll want to look for the weapons. We must execute them all before more danger enters our city."

"We have nothing *they* want in this place. Nothing to fear," says my dad, his voice heavy and dark. "The city is protected. Old, indestructible spells—"

"The spells have been broken. Our perimeters are unprotected." Ulrik's voice causes an outrage.

The whispers grow into growls and anger. I hear, "They are here to take our land and destroy our city. War will be upon us. We must rid ourselves of the intruders. It's the law of the City."

My dad waits until the whispers die down. "This land was forged by the gods to protect the last true Vikings," he says. "We've built it and recreated what was once lost. We will not give it up. Not now, not ever. This is our city. This land is ours. Our blood is in the red soil; our bones brace every pillar and every great wooden hall raised on these grounds. My fellow Vikings, you must trust me when I say my daughter, Nora, comes in peace and shall leave in peace."

"What about the gate that leads into Arres?" says Ulrik, crouching. "What if *they* get out?" He looks small, like he is shrinking out of fear.

"*They* will not. The Garm creatures possess the power to decide who leaves and who stays. Without their permission, no one walks through the time portal. It's a promise they are bound to." His hand brushes the sword to his side—*my* sword, which was taken from me. His fingers drum against it impatiently. The gleam in my eyes is visible in the metal's shiny reflection. It belongs to me. I have every right to take the first ever Viking assassin weapons forged.

While I watch, he gives it to Grethe. I hold my breath so I don't explode. Duchess or no Duchess, I am not leaving without the rest of the weapons. Nor will I leave till my dad tells me the truth he owes me. I have a feeling none of it is going to be easy.

If the whispers from the crowd are true, I can expect something far more dangerous waiting ahead. The young Duchess they refer to can of course only be Grethe. I'll have to fight her if the rumors turn out to be true. Perhaps even kill her. A cold chill spirals down my spine. I do not want to kill anyone. The taste of blood doesn't thrill me. My ambition reaches higher, all the way to the assassin weapons. That's where I have to go.

My dad eyes the crowd like a hawk. He holds out his arm as if unfolding a deep dark secret from the dawn of the world to the twilight of the Norse gods. The power of his prayer still echoes in my ears. Strange expressions travels across his face—suspicion or perhaps hope. He jerks his head and takes one step toward me, eyes cutting.

"The people of the city are hungry for answers, and I, alone, cannot satisfy their appetite for much longer. Soon they want battle for Vikings believe in battle and they believe in shedding blood against those they see a threat. They know why you have come, and although I cannot stop you from claiming the keep that's your cursed heritage, I can tell you what doom it will bring."

"That's not why I have come," I say. Why would he just

assume the only reason I'm here is to look for the weapons? Before we've had a chance to speak together as father and daughter, before the chaos that surrounds us now, and before asking me? "I came here to see you. I've been waiting for this moment my entire life. Everything else can wait."

"Why?" he says, and the question hits me like daggers. "Why would you make such an asinine decision?"

I'm mute, and every attempt I make to gather words withers. He doesn't want me here. He doesn't care about me. His fatherly embrace minutes ago, was that all just a moment of weakness or an act? I want to scream. I am furious. But instead I choke on a sudden onset of nausea. *Contain yourself, Nora.*

"I—" The question feels like pain, and I can barely manage a croak. "Didn't know…" Why would he say such a thing? He's my dad; of course I'd come looking for him. He owes me an explanation for *everything.* For all the lies and deceit.

"You must come with me this instant," he says when I don't go on.

The assembly breaks up, and only we stand behind like wraiths caught in an eternal burning flame. The Earl motions for Balder to leave the gates with Frederick and Mina. I catch a glimpse of Frederick's soft blue eyes. He swiftly turns and places both his hands to his heart, and I, too, lay both hands on my heart—a symbol of affection we've built between ourselves.

Look after my heart Frederick, as I will look after yours. I let go of him, my soul aching. My caged emotions have been set free and for the first time in my life. I am afraid to lose the one that I have foolishly come to love so much. *Frederick, Frederick.* His name is a gentle whisper in my ear, and I know I will see him soon again. It's only a matter of time. When I turn, my senses tell me something is wrong. Frederick's mind feels elsewhere, distant. He knows something that I don't.

2

The Secret Meeting

WE WALK OUT of the back door, leaving the assembly behind. I continue to hold my tongue instead of lashing out with questions I should be asking my dad. I think back to my recruitment in the East when Dan, the recruiter told me, *"all the answers are coming. Be patient, Nora."* I need to be patient and wait just a little longer. I hope the truth that was kept from me is soon to unravel. The truth about who I am, and what I still don't know about myself. Why did my dad leave me?

We pass through a door crossing the corridor. It leads us down to a secret dark tunnel. I walk with my dad and Grethe in silence, wading through the low vaulted shaft. We're underground in some kind of catacomb. We wade among rats and other vermin hiding in the shadows.

I force myself to adhere to the rules of this place–those that say don't start an argument with your dad who is a respected Viking Earl. I admit having trouble accepting rules in general. There are nuisances of being raised under the Triangle's repression and coming from the East I have no privileges. Not like those raised in the West. What norms govern this city? I do not know. They call themselves true Vikings. Hungry for battle they seize any chance they get to fight.

For a brief while, I stop. My dad turns around, and Grethe follows closer than his own curled up shadow.

"We have much to talk about," he says. "I know you must be tired and overwhelmed, but you have to trust me. I am taking you to a safe place." He motions with his hand, big and strong. His arm is covered in dark green inked Viking tattoos—the eagle crest of the Jarl raider dynasty and a symbol of courage, intelligence, and tenacity. Once he was also a raider, and now I may never know who he is or what he has become. I don't say anything. I follow their trail in the tunnel. But he knows I have an urge to speak with him, and I can't hold back for much longer.

As we leave the catacombs, a strange sight meets me. A winter sky is above me and sprinkles of ice land softly in my hair. Yet the sun is warm and it feels like summer. Underneath my feet, each step crunches brown, yellow and red autumn leaves. And yet the air is fused with spring birds chirping and tweeting, and I hear the sound of a distant ticking tab of a woodpecker.

Four seasons seem to melt into one like a conscious spell of magic. Could we be in a multi-season forest? I have heard of magical places like this one in Viking tales. I never thought I would live to be in one. The feeling is sensational. Overwhelming. I wish that Frederick were here with me to experience this moment. I hope he and Mina are safe in the Ashes. I hope Knud Forkbeard gives them the reception they deserve.

"Where are we?" I say and turn my eyes to the electric blue sky.

"This place belongs to Alfrothul Gunnlaug," says Grethe. "He calls it Jølsig, which means, Peak of the World."

"It's beautiful." I say as I look around. I forget about the troubles that haunt my mind, and about the quest for the weapons. The eternal pressing need to speak with my dad pauses. The forest has enchanted me with its spell. I unwind, and after days of being on a dangerous journey I let my mind wander.

"There is lots more," says Grethe. "You've only just seen the beginning of Jølsig." Her voice is soothing and seductive as if she wants me to follow the long winding trail in front of me. I can hear her whisper. *It's all right don't be afraid. Go on and explore the woods. Go that way...*

I nearly pass a threshold that leads to the darker side of the forest when my dad pulls me close. The warmth from his hand feels like sparks of ember.

"Nora, come with me." He gives Grethe a hard stare. She looks away.

We enter a great long house with rough wooden walls thatched with stout beams and a dais. Light slithers from the candles in the walls. The room at the end is dark and gritty with handcrafted furniture. Antlers and skulls are pinned against the walls, from large, rare animals.

This world begins to feel very different from the comfort of the Triangle.

The wizard makes his appearance. His spoken words of wisdom when he came to see me upon entering the city still linger in my head. He cannot possibly know how I feel after that. The anger and hurt I carry. The disgust, surprise and even fear, or does he? It doesn't matter. I take in the angle of the room, where the wizard appears. It looks like an old barn with tall double doors, straw tucked into the corners. It carries a sweet smell of grain, hay, and wood. There are no animals in here, just us and outside the four seasons furiously dancing with one another.

Jølsig feels like a dream within a dream, and the City of Vikings is an unreal place full of magic and spells. I never had any expectations of what it would be like coming here. All this while I have been focused on what I came for.

"What now?" I say. I can't contain myself when I look around. The edges of the hall are timber platforms. The bracken-strewn floors below are like slopes of a rocky inlet. But there's no answer. I know this place was built to meet the needs of the fabled wizard who is as quirky as a midnight mystery. And I am here waiting for all the secrets to unfold from his and my dad's keep. "Is this place supposed to make me feel better?"

"You are safe here, Nora," says Alfrothul Gunnlaug boring his eyes into mine. He shows no emotions. His face is as hard as a winter gale. He gives away nothing that leads me to believe I am safe, and it worries me.

"Safe from what?"

"From the curiosity of the people of this city, child," the wizard says. "Rest now and save your strength. That's why you have been brought here. And if you cannot rest, then go you shall."

"Rest?" I say. "I didn't come here to rest. You know that as well as I do."

There's silence. No one says anything. I can see why this place should ease me and make me want to trust them. It's beautiful, enchanting and free of any worries. But how can I turn down the noise inside my head? When I first met Alfrothul Gunnlaug he told me that the quest for the weapons would cost me every single drop of strength in my bones. I'm not sure what he meant then, and I am not sure what he means now.

I've also come here to meet my dad—a man of honor with a strong sense of duty. A respected man among his people. I glance at him from the corner of my eye. He appears harsh, with clothes that mask his powerful presence. Does he always strive to be this tough looking, regardless of how he actually might feel? How does he look when he is happy? I want to speak to him, get to know him, but that's clearly not why I was brought here.

While walking slowly across the room my dad moves his hands across old and rusty swords and shields, which are kept in the room we are in. He is sending me a clear message. *I know why you have come here.* I am eager to get to know more of him and want to break the cold silence between us. I partly blame Grethe for it, because I am jealous of her. Envious that she has her place in my dad's heart whereas I do not. I may never have what she possesses and for that I resent her.

I've been carrying so much love and devotion for him for so long that I do not have the courage to go against what he wants. *"Nora has come in peace and shall leave in peace."* By the gods if he wants me to leave, then why am I even here? Perhaps I made a stupid decision. The Goths want the weapons, and I, I just want to be my father's daughter. I can't help thinking maybe it was a mistake traveling through the dangerous woods to get here. And for what? I've risked not just my own life, but also Frederick and Mina's lives.

We sit in the dark wooden chairs covered in animal skins in the main hall of the long house in which I am meant to be resting. Grethe's face is an unreadable mask, but her body language speaks. She drums the tips of her beautiful fingers, which are dressed in golden rings with ruby, emerald, and sapphire stones. I can tell she's nervous, like she doesn't want to believe that I am also the Earl's daughter.

"How did you know it was me?" I say, addressing my dad. "When you first saw me."

"I recognize my own blood," he says and gives me an honest smile. The green forest in his eyes turns dark and mysterious. His face is a dim torch against the night. "When I saw you, I knew..." He doesn't wipe the tears that fill his eyes. Instead, they stream down his cheeks and reach his lips. He looks gaunt; deep wrinkles cutting his forehead and the small, faint lines around his lips become visible, even sitting here in the dark room. It's like he's aged from one second to the other. His sudden sorrow is deep, visible.

"Knew what?" I want to hear him say the words that I have longed for all my life.

"That you, Nora Hunt, are a courageous and brave young girl who carries the spirit of a warrior and the soul of a true Viking. You are *my* daughter, and I should have known you'd come looking for me one day." Grethe stops drumming her fingers and glares at him. "When I heard from Alfrothul Gunnlaug of your arrival, I couldn't believe it. How you made it past the time lapse and defeated Noddabah is a testament of who you really are."

"Who am I?" Broken with sorrow, I am more driven than ever to discover the truth about myself. Am I the cursed child carrying a doomed legacy? And is my purpose to serve the

Goths and to rise against the Verans, against the boy that I love? Should I too, kill for my clan? For freedom? For fear our enemy might wipe us out?

"Tell me, Earl Robert Hunt, who am I?" My voice nearly breaks as I hold back the grief my heart has been carrying for all these years. But I can't let this moment of weakness wash over me and distract me from what I need to hear. The temptation to bury my face in my hands and weep is greater than ever but I won't. I can't.

Not in front of her—the sister who carries murder in her eyes.

"Nora, my child, I cannot tell you who you are." He rises like a lean lion and walks to the glowing and cracking flames in the fireplace. Grethe's hawk eyes follow him. "Yes, you are my blood, and have to honor your duty to *your* clan, to *your* dynasty, but being my daughter does not define who you are."

"I am an assassin, cursed to kill just like my ancestors before me," I say, my voice thinning out. "That's all I will ever be, a killer." The smell of Maja's blood reaches my nostrils and I feel disgusted by what I did to her.

"Vikings are not cursed to kill," he says. "We are warriors and believe in battle. It's a tradition we must honor. You must confront the battles you are faced with. Set yourself free. You must either act upon your duty or—"

"A duty you wouldn't take on?" I say cutting him. "And the reason you chose to build a new life here in exile." He throws me a sharp look. His face is severe. The fire in the hearth slowly dies out and the gray smoke rises like a dragon's tale from the ashes and blends with the shadows in the room.

"Nora—"

"I was left to rot in the East. I was kept in the darkness my entire life and knew nothing of my Viking legacy." My voice trembles with anger. I don't care what he thinks my feelings are *mine*. I need to share the pain, the frustration I have been carrying for all this time. *Damn you!* I want to shout. Now, I've done it. I've let out the rage. Broken the rule. I notice the surprise in Grethe's eyes slowly turning joyful, like she gets pleasure from the tension between the Earl and me.

"The Goths were once glorious and magnificent Viking rulers, but their legacy is long gone," he says. "What do you—"

"I need to know the truth about myself," I say.

"I am sorry the truth was kept from you, but it was for your own good. I did what I had to because I was trying to protect you—"

"Save your words," I say bitterly. "I've heard it all before."

"Listen to me," he says. "Serving the Goths was a choice that I chose against. I made my peace with Benedikte, but I couldn't save what was chosen for you. By the gods, I wish there was a way I could have changed your fate but your—"

"Leader of the Goths, Benedikte is dead." I say and looked into his bright green eyes.

"The news reached me and I am sad to hear she is gone. She was a great and honorable woman," he says. "The Veran Lords finally defeated her after years of pursuing her."

"Still, you do nothing to serve our people, our clan? Nothing to defend Goths from our enemy? You just sit here in your little world, safe and content with your daughter." His silence feels like fire from Helheim. Burning, just burning, and I can't contain myself. I want to rage at him because I see a coward, a selfish man. A man uninterested in the needs of others, except for those he cares for—the city he has built and its people. I feel ashamed to call him Dad.

"It's not my battle anymore; you wouldn't understand."

"Why are you hiding? Isn't that why you are in this place? Shutting everyone out so *you* can live the life *you* chose for yourself?"

"I am here because I made a choice your mother didn't want to make." His voice lacks compassion. "But let us not make this about me. Okay?" He bellows, his face scarlet.

"It is about you." I raise my voice. "Don't you understand why I have come?"

"I am sorry for what you must have been through growing up. Feeling different and knowing you carry something inside you, a burning torch against fading candles."

"You have no idea," I say. "I'm here because I've been waiting to meet you." My breath falls short. Why doesn't he take me into his arms, hold me close? That's all I want. But he's as cold as the winter of Jølsig.

"Nora, although I've dreamed of seeing you again, you should never have set foot here. You have no idea what danger you could unleash. There's so much you still have to learn." He turns around, twisting his hands nervously. "You have grown more beautiful and courageous than the gifts the gods blessed you with. The gifts of bravery, beauty, and strength."

"What about freedom?" I say. Grethe stands and takes a place next to him. She clearly respects the Earl and is unquestionably devoted to him. I sense the vanity that surrounds her. Grethe knows her place and she knows who she is, and she is outraged that I dare to question the world surrounding us. I question the things that she never would. Why should she? She was raised in a time and in a place that is sealed from reality and for that, I pity her.

"Nora," she says, her voice thin as if it was a flickering thread.

24

"No one is ever truly free. We are all slaves to either our own mind or the minds of others. When we cannot live up to our own expectations, we fulfill the hopes and dreams of others, and through that we find freedom."

"Your sister is right, Nora," says the Earl and shifts his glance toward Grethe. "You must take her advice and settle your inner battle."

"Is that what you're doing here?" I say. My voice filled with anger. "Fulfilling dreams of others so you can be *free*? And you dare tell me I am the one with a fight?"

"We are Vikings, and we are born free," Grethe says. "We carry the legacy of our gods and live the values of our ancestors. Call it fulfilling dreams if you like. But where you come from, the Triangle, people are scattered among different beliefs and clans. It's a place run by dangerous Vikings, and two you have brought with you—"

"And the Goths?" I say. "Why don't you serve them? They want to reinstate the old Viking rules, don't they?" The guise in my dad's eyes is deeper than the evil shadows that haunt the Forbidden Areas. What stops him from telling me the secrets he so obviously holds back? Perhaps he cares only about the world he's built in the City of Vikings, and cares only about the daughter he's replaced me with. Grethe seems like a dangerously wise girl who I sense guides him in his decisions. The way she shadows him, looks at him. They depend on one another.

"Soon you will know what the Goths are," he says. "I don't have to tell you."

"Tell me what?" I feel a sting on my wrist. A message is transmitting to my chip, which has had no signal until now. I take a moment to stare at the red flash, and then tab it to read the text from Magnus hoping he sends good news.

I glance at my dad. He's silent as a grave. I wonder if he knows...

The message says, "When you find your father, you must kill him."

3

Trapped

THE RED FLASH dies and the message from Magnus melts like molten brass. The air around me feels hot and the smell of death closer than my own scent of fear. The message doesn't hit me immediately and when it does, I find it hard not to believe it's a mistake. I feel hurt and betrayed. Did Magnus send me here to kill my dad?

He must be out of his mind to suggest that I should commit such a crime and murder my dad in cold blood without any questions being asked. How can he tell me to do this? Being an assassin doesn't mean I don't feel or don't dare question orders from the Goths, or does it?

Killing Maja may have seemed easy, but it wasn't. Her blood still taints my skin with the smell of rotten flesh from when I took off her head. Although I know Maja deserved to die, but the Earl has done nothing except serve his own needs. That doesn't mean he needs to die. Does Magnus know something I don't? Is he keeping secrets from me?

What does Karen have to say about all this? Maybe she doesn't care. She hasn't seen her own husband for fourteen years. What difference does it make if he lives or dies? He's been away for reasons he's kept secret and stayed away to serve *his* purpose—becoming an Earl of the City of Vikings. And what a purpose that is.

When I look up, Alfrothul Gunnlaug, the great Viking wizard—also known as Åse Almvej—sits with his other face confronting me, as if I was on trial. His back is twisted badly. Unnatural. Unnerving. I did not see him come my way. Like a wraith, he appears out of nowhere. The two masked faces on his front and back guide him, and it is Åse, the face of tragedy I fear the most. I nestle in the stiff wooden chair, shifting the animal skin underneath.

Instead of feeling comfortable and safe, I feel distressed and threatened by everything in this room. I wish Frederick were by my side. His love is my strength and without it, I feel weak and frail, as if some ancient spell is overpowering me.

I don't exchange another word with my dad, but the look in his eyes tells me he knows about the message. *Soon you will know what the Goths are.* He'd said. I am committed to serving the Jarl Dynasty, and Magnus is not cruel or heartless. He's my friend and I trust him. I've sworn my loyalty to him and promised I'd get the weapons to strengthen our forces against the rising threat from Lord Nourusa.

But how does killing my dad help me defeat the enemy?

For all these years, my dad has been a fantasy figure. Am I to just kill him without questioning Magnus? He knows I am not the killer the Goths need me to be. I may be fearless, courageous, and brave in his eyes, but I am not heartless. I do what I must when I have to and guard my feelings against the world. For it has given me nothing except questions that still lead me astray like a dog searching for its one true master.

I still want to confront the Earl with all my questions. They are like a deadly poison dripping into my veins. The only reason I don't entirely resent him is because I know hiding me in the East wasn't his choice. It was Karen's—the woman who calls herself my mother and dedicates her true loyalty to serve the Goth clan.

"I hope the news you received is pleasant?" says Alfrothul. He pulls up his comedy face and smiles at me. He knows what stings my mind. The message from Magnus is hard to erase. I dig my nails into the arm of the chair to release my stress, but instead it circles and explodes on the inside. I have no place to hide. I feel naked and exposed like the wizard can read my fears and anxieties before they rise.

"Very pleasant," I say curling my lip. I keep a straight face. But Alfrothul is a wise wizard. He's seen past the awful face of a liar.

"I think the young lady needs to rest now, Earl Robert, wouldn't you agree?"

"I'm perfectly rested thank you," I say crisply. They've brought me here to tame me. What else are they to do with me? I know the ugly news Alfrothul is about to announce.

"Very well, Nora," says Alfrothul. "You may want to reconsider my offer when I say that you need to rest, because you're expected to be in battle by the break of dawn."

"I've not come here to fight," I say. "I've come here to get answers and the weapons that are my right to claim." I want answers that will give me hope that my purpose to serve the Goths is good as I am beginning to lose faith. But Magnus's message suddenly changed everything. I am avoiding the question circling in my mind.

"Vikings always fight," says Grethe, her smile full of mischief.

"And fight you shall, dear sister. Only then will you get what you came for. You didn't expect to walk out of here just like that, did you?"

"Fight against whom if I may ask?" I sound condescending, and I don't hide it. What do I really know about this place, other than my dad has been hiding in it? Do I trust that he alone holds all the answers to what I'm looking for? And now this. "Who do I have to kill to get what I came looking for?" I say to provoke Grethe.

"Me of course," says Grethe. "But don't be so sure about killing me. You're not the only assassin under this roof."

"What?" I say angrily. "I never wanted—"

"But you are," says my dad. "You know very well who you are loyal to."

"Why is that such a crime?" I say. "It's not like the choice was mine."

"But it was, my daughter," he says. "When you selected Jarls you chose the side you wanted to be on."

"And why do you think I did that?" I say furiously. "Did *you* not submit to them?"

"That was different." he says.

"Why?" I ask. "When I was taken by the recruiters I wasn't exactly given a choice. I was told what to do. Do you do what others tell you? No! You give orders. You don't take them."

"Nora," says my dad. "You're in my territory. Contain yourself."

"What if I don't?" I say. I want to roar and unleash my blazing anger. "And what if I refuse this battle with Grethe? What will you do to me? Imprison me? Poison me? Stab me to death?"

"Our rules are not bound by the Triangle or dynasty code

of ethics. We do not serve the Goths or the Verans. We fulfill our duties to the gods, and the gods believe in battle. Grethe is a Viking assassin and has trained since the age of four. She's clever, quick, and merciless. She's the sworn protector of our city—a city that rose from nothing and became a place for the true believing Vikings. You will fight her because that's the only way you're getting access to Arres."

"What is this place?" I say.

"We call it the City of Assassins."

I take a deep breath. "You speak as if I am just here for the weapons."

"You come here seeking death, my daughter, because nothing else awaits you. You must fight Grethe."

"I'd never—"

"You don't know that," says Alfrothul. He turns his back to keep Åse Almvej, the female side, from speaking but fails. "You will kill for the Goths," she cries. "That's why you've come. You will kill your family to get past the gate that will lead you to the past world."

"Do you mean Arres? No! That's not why I am here, I swear." I seek comfort in the eyes of my dad. I read the worry on his mind.

"Grethe will do what she must to protect us," says Alfrothul. "And so must you."

"I don't want to fight her," I say. "I'm here as your daughter, not as an assassin." Do they see me as a deadly threat? Is that all I am to them? An assassin...

"You have no choice," my dad says. "You need to fight if you want access to the weapons."

I stare at him and see cruelty in his eyes. He's been waiting for this moment. He's known I would come and has prepared himself with his own personal missile–Grethe. The Earl is guarding the weapons. He has reason to. I am not leaving here without them.

"You'd rather see your two daughters fight to the death?" I say. "And what for?"

"It's the will of the gods," he says and draws out my missing sword. I reach for it at the same time as Grethe, but the sword lingers in the air, the blade changing color from blood red to crystal blue.

"It will need to return only to its true masters," Alfrothul says. "It's the only way to activate the power of the other weapons."

"The sword was given to me, and it is mine to keep," I say, my voice raising. I can't control my rage. I do not want to follow the old Viking rules of battle, bravery, and honor.

"All the weapons belong to the assassins of Arres, including the sword you claim to be yours," Alfrothul says. "Take my advice and rest now, child, for tomorrow you will need strength if prayers can't keep your mind calm."

"Wait!" I say. "Why must the sword return to its true masters?"

"The sword was given to Karen in return for…" Alfrothul pauses. "I will not talk about these matters anymore. This conversation is going to end now." And just like that he begins to fade quicker than the night breaks into dawn. I want him to stay and answer all the darting questions on my mind. Why was the sword given to Karen? What did she get in return? I reach out to grab hold of his cloak, but my fingers hold nothing except a thick, smoky air.

It is late in the evening, and I've been brought back to the same room I was in when I first arrived here. So much for resting and gathering strength. My head throbs and my body feels heavy as if my bones were made out of metal. I am confused. I find myself in a web of mysterious riddles unraveling, one after the other. I wish I were born into the truth. I wish my dad had never abandoned me. I wish Karen had raised me in the West.

My wishful thinking will not change things. It's too late for that now. All I need to do is follow the rules. Fight Grethe. Earn the respect of my dad. He loves me. I feel it deep inside my heart. Why else would he be so emotional when I asked him how he knew I was his daughter. He's afraid and seals his feelings to please Grethe and his people. The Earl has his duties to carry out, his role to play.

It feels as if everyone is against me and detests me for what I stand for. They hate me for wanting the weapons, and for bringing Frederick and Mina with me. I came here thinking my dad would hold me in his arms, be happy to see me, show me what way I need to go, and offer advice. Nothing has worked out the way I'd hoped.

My dad disobeyed every rule and fled. He now obeys silly rules that have entrapped him. He has been in exile for all those years, and I get it. He is wanted for treason against the Triangle for leaving his duties. I was sent to kill him; I understand that now. He knew that all this would happen. He has been preparing for the battle. One assassin against another. It makes me feel like a pawn in game of chess. Are those I trust using me?

My dad has created his own deadly weapon and trusts no one, least of all me, because I am a stranger to him, someone who serves the enemy. Could it be that he is torn between his obligation and his belief and maybe even his old feelings from the past?

But the real question is why did he leave his duties in the first place? Robert Hunt started out as a raider just like me, on a mission to find the ancient Viking artifacts. What changed? What made him leave and become a deserter?

I have to speak to him. He can't just send me into battle against Grethe with a confused and tortured mind. He must know that my heart sits with Frederick. The powers I have allow me to heal fast. I have dodged the sweet taste of death before. Yggdrasil will protect me; she always does. She is my shield just for a little longer. In a few days I turn seventeen, and that's when the real magic happens—the symbols that unlock the nine Viking worlds.

I know nothing of Grethe, except that she is my halfblooded sister. To defend myself I will have to kill her. I'm sure she has no problem killing me. The hatred in her eyes, the resentment she feels for me is obvious. It's like she's been waiting for me her entire life guarding the secret that leads into the City of Assassins. That's the only logical explanation I can think of when Åse Almvej screamed that I was here for the secret key to the world hidden in the past.

But I need answers from my dad before I face Grethe in battle. If I die, I want to die knowing the truth. What grudge does the Earl hold against those he considered his own? Against his wife? I've always had a strong spirit in spite of my upbringing in the East. I feel something deeply rooted inside my heart. *"A torch against the fading candles"* like my dad pointed out. I have to keep the flame alive and do what I believe is right.

If I'd sworn loyalty to the Verans, I would have chosen Rognvald. Dark raiders who believe in battle, rivalry, and merciless killings to get what they want. Just like Mona and

34

Peter who nearly killed me when we raided Eldor. Frederick was never like them. He was different from the start and battles every day between what his mind tells him and what his heart tells him. There's a risk he could betray me. The dark side is like a shadow. It follows. It takes over people's will when it is weak and broken.

As Jarl, I've had to take responsibility to lead the dynasty. I've had to submit to my duty as an assassin and protect the Goths against its enemies, the Verans, Lord Nourusa, and even the people of this city.

With Magnus as the new leader, things will change. They have to. The sedition against the Verans is happening, and the alliance with the senate is getting stronger. I don't want to fight the wrong side. I can't escape the feeling that that is what I am doing. Ever since coming here that feeling is growing like a tumor in my mind. Karen warned me if I fail to take up my duty, my fate will be written in blood.

Magnus will have me killed should I disobey orders and go against him. He is counting on me. Treason is frowned upon in the Triangle. Where does that leave Frederick? He will be wanted for sedition. He's betrayed his clan and dynasty for me. I shake off a cold shiver. Was Frederick sent to the Ashes to redeem himself?

Before I go to sleep, I think of a way to avoid going into battle. I have no vision from Yggdrasil. I don't know what I am up against. A young Duchess, yes, but is she as undefeatable as I am? Will I be fighting against my own shadow? If only there was a way I could reason with her. But she's as loyal as the assassin's blade. I'll have to try and speak to my dad alone in the morning.

Yggdrasil holds the worlds of the Vikings: Asgard, a divine

place and home to the gods; Niflheim, a place of dead souls, dark and daunting; Alfheim, land of the powerful and wise elves; Jotunheim, home of the giants; Midgard, home to mankind; Svart Alfaheim, home to the dwarves; Vanaheim, a land claimed by the Verans; Muspelheim, a land of fire where the demons reside; and Helheim, a grim and cold place for killers, and dishonorable people.

The nine divine worlds are powerful and for the Goths to rule, it will take a battle greater than Ragnarok. With that in mind, I have my own battles to fight, against myself, my heart, and against the world that I cannot escape. Nothing feels safe in the Triangle. Although I have one alliance I can count on. A person no one will suspect–Andreas. He is in the West, and he will help me. I am certain. With a restless mind, I fall into a dreamless sleep.

Some time later at night the sound of music wakes me. I get up and look outside my window and catch a glimpse of the large barn across the main yard. There's little light coming from the corners of the doors and windows. I sharpen my ears and hear a thumping. I cannot believe it. They're having a fest.

I get dressed and grab the handle of the door, but it's locked. I shake it, but the handle doesn't budge. I can't believe I'm being kept captive while there's a fest in full swing on the other side. If I've learned anything since leaving the East, it's to make friends, seek alliances, smile, and don't piss people off. Unfortunately, I am not good at playing by these rules. But I am sincere and honest—qualities less preferred in the Triangle. Qualities that seem to be accepted in this place, which is why I have to get to that fest.

I shake the handle again, but it is still not budging.

Out of frustration I squat, holding my head between my hands. I'm staring angrily at the thick oak door. There has to be a way out of here. I lie on my back, staring at the ceiling. There's a slit in the roof, which is made out of turf. A smile creeps up my face. I get to my feet, grab the chair, and swing onto a steady beam. I smack my legs over it and sit in an upright position. Then I get up and balance my weight, my arms spreading out like an eagle's wings, just like the proud Jarl tattoo on my arm.

With my hands, I shove some of the hard turf from the top away to widen the slit. But it's still not big enough to get through. I swallow a scream against my fist. The sound of music and singing is getting louder. I refuse to sit in here and miss out on what could be an opportunity to meet the very people who call themselves the *real* Vikings.

If I could just get to the other side I might get answers to the questions that I heard in assembly earlier. I'm the intruder who brought the Verans in, and broke the spell that kept this secret city protected. They hate me and from what the Wizard warned, they want to see me dead, a wish Grethe wants to grant them. A wish my dad fully supports after seeing his daughter after almost fifteen years.

I form a fist and keep punching it against the roof. It takes me twenty attempts before the top starts to break. My knuckles ache. They've cracked a little and are bleeding. Thick dust motes and hay straws fall onto me. I sneeze hard and lose my balance from the beamer falling flat on my back.

I crush the necklace carrying red soil from the East. My hand feels the softness of the earth crawling between my fingers. I've been carrying the chain since I left home. Someone that used to be my friend, Gustav, gave it to me. Why can't I recall the way he looks? I remember other faces and places from the East in a blur.

I remember that I tested my courage by entering the Forbidden Areas—a god forsaken place ruled by trolls, fairies, giants, and other mystical creatures. It existed ever since our world turned dark after Ragnarok. How else would the birth of the Triangle have been possible?

When I come to think of it, I despise the rules of the Triangle. They swore they'd find the Nine Worlds. When things changed alliances were formed and broken. I don't know why

the Verans are siding with Lord Nourusa. What has the dark lord promised them? Immortality? Power, wealth? They already have all that.

The peace we've preserved in the Triangle for so long means nothing. The enemy is doing what it needs to; eliminating threat. Raiders do not have the strength alone to defeat the old powerful Viking wizards. And certainly, not commoners. It is not what they are trained to do.

Rarely commoners obtain elite status among raiders and those that do, like Maja Gustafson, can become incredibly powerful, using black magic and death spells to harm their enemy. But magic among Jarl raiders is against our code of ethics.

I was lucky I survived an attempt on my life in the Tower of Swords. Maja was not just thirsty for my blood; she also desired Magnus's love. Soon Magnus will rule, but he needs my help to defeat Nourusa—a vicious and powerful, ancient lord from our past that's gathering his strength from the Veran worshippers summoning him from the dead. I cannot leave without the weapons. If I do the Triangle and Midgard will fall into darkness. I need to get the weapons.

In my dreams, Midgard is nothing like the Triangle. It is a world apart where people live freely and in peace. A world with lush green forests and silver peak mountains. In my vision rivers run wild and blue. I can almost touch it. The taste of freedom.

The burden I carry on my back feels heavy. Some might think it's a privilege to have such great responsibility. To carry the map for all those years, until Yggdrasil makes her journey through time, to be awakened and give us what we've been waiting for. Sometimes I don't think I can do what I was chosen to do. What will happen if our worlds fall into darkness? Will all hope of free worlds be gone forever?

I remind myself over and over why I am here and what I must do. I am afraid if I don't, I will fall weak and lose my sense of purpose. I still wish I had Frederick by my side.

What's he doing in the Ashes? Will he turn against me now that he's back with those from his own clan? Is that why the Earl was so stubborn about sending him and Mina there?

I try to defeat my negative thoughts and curl up like a ball on the floor where I am kept. I'm in agony, and the bones in my body crack and rattle. *I think I am okay.* I want out of here and rise to my feet to try the door again. Only this time someone opens it for me.

"Going somewhere, Nora?" the Earl asks with a smile in his eyes.

4

News

MY EXPRESSION REVEALS nothing I hope. I want him to know I am furious but realize he probably recognizes that by now. He walks into the room and searches for the truth in my eyes. *I have nothing to hide.* He can search all he wants and he does, like a serpent twisting around its prey. Will he see who I truly am? His blood and bone.

He thinks he knows me because I am his daughter, but the truth is he knows nothing about me. All he carries are ideas about who I am from what little he's seen. He leans against the wall. At least he's come alone to see me. He didn't bring his young bodyguard. I wonder if he can read my thoughts and gauge my feelings.

"Yes," he says and looks away as if shy. I can't imagine a man like him timid or fearful. Perhaps he's nervous and doesn't know how to handle my expected arrival. He's short of words, but something tells me tonight he'll not be sparse. "I can read some of your thoughts. Not all, and certainly not your feelings."

"Still, you think I am dangerous and should be treated like a captive, keeping me locked in this room against my will."

"You're here out of free will. No one is holding you a captive. The door was locked to protect you from people in this city—people who want answers and have been long waiting for the battle you've invited yourself into."

"I have?" I want to laugh out loud. "You should know I hate battle."

"You can't; you are an assassin."

"So is Grethe, and so were you." I say. "Just because I am one doesn't mean I like what I do. Killing someone, anyone, whether it's a long-lost sister or an enemy is not something that I take pleasure in."

"Grethe is an assassin with a purpose. There's a difference," he says. "Her mind is trained to believe in battle, unlike yours."

"My purpose is no different. Grethe serves you and your city, and I protect the people I have sworn loyalty to. She carries the tattoos of our clan, and the same blood runs in her veins as it does in mine."

"Grethe has been tasked to protect the key to the gate that leads to another world where the Viking weapons are kept. She's taken a blood oath."

"Then I just have to fight her." I sound like a bloodthirsty assassin. "Killing someone that wants me dead is a familiar feeling."

"Have you ever wondered why people want you dead?" He furrows his brow.

"They see me as a threat."

"Still you feel it is safe to break into the City of Vikings and snatch up the key that will grant you access to a place in the past where the weapons are kept?"

"Point taken, *Father*," I say. "I am not welcome here."

"I am not your enemy, Nora."

"You aren't my friend either."

"I don't want you to suffer more than you already have. I know one part of you came looking for the father you never knew. I do not blame you, but I cannot live up to your expectations. I will disappoint you."

"Is it that awful to have me as your daughter?" I hold back the tears welling in my eyes. *Bastard,* I want to shout.

"I'm sorry I couldn't be your father, Nora. I will not stand here and pretend I know what it feels like to be in your shoes. But I needed for you to grow up knowing of me—"

"Because you wanted me to come look for you?"

"No, I knew you'd seek the truth yourself. I never wanted you to find me. I made that clear to your mother when I left her."

"What truth are you talking about? Or should I say lie. I have discovered many." I break down in tears and fall to the ground. I feel weak, vulnerable, and lost. The love I longed for from my dad is denied to me. He never wanted me to be his daughter. *Why?*

"Because..." He squats down before me and lifts up my chin with his finger. The green of first spring in his eyes feels warm. "We both know what you must do to me."

"I'd never—" He wipes away the tears in my eyes. "—Kill my own father."

"You may not like this," he says firmly. "But it is the wizard's foretelling. I never wanted to leave you. I had to because of your mother."

"Karen?"

"We used to think alike, until she didn't. She lied to me and deceived me. If I knew what she was plotting, you'd not be here. You'd never have been born."

"What do you mean?" I say. "I beg you. Tell me the truth about what happened. Why did you leave and choose a life in exile?"

"I will, Nora. It's your right to know."

"Was it because I was chosen by the gods?"

"That's what she told you?" he says, curling his lip. I sense I will miss out on the fest, but I'd miss out on any Viking fest to stay up all night to hear what he has to say. At this moment, nothing else in the world matters more than his words.

He crosses his arms over his chest. His head is bowed. He doesn't seem willing to tell me anything. Just when I am about to raise my voice, the cords in his throat release a sound colder than the winter season outside the wizard's barn.

"It all began before you were born. Karen and I were young, in love, and life in the Triangle was peaceful. We knew who we were and had sworn allegiance to serve the Goths under their glory days. But it all changed. A year before you were born, it became the hardest time of our lives. It was during the inquisition that the legend of your ancestors, a hidden seal, was broken. The sword you brought was taken from Arres, also known as the City of Assassins. Karen was with child, but you were not the baby living inside your mother's womb. You had a sibling. We lost the child during the interrogation the day the Verans came to power. They had gathered a strong army of men led by Lord Wilhelm. The Goth fell and Benedikte saw her husband ruthlessly murdered. She decided to hide her son and daughters from the eyes of the enemy when she saw what they did to Karen.

The Verans took the child from your mother's womb before she ever held it. It was a miracle she survived after they left her

43

in a pool of her own blood to die. Karen is a strong woman. She insisted we have another child after our baby was taken from us, and that's when you were conceived. The gods know we had no trace of our lost child, as if the Verans had erased it from the heavens and from the earth. We used every forbidden spell we could find in the Viking books, but not a single clue led to our child's existence. I started to believe it was dead and after a while, so did Karen. She never said anything of course because she didn't want to believe it at first." Tears fill his eyes.

"Why did the Verans take the child from you?" I ask.

"Because the foretelling had reached the Veran Lords. The birth of a child chosen by the gods would lead us all to the Nine Worlds of the Vikings. It was not just any child, but a descendant from a Viking assassin clan. The scoundrels began their search. And it wasn't long before they tracked us down. Nora, I am sorry that all this was kept secret from you. Sometimes not knowing the truth is better than a blissful kiss from the gods. I don't want to think about the past. Much grief lies there and much sorrow. I am telling you all of this because it is the truth you came seeking."

"Did you ever care about me?" I say, my voice trembling. The tears stream down my cheeks. If he says no, I will have to find a way to live with it.

"Of course, I did. I still do. Nora, you're my own flesh and blood. You deserve to know the whole truth about what happened. Why I chose to leave, and had nothing to do with you." He pauses for a while before continuing.

"A year after we lost our child, the Verans began undertaking their own missions, but the raiders found nothing among the ruins in the Forbidden Areas. No clues of any kind, only death and deadly creatures. My soul was restless after everything that had happened. I had no purpose in life and decided to become an elite raider for the Jarl dynasty. The life of a raider gave me no purpose. It only distracted me for a while. I knew I had to escape, although some part of me wanted to die. Perhaps the part that chose to become raider. I didn't graduate from Dock Harbor because Verans controlled it. Benedikte went against all odds. She used her ancient wisdom and power and granted me elite status. I led a mission of my own into the Forbidden Areas hoping I would find our child. Something I did not expect happened. A secret passage led me into this sacred land, which became the City of Vikings. I knew it was an opportunity for Karen, you, and me to escape the tyranny that had taken over the Triangle. This would be a fresh start for us, leaving it all behind, building a free place."

He stops talking and the expression on his face is a mix of sadness and grief. Is he sad that he left me behind? I don't know. The truth is hard to swallow, hard to understand. All this was kept from me. Why? Because he was devastated to lose his child that was taken? When I look at my dad I feel anger. I want to distance myself from him and from his story. He left me, left his clan, left everything behind, even his own wife. What do I expect now that I know the truth? An apology? It's too late for that. I've seen and heard just about enough. Yet I'm curious about one more thing.

"What about the child you lost. Did you ever find them?"

My dad shakes his head.

"After spending months in the Forbidden Areas, I returned to the West. Everything was different. The Triangle had become the new and rising land and the City of Skies was now the capital and rose faster than any other place. The Triangle was considered a place of the future."

"What about me?"

"You had turned two that year and were living in the West with Karen. That's when things changed for us again. The search for Viking worlds was suddenly banned. The foretelling was reinstated. Raiders were only to search for the ancient artifacts: Thor's hammer, Mjölnir, and the golden horn, Gjallerhorn, which awakens Yggdrasil. It is said that when the tree is awake, she will sow her roots into the Nine Worlds, and a child chosen by the gods will lead us. This was supposed to be another descendant from a Viking assassin clan. This child would carry the key that unlocks the nine realms. The recruitments of raiders began. The search for the artifacts was enforced across the West, slowly spreading to the North and giving birth to the Orkeney dynasty, which was ruled by intellectuals and their wisdom. Rognvald's dark raiders were controlled by the Verans and led by Lord Wilhelm. Jarl fell under the Goths, but they were weak. Benedikte had no power, no authority left. No one wanted to recruit raiders from the East, who they considered a secluded and primitive people. It was the only place where you could be kept safe."

"What happened then?"

"It became clear why your mother wanted to have another child. My own wife betrayed me. She knew of the second foretelling long before me. She wanted our legacy to lead the Goths back to power. Karen was determined to raise you against my wishes. I wanted a free life for you, for us, built on old Viking traditions. Karen made her choice and hid you in the East, where Verans never set foot. They were unable to track the chosen child. Because the more you'd know, the quicker they'd find you. Karen has put all her faith in the Goths more than anything and wants revenge for what they did to her. I wanted nothing to do with it. I had seen enough death and destruction during the invasion. I left when you were two years old. I used my new mission as raider to pretend I was searching for the ancient artifacts. But I set out to create the City of Vikings. Benedikte reluctantly allowed me to leave, but I was never to return. Karen became obsessed with the idea that the Goths should regain power. I had every reason to leave the West, my dynasty, clan, and Karen. Our ways changed under the new rule. The senate was useless, and the chancellors and ombudsmen did nothing to restore an alliance with the opposition. The Goths became submissive and needy, obeying everything the Verans demanded. They used their power of manipulation to get what they wanted from commoners. The essence and ethos of our Viking clan disappeared. It hadn't always been this way. We'd die and defy those who'd oppress us, but our enemy broke us. I couldn't fight, because I was in anguish. Everything I needed was lost. Karen preserved what was left of the Hunt family's legacy. Behind closed doors, she ran sedition against the enemy. She broke our ancestor's seal. She took the sword from the past world of Arres and gave it to you. Karen knew what it meant and that you would bring it here with you in search for the other weapons. We believe it was after the first foretelling that she entered the City of Assassins and somehow got hold of the sword in return for something else that only the devil only knows about."

"The curse to kill," I say my voice low. He looks at me warily. There's a quiet death in the air. "I can't explain it, but when I hold it, I feel a need to kill."

"Karen may have unleashed the curse of the assassins bringing the sword. I can't piece together why they let her have it. The weapons are powerful but only when kept united. Without the sword, the remaining weapons are powerless. They were forged to destroy, and if they fall into the wrong hands, it could be disastrous for the Triangle. Legend has it your ancestors were merciless killers of the oldest Viking clan. They traveled outside their realm to discover a new world. But it wasn't new. It was a world of the past called Arres. Their only wish was to break free from Justus Markus's spell, and return to Midgard."

"Why did he put a spell on them?" I ask.

"He needs them to build and maintain an army to protect his world. This is a place that never moves into the present or the future. It just remains as it was five hundred years ago."

"Protection against what?" I say. "What is this place?"

"It is nothing but wasteland, and it gained its name, the City of Assassins, after the assassins came to be. Arres was originally the promised land of the Garm Klan, given to them by the Goths in return for their eternal loyalty. No one saw its fate turn when it fell under the Mad Emperor."

"Mulhog," I say. "That's why he didn't eat me that day in the Forbidden Areas."

"They are never to harm us."

"Nora, your ancestors have no land, no belongings, and no purpose. They are the worse kind of killers—evil to the core. It has taken us generations to clean the filthy blood that runs in your veins. They don't care about who you are. They'd skin you alive just for fun. If you ever decide to enter the time portal, be aware of the dire consequences.

"How did Karen do it?" I say.

"Karen had no other choice given she'd lost everything—her child, her husband. She had to give you up to protect you.

I'm not justifying her doings. You were sent here to get the weapons out of Arres, and she is using you, her own daughter, to get to what she wants. She is obsessed with hatred, revenge, power, and greed."

"Why is she using me?"

"Because she knew of the second foretelling. Her only purpose in breeding another child was to fulfill the wish of the prophecy that would put her in a powerful position. She wasn't the same Karen after we lost our firstborn. She became resentful and angry. She wanted vengeance. But the Verans were one step ahead of everyone. They increased the raids, hired more raiders, and expanded the recruitments to the East. They were desperate to get more raiders as they were fading faster than autumn leaves. Of course, they recruited you, a diamond in the rough. You could have taken down the entire Dock Harbor Academy if you wanted to, making use of the power you still know so little about. I knew you'd find the ancient artifacts that awaken Yggdrasil. It was only a matter of time before the Verans took the weapons. And the map in the form of the tattoo you carry on your back is an emblem of who you are—a carrier, a key holder. The Verans are just waiting. They will awaken the tree only when you turn seventeen. That's when Yggdrasil will spread her roots to the Nine Worlds. You will receive the encrypted runes, which are the key that opens the Nine Worlds. It's all about to happen. When I first saw you here, I didn't know how to feel. All you have to do is wait, and everything will happen. Coming here, you've risked far more than you can imagine. You don't need the weapons. You have enough power within you to fight the evil threatening the Triangle"

"I don't believe you," I say. He looks me straight in the

eyes—a hard, unnerving glare. "I've felt the power of the sword. I know what it can do. And that has nothing to do with my inner strength."

"You may not succeed in the City of Assassins. You and your powers may have no significance there. It's a dangerous place. I will not lie to you. The assassins will want you dead unless you give them what they want."

"What do they want?" I say.

"Midgard." He looks at me, his expression soft. "They cannot leave unless the spell they are under is broken. The Garm Klan has been trying to break the spell. They want the assassins gone, and the Mad Emperor dead."

"What would happen if they were to escape this past world?" I say.

"We cannot predict what is kept in the past, only the future. But then what happens when you unleash evil anywhere? It breeds, and it destroys."

"But Karen, she had a painting in her house. She takes pride in our ancestors." I sigh; frustration takes a toll on me. "Why would she keep that portrait if they're vicious killers?"

"She thinks our assassin legacy is glorious."

"Isn't it?" I say. "Isn't that why the gods—"

"No one knows what the gods want. No one knows why they chose a child from our bloodline. We are descendants of the oldest Vikings that have lived."

"Whatever the reason, I was chosen. I still have a purpose—a calling I need to fulfill. I don't take pride in any of my heritage or bloodline. But I've been cursed from the day I took that sword into my hands."

"You're still a novice at killing, but they have killed thousands of people. You mustn't kill innocent people. Kill only to protect, and kill those you must. Arres has far too much evil. Learn to understand who you kill and why. Never make hasty decisions, Nora. Weapons do not protect, they destroy."

"What do you expect of me now that I know the truth?" I say.

"That's for you to discover," he says. "You will learn new ways of life. You're just a child, a girl. Don't give your ancestors what they want."

"What do they really want?" I ask. "I am not sure I understand all this."

"What we all want. Midgard. The world to rule them all."

"Midgard," I say. "The battle is all about Midgard." I take a deep breath. The weapons are all that matter. I cannot leave without them. If I do, the Goths will lose and become enslaved by evil lurking from outside the Triangle.

My dad looks at me.

"I remember when you were born, and I saw myself in you. I saw your courage, your bravery, and your thoughts. The gifts the gods had bestowed upon you and your legacy became apparent. I knew why you had come. To seek the weapons that would lead the world into another Ragnarok. When your blood spoke to me and you were looking for answers, I knew I could no longer deny you the truth. Your fate to become a killer had already been written—a deadly weapon for the Goths who need you now after the passing of Benedikte. She gave you a powerful raider weapon to defeat the enemy. But that weapon only works when you show true loyalty to your clan. I see doubt in you, and that's why your weapon has faded. You see, Nora, your life was chosen for you, and you must do what you were designed for. Your purpose is not your own. You may not even know what it is."

"There is still hope, with Magnus—"

"Yes, Magnus is strong willed. He carries his father's heritage. I can see why he chose you to lead Jarls, and why he trusts you. I also know why he wants me dead. The Goth law falls against traitors like me. I'm an outlaw. I should redeem myself and grant you access to Arres, but I can't. The decision does not sit with me anymore. I have passed my responsibilities on, and Grethe is the gatekeeper to the port. You'll have to defeat her first to get to the City of Assassins, which is set five hundred years back in time. Even the best of raiders have not returned from that world. As for me, I no longer care if I live or if I die. My time has come, and I am not afraid anymore. I should have seen this coming. But if you should die, everything you were chosen to carry will fall into the hands of the Verans. I cannot say that is what I wish for, but I cannot let you come here and demand the weapons the way you have, not without a battle. Who knows why the gods test us in the ways they do? Shall my own blood kill me for deserting my clan? For banishing? The City of Vikings is my legacy. The Norsemen and descendants from every race have a seat on my council. The people of this city live openly in transparency, in trust, and in harmony. This is not another East; this is the only East. And I, as Earl, must serve justice to my people. Do what is right. They know why you have come. They have been waiting and are afraid of what comes next. I don't have to tell you Grethe is a fierce and ruthless assassin. She's killed an army of men with the flash of blades and daggers when they tried to enter past our gates. The wizard and myself trained her. Yes, she knows magic, and unlike the Goths, she is not afraid to use it. I urge you to get some rest, body and soul, but if you'd rather attend the Viking fest on the other side and mingle with people who do not welcome you, I'll leave the door open. You are free and no prisoner in my city. This may, after all, be your last night alive."

He wanders around nervously and glances at me from the corner of his eye. I've listened to all that he said, but I didn't expect it to be this difficult. He speaks of battle, honor and duty. What do I know of all this? I feel like the wild untamed animal from the outside that has come here to destroy what he's spent his life building. I've not come here to destroy their world or to obstruct peace.

"Robert," I say, my voice cold. "You said sometimes not knowing the truth is better than a blissful kiss from the gods. What did you mean when you said that?"

"It is my firm belief that the child Karen and I thought was dead lives."

"What are you saying?" I chew my lip. I begin to resent where this is going, and his long silence stings me like a swarm of wild bees. I know what he is about to say next and I do not like it. "Tell me, who—"

"— His name would have been William Janus Hunt." The words pull out slowly from his mouth. He turns his back on me.

"And who is *he*?" I say. "Is he here?" I am relieved and excited. If I have a brother and he lives, I want to meet him.

"It's Frederick. He's your brother."

5

The Fest

WHEN HE LEAVES, the heaviness in my body pulls me into a black ocean. I don't know how I feel after all that has been said between us. Father or daughter? Friend or foe? Ally or opponent? I don't know. I wish he'd not judged me for coming here and seeking what is mine. I don't believe the last thing he said to me. It's not possible.

Frederick can't be my brother. I refuse to believe it for the simple reason that I am in love with him. How can anyone be in love with their own brother? I push the thoughts away, but they keep invading my mind. His deep blue eyes, his honey blond locks. Frederick bears no resemblance to his brother, Tommy, or to his father, Lord Wilhelm.

No! I don't want to believe it. It's a mistake. There's been a mistake; that's all. The Earl thinks Frederick is his son because the Verans took him and because he bears a striking resemblance to me. But that doesn't mean he's my brother. It doesn't mean anything. Most Vikings are blond and blue-eyed, although not everyone in the Triangle. It's a trick to keep me away from him. Robert is lying. He must have sensed the strong bond that binds me to Frederick, and he doesn't want us to be together. He spun up this lie just so he can separate us. How can something so absurd really be the truth?

Each thought hits me harder than the next: Frederick, Karen, Grethe, and Robert. One big happy family. I should be filled with joy. Reunite, celebrate. Join the Viking fest. Tomorrow, Robert tells me I may not even be alive, so much for the foretelling. Where does that leave Karen? Where does that leave any of us hunting the shadows of Viking worlds?

What difference does it make if Frederick is my brother? None. He was always forbidden to me, my enemy in blood and in dynasty. If anyone should know the truth, it's the snake, Lord Wilhelm. I can't trust him; he'd say anything to get what he wants. He is eager to scrape his nails against my back, his fingers melting with my flesh just so he can get his hands on the map. The damned map. The curse Karen put on me and pushed me into the world for and for what? So she can give me up and *use* me? Get me killed for not following orders? How could she? She's been using me all this time. I feel sick, disgusted.

The web of lies never ends. It continues like an evil spiral.

I'd rather die than give in to what the Goths want. I will not be their slave and obey their rules. I feel betrayed; shocked at how far Karen is willing to go to get what she wants. Her obsessive need for power and control. And the order to kill my own father from Magnus. But what did Robert mean when he said it's the will of the gods? Does he want to die? Has he given up before the battle has begun? Robert knows things. He knows what's on my mind, and he knows of the past. He knows even more of the future. He's been watching me, following my every move from his little realm.

He said they use magic, and Grethe has the power. They seal their borders with spells, which is why trespassing the Forbidden Areas to get to the City of Vikings feels like an illusion. Frederick knows magic and manipulation. I have to get to him, get to the Ashes. Together, we need a way into the City of Assassins, so that we can find the weapons to protect ourselves against both our clans before they claim Midgard in a bloodbath.

But I will not go into battle against my own sister. I may not like Grethe, the charming little bird that she is, but that doesn't mean I should abuse my powers and rid myself of her. There are other ways—reasoning, logic, and plain common sense. Perhaps I could talk to her, convince her that I am not her enemy. But she'll not want anyone to get access to the weapons. It's what she is tasked to do, to be a deadly gatekeeper. It's her sole purpose, is it not?

By the gods, if Robert is right and Frederick is my brother—*William*—he should have a say in all this as a third heir to the legacy of the weapons. So there are three Viking assassins carrying the eternal curse to kill. Together we can protect ourselves from the outside threats. What frightens me is Lord Nourusa, but Frederick will know how to defeat him. He knows of the dark ways and the ways of the Verans. Suddenly, I understand that I need the weapons to win the battles that I face and to be free with Frederick to live in Midgard. I need Frederick's help.

The warm evening wind blows and my eyes turn to the creaking door. The sound from the fest is getting louder: music, chatter, and laughing. I leave the room. Maybe Frederick is there. Grethe might also be there. I have to convince her that the battle tomorrow morning is a bad idea.

She may not want to listen to me, the devout daughter that she is, but I have to try at least reasoning with her. I don't want Grethe to believe she's a fool for letting me take the weapons. Is she really willing to let the City of Vikings face battle from the enemy?

I need to find Frederick and tell him the news. Something tells me he already knows. I look down at my chip and tap it. Maybe there's a way I can connect with him. I desperately keep tapping my chip, but I can't get a signal. How did Magnus's message reach me?

I slip down the stairs and face the main square. I see a black rose bush with unusually long claw-like thorns. I don't remember seeing it before and hope it's not a magic spell to distract me from going to the fest. Something about the deep, dark blackness of the roses shining in the moonlight is arresting. Rotten leaves infuse my airways.

I stretch out my hand, as if spellbound to pick a rose, and feel Frederick's whisper tickle my neck. I turn, but no one is there except my own shadow. I step back. The petals fall to the ground and begin to wither. I see snakes mangling around my legs. It's an illusion. It can't be real. My limbs freeze. I try to focus on something else, anything except the snakes crowding my legs, hissing at me.

I close my eyes. I try to think about the memories I've lost of the East. I'm with someone. He's tall, muscular and dark skinned. Who is this person? And why don't I see his face? The faint vision of the person from my past flickers in my mind. I look down. The snakes are no longer there. The black rose bush lights up in blazing flames. I step back and scurry into the courtyard when a strong wind blows my way. I peer up a dwindling pathway. A shadow is approaching.

"Frederick?" I whisper. "Is that you?"

"Nora?"

It is him. His eyes are dim and dark.

"You've come for me." I run to him and hold him close. I breathe in his scent. He is cold to the bone and his arms are hanging to his side instead of holding me. "What's wrong?" I look up to find his face as gray as the midnight moon. He turns toward the darkness becoming almost invisible. I know what stings his mind. I can almost gaze into it. He's had the news Robert gave me. He knows, about *the lie*.

"You don't believe it, do you? I've never heard anything more—" He turns around. "What's wrong? Don't tell me you believe we are brother and sister."

"Whether I believe it or not doesn't matter," he says, his tone stone cold. "It's whether it's the truth."

"It's not," I say. "We're the same age. I was born sixteen winters ago, and you must have been born—"

"Two years earlier than you. I turned eighteen this year."

"That doesn't prove anything," I say. "Frederick, listen. They're turning us against one another. Together we're strong, but apart we become weak, enemies. We need to work as one regardless of what Robert claims."

"I want to believe you. By the gods, you are my soul, Nora. But I'm no fool either. If you are my sister, I'd honor it the way we're supposed to and love you like one."

"Don't speak to me like that," I hiss. "It's upsetting."

"If it's true, and I hope by Odin it is not—"

"It's not the truth—"

"Stop saying that," Frederick says, with a sharp a edge to his voice. "Saying it over and over doesn't make it disappear."

"Why are you this way?" I say. "It's like you've accepted

whatever they told you in the Ashes. How was it there anyway? I was worried about you. Where is Mina?"

"Mina is still there." His voice doesn't change much; it's flat as the cold ground beneath me. "It's safer for her to stay there. Out here she will be at risk for being attacked. She is not able to defend herself the way we are." He wears a brown cloak.

"What's this?" I say. He hands me a similar looking cloak.

"Wear it. We're going to the fest." He marches ahead of me. The wind flares behind his cloak and hits me. It is cold and detached like Frederick. Just the way he was, when I saw him for the first time. What a moment that was. The sight of him consumed me; it still does and no matter how weak my heart feels, Frederick is right. We need to get to the bottom of everything first. The Earl has no interest of his own to make up such a lie. Karen, on the other hand, I never trusted.

I throw my body into the mantle and hide my face in the cowl. I follow Frederick into the long house where music and heavy thumping can be heard from the creak of the door. Standing just behind him, I see some of the faces from the assembly. They are red and blotchy. Others are old and tired, as if they've returned from years of battle.

"Stay next to me," says Frederick. He yanks his hood to cover his face as we walk into the dank hall. We do not go unnoticed. Curious eyes gaze at us. I instantly look away. In the middle of the room sits a long table. It has bread, cheese, and dry meat with pitchers of beer and wine. Big-chested women sit next to smaller and slender ones, and beefy, wide-shouldered men chortle loudly as if they have no worries.

One man, with a patch on his eye, peers at me from the corner bench. He slams his fist hard into the table. He growls like a wild beast. I look away and pull Frederick's arm. We find an empty table and sit down. The scent of jasmine reaches my nostrils. I turn as Grethe approaches our table. Her golden hawk eyes never stray from mine.

"Didn't expect to see you both here," says Grethe with a hint of amusement. Her cheeks are rosy, and she wears a different dress. Black silk hugged tightly to her small frame, snaked up to cover her long swanlike neck.

"We thought we'd join you to learn about some ancient Viking customs," says Frederick. "It's so different here. Don't you agree, Nora?"

I glare at him and nod.

Grethe sneers. "The Ashes wasn't convenient enough to learn about Vikings?"

"It was very convenient. But I am not *here* to learn about the Vikings. I know everything about them. I am here to learn about *your* customs, weapons in particular."

"What is there to learn from a civilization like us?" Grethe says. "We're considered primitive when compared to where you are from, are we not?"

"Ancient secrets of the past, sister," I intervene. "Why don't you share them with us; we are no strangers to you. Not anymore."

"Secrets are only to be shared with those you trust. And I cannot say that for you two," says Grethe and smiles. "Father warned me about you, Nora. He said you carry the beauty of the gods, their strength and their will. All which can be broken."

"Grethe, listen," I whisper. "Before I came here, I knew nothing of your existence. I didn't come here to cause trouble to your way of life. Both you and I know there's no way I am leaving without getting access to Arres." Frederick grabs my

60

arm as I stand to get close to Grethe. I know he wants to tell me to take it easy, and I think I've done it again. I've made a foe of the one person I wanted to be my ally. Grethe's smile fades, replaced with the murderous look of an assassin.

"You'd better be prepared for battle tomorrow," she says and before she walks off, she stares at me, eyes bleary as if veiled behind a fog. "And fight if you want what you *really* came here for." She shifts her shoulders with pride. Her gait is that of a dangerous lion. Grethe has no intention of helping me; she has been waiting for this moment. I will make sure to make it worth her while.

The music amplifies. Its sharp tones are coming from pan flutes, bagpipes, and a lyre. The man playing the flute steps forward. The flow of air pushes through the instrument. He taps his foot onto the floor. The crowd is clapping, cheering. I can taste the sweat in the air. It's bitter and salty. Frederick pinches my arm, indicating we should make a move. But I don't want to leave. I walk across the hall and take a seat in the corner of an empty table. He follows me sharply, and sits across from me. He stares at me wildly with his heavenly blue eyes from the shadow of his cowl.

"What are you going to do?" I swallow the word, "*you.*" What happened to us?"

"You can't fight against your own sister. I mean, look at her." He glances back. Grethe is watching us carefully.

"What do you mean?" I feel the heat rising to my face. An incontrollable energy builds. I want to explode. "How do you suggest we get the weapons?"

"I don't know," Frederick's voice is condescending. "Killing one another in battle is not what I had in mind. It's stupid and dangerous." He reminds me of Robert.

"It's the only way," I say.

"What father wants his two daughters in a death match?" says Frederick.

"The cowardly kind," I say. "The kind that would leave his young daughter with her revenge sick mother to pursue a life of his own."

"Nora." Frederick puts his hand onto mine. "I—"

"Don't." I say.

He sighs. He looks at me for a while before he says, "Think about your inner strength. Everyone here is afraid of you. Of us. We're the intruders from the outside. You, me, Mina. Could we take them down?"

"What do you have in mind?" I say.

"Don't go into battle tomorrow. Be brave and strong."

"I'm tired of always being the brave and strong, Frederick. Where will that lead us?"

"Exactly where we want to be," he answers. "In control."

"If I don't fight her, she's going to kill me. Is that what you want?"

He shakes his head. His eyes don't leave mine.

"I would never let anyone hurt you."

"You can't protect me, Frederick."

For a moment, Frederick reminds me of Helena. I miss her. What would she say if she was here? What would she do? Helena is a wise Orkeney. She always knows how to create an alliance. Why can't I be like that? Why do I always have to piss people off until they want me dead?

Suddenly people in the crowd point fingers at us. They are whispering. They know who we are. I motion for Frederick to make a move. We start to walk toward the doors leading out of the hall. The music is still pounding. Someone grabs hold of my arm. It's Ulrik from the assembly this morning. Next to him is the man who stammered his words.

"Why don't you stay a little longer with your friend?" says Ulrik, and closes the door hard with the palm of his hand. He drums his fingers against the knife sitting in his belt. My heart flutters like a trapped bird in my chest. My throat feels tight, dry. We should never have set foot in here. What were we thinking?

I stay quiet and wait for Frederick to say something. Why isn't he saying anything? I look away and brush the sweat and hair from my face.

"We really must be going," I say and turn the handle, but his hand stays pressed against the door, slamming it shut as I open it. That's when I realize the music has stopped, and we're surrounded by a mob of tall men and women, with sweaty red faces and heavy breathing.

There's no reason pretending; they know who we are. I remove my hood and reveal my face for the spectators to get a clear view. I sense their need for answers in their hostile glares. If they could toss us beyond the tall walls of the city, they would. We are not welcome.

"Come on," says Frederick and takes my hand. He stands broadening his shoulders in front of Ulrik. He pushes his way forward. Ulrik budges a little. Swiftly, Frederick and I slip out, slinking through the dark night and scuttling across to main courtyard. He stops at the beginning of the dwindling road leading to the Ashes. He looks at the sky. The silver moonlight shines on his face. Frederick looks exhausted as if he's going to faint at any minute.

"I shouldn't be leaving you behind, Nora. But it's not a good idea to bring you with me to the Ashes either. Knud Forkbeard is a heavy old man who doesn't say much. He just glares and breaks into people's minds and steals their thoughts."

"At least we would be together in the Ashes," I say, detecting the fading emotions from his face. Is this the face of my brother or or my lover, or my enemy? *What difference does it make?* Maybe we were not meant to be. All odds stand against us.

"I can't bring you with me. It might cause more trouble." There's certainty in Frederick's voice. He's not even trying to tell me how he feels; it's obvious. The cold distance, the stern glance he throws at me, as if I was poison, slowly killing him. "I have to go now. You will be okay. You always are."

"Frederick?" I can't believe it. He's leaving me alone.

He turns around, shifting his cloak in the silent night. He walks up the steep hill along a black trail among flowers. I stand behind long enough to see him turn into a tiny dot and disappear. I don't want to think about why Frederick is behaving this way. It's obvious that he thinks of me as his sister. It upsets me to see how effortlessly he's accepted the lie Robert is spreading. I know Robert may have wanted a son, and that he's traumatized about what happened to him. But telling me Frederick is my brother doesn't change the past.

When I turn to walk back to my room I see a shadow. It is Ulrik. He has followed me. I notice a knife in his hand and anger on his face. Before I have a chance to run away from him the hot, burning sting of his knife pierces through my shoulder. I slump to me knees, barely able to hold my own weight. My breath falls short. The sharp pain connects with my senses so unexpectedly and leads me into darkness.

6

The Battle

WHEN I OPEN my eyes, bright light blinds my vision. I feel comfort in the softness underneath me. I am safe from the knife that stabbed me. *But where am I?* The light fades and when I take in my surroundings, I find myself in the presence of Robert, the Wizard, and Grethe—the three people that made it clear who I am and what they want me to do.

The memory from last night hits me. Ulrik? I touch my shoulder where the wound is still fresh. He stabbed me. Why didn't the tree protect me? Or give me a sign or a vision? She usually does. What *is* happening?

"Ulrik poisoned the knife he stabbed you with. He put a spell on the cut. It will eventually heal, but it will just take longer for someone like you." The Wizard stares at me.

"Spell? What the—"

"I broke the spell. The scar may remain forever." The Wizard pauses. "What in the name of Odin were you doing out of your chamber last night? You must understand the danger you've put yourself in. *You* are not safe here. Good thing Ulrik only injured you—"

"He didn't injure me," I croak weakly. "He tried to *kill* me. Don't make it sound so innocent. The man is dangerous and wants me dead."

"Every man and woman in this city wants you dead, Nora," says Robert. "You are an intruder. Under normal circumstances, you and your companions would get the death penalty for entering. Because you're my—" he swallows hard. His Adam's apple bobs as if sinking into his stomach.

"Daughter?" I remind him. I shift my head and give him a hard stare. "I get it," I say. "I am unwanted, in which case I will be on my way as soon as I get access to the City of Assassins. That counts for the sword, too, that was taken from me."

"You must get past the gatekeeper," says the wizard and motions toward Grethe.

"What if my brother, what if *William* felt the same way? He and I have a right to know where the weapons are." There's a deep, dark silence.

The muscles in Grethe's face shift like an evil black tide. She wants to say something. Her golden eyes hunt mine with a killer's instinct. Her nose twitches. "Has he said—"

"He wants what I want. That's the reason he accompanied me on this journey."

"Frederick is still considered to be a Veran," Robert says.

"No, he's not." I outplay him. "If you're right about what you said to me, Goth blood runs in his veins."

"To the world, he's still a Veran." he says darkly.

"What difference does it make?" I say. "What matters is that he is heir to the legacy as much as I am. You may have chosen Grethe as gatekeeper, but that doesn't give her any special powers over *William* and me." I feel dirty using Frederick. But I need to be smarter than them.

There's a naked silence, as if someone stripped them bare. And I don't know where my words suddenly come from, or how the idea entered my mind, but it's the only rationale I can use against them to get to the weapons. Frederick would want to play along. He'd want to get the hell out of here.

I can't hide the glee in my eyes when the silence turns into insecurity and anxiety flashing across their worried faces. Did he see this coming? He seems to know so much, even the prediction to his own death. I will not give him the pleasure of dying, because he thinks his time is up, and leave me with the guilt. I'd be a fool if I wanted to kill my dad. And for what reason?

He's still my blood, and deep inside my heart, I feel love for him. If I could only fall into his arms and stay there and weep for all the dreams he had that were torn apart. All the time that separated us will never return. For that I feel broken and devastated. Does he not feel my longing, my pain?

Does he want me gone, or is he protecting me? He guards his emotions against me. I think he knows that I will easily defeat Grethe. He's seen the future, and he is afraid of what it holds—death. I will not give in. I would rather change the course of the future to allow him to live. I understand he cannot give me what I want: love, protection, comfort, and safety, at least not for much longer.

Robert steps forward, his gaze soft and resting on mine. He lets out a heavy sigh. I have the wizard on check with one eye and Grethe with the other

"The gatekeeper was chosen before my knowledge of you and William came about."

"You knew about me," I say containing my anger. "You left me behind."

"In this world, what matters are the decisions we've made."

"Robert!" I say. "I am not going into battle to kill Grethe to amuse you and your people. There must be another way to get to the weapons. After all I have a right to them." I get out of the bed and stand. I feel weak and vulnerable.

"The law is the law," says the wizard. "If we break the rules, every man in the city will start doing the same. It will lead to chaos and our doom. The people of this city want battle. Only then is justice served."

"They're expecting it," says Grethe. "Unlike life in the Triangle, our city is built on the foundation of transparency. We live and abide by the rules we've set. We are hostile toward intruders, as they know nothing about our customs. You will face battle. You are also the Earl's daughter, and you brought enemies into our territory. Rumor has it there will be more—"

"Enemy?" I say. "*William* is the Earl's son." I make the statement believable, and I hate myself for it. But I am convinced if I play my cards right and have Frederick appear as an ally or even my brother, things could work out favorably for us.

"No one here knows that," says Grethe in a low voice. "No one needs to know about all the Earl's *lost* children."

"I was never lost. I was abandoned."

Robert's eyes meet mine. He turns and drifts away as if abducted by guilt. "Enough of this," he says. "Our rules cannot be changed."

"Rules were made to be broken, and you also broke them, didn't you?" My voice is sharp like the assassin's blade.

"I did, and I've been suffering the consequences. Even if I wanted to, I could not have come back for you. I didn't have a choice."

68

I laugh. "There's always a choice, Father. You just chose to benefit yourself because you didn't care about me or your wife."

"That's not true. I care and at the time, I had to do what was necessary," he says.

I sense the disappointment that takes its toll on him, but I don't feel guilty. This is my moment to tell him how I feel now that I've had time to digest everything he's said to me. I am wiser and soon I'll be seventeen. He has done nothing for me, except making it more difficult to get the weapons. He rules the city, and if he wanted, he could grant me access. What would all his loyal followers do? They want to kill me, and he doesn't even care. *Nora shall leave in peace*. Why should I? I'm furious, hurt, and angry, and I want him to know.

"Nora!" The wizard approaches me. "Bury your hatchets. Forget about the past. For what has been done cannot be undone."

My blood runs cold. He could as well have drawn a line across my throat. What about atonement? Everything else is madness. Just madness.

"Well," I say behind gritted teeth. "I'll just have to kill to get what I want. After all I'm an assassin." My heart pulsing faster than usual while Frederick's words whisper in my ears. *"There's no glory without danger."* I stalk off, composing my trembling body still weak from the attempt on my life. I stop and turn around. I realize I want neither—neither glory nor danger.

I'm facing Grethe, standing in the battleground surrounded by the people of the city, along with my dad and Frederick. The pale blue dusk plays with the furious wind. The atmosphere is dense, twanging with crickets. Torches flicker in the northern breeze. Underneath my feet, I feel the cold black earth. I look at the mauve, purple and blue sky against tall, swaying trees. The evening feels vivid. Dangerous. Mad.

To my right I see Frederick and Mina. Their faces are awash with fear. Frederick's eyes are restless. Mina's appearance is in tatters. Her dark hair is tufty, and her hands and feet are dirty. To my left I see my dad's angular face, shadows darken his green eyes. Next to him is the wizard, scratching his chin with his hair flaring around his face. The people of the city surround me. Their eyes stare straight at me. Standing right in front of me is Grethe in all white, giving her the appearance of an angel. Her blonde hair is pulled tightly into a crown, her forehead is glowing.

As I crack my fingers I'm pelted by my own thoughts. *Don't do this. Run, defy, fight, but don't kill for what is yours.* I silence my mind and face my sister. A fine strand of her blonde hair whips free with a gust of wind and lands across her cheek, and she gapes at me with eternity in her eyes. For a moment, I see myself in Grethe. It's terrifying. As if I am facing myself in battle.

Grethe's lips purse, her head tilts to the side as if to say, *"the pleasure to kill you will be all mine."* I stifle a snort when I hear Robert speak.

"The seal, which was once broken to protect the ancient keep and the assassin's weapons, is compromised but not without reason or intent. Nora, my daughter, has come here seeking what is hers. As Vikings, we believe in battle and will honor the intrusion with battle. Shall Grethe succeed Nora's companions will leave with nothing." He looks at me, his expression blank.

"I will succeed." I hear Grethe murmur with a smug smile

creeping onto her face.

"Shall Grethe not succeed," my father says, pausing, and looking at his other daughter. "Nora and her companions will be granted access to the City of Assassins."

Loud hisses and anger swirl all around me, and it does nothing to me. I am not afraid to claim the weapons. Except what my dad fails to understand is that I lose no matter what. I will leave without his love and without knowing if I will ever see him again. It breaks something inside me. Something he'll never know.

"Let the battle begin," Balder says and steps back from the main court where I'm facing the fine looking Duchess, Grethe.

She gives me a pointed look and strides back. Grethe uses magic to pull me to the ground. When I fall the black earth underneath my feet dissolves and turns into hot desert sand. My hands tremble. The cool night turns into a blazing hot day. *It's an illusion.* Grethe is using her magical powers, the clever little witch. I don't know what is real. I am trapped in the vision she's created around me.

I shield my eyes from the sun and look around. Nothing but sand and rock is in sight. I don't see Grethe, but I feel her presence. She is the wind shifting around me, the salty sweat coating my lips. She is the numbness I feel in my legs, the dizziness from the sun's merciless kiss. Something stings my skin, and smoke rises from my body as if it is in flames. I scream, but the sound is muffled. There's no escape. She's imprisoned me in this hell with rippling dunes, whispering death in my ears. My body withers, the flames turning into ashes. I snatch a breath, but the air is dry and feels like hot coal in my lungs. I hold my ground, so I don't disappear, but that seems impossible. All I want is to disappear.

The tattoo on my back wiggles and writhes. I feel some life coming to my bones and the blood rushing through my veins. I see Grethe's wan face—the wind howling with her scream as she strikes me with daggers. But her aim is in vain as she attacks me hitting nothing but thin air as I crouch down.

I haven't felt Yggdrasil for a while, but her branches embrace me like a thick metal shield, the cool twigs scraping my skin, and the soft leaves cushioning my frame. Grethe rages, and I hear her screams and laughter. She's not giving up easily. She may have the power of magic, but I have the power of the gods. The world tree protects me.

"Come on," I shout. "Show me what you have, witch."

I pull myself out of the vision she created; it scatters around me like shards from a mirror. I rub my eyes from the fake sand grating my skin. Nothing is there. An empty vacuum.

"Assassin," a whisper lingers. "You have to finish her. Do you hear me? Finish her before she finishes you." It's Frederick's voice.

Grethe's hands grab the back of my shoulders, her knee astride my spine, and I fall. The cool black earth underneath me is visible. A cold blade prickles my back and breaks into pieces. I don't feel anything except relief. Had it not been for Yggdrasil Grethe's blade would have had me.

My body rolls over and I scramble to my feet facing Grethe. The mob around us is thick. Among the faces, Frederick's eyes watch me, and that's when I realize how much he resembles Karen.

The same pale skin, blue eyes, and warm blond hair. *Deny it for as long as you want, but you know he's your brother.* I realize in this hazy moment Frederick will never be mine, and perhaps he never was. I borrowed him against all the odds, and now I must face him as my brother, while I stand face to face with my sister whom I do not want to kill.

"It's sickening that you desire your own blood," she whispers at me. "You see it now, don't you, Nora? How desperate you must be for love to want your own—"

I raise my hand in the air, stretching it to the black sky, and the sword flies out from my dad's sheath and into my hand. Firmly, I curl my fingers around the pommel and strike the sword aiming at Grethe's long neck. I see blood coating her white attire, her face horrid and screaming, but it is not Grethe's blood. It is Robert's.

My dad's green eyes flash despair, and the steel glows gloriously. He drops like a stone and in the moment, I feel nothing as if my emotions have stopped functioning. Grethe's scream fills the air like a storm. She wipes off his blood from her face. The crowd holds their breath, their eyes wide, their jaws dropped.

What have I done? I should have seen this coming; I should have known this is what he meant. Is that why he wanted me to go to battle? Did he frame me? The air smells of iron and salt, thick and humid. I turn to look up, and the skies are bleeding. Death is everywhere. It has surrounded me, and I cannot run or escape.

My knees turn soft. *This can't be. No, no!* I stumble to the ground. Frederick rushes to my side looking at me with shock and disbelief. Grethe yanks me to the side. Her voice is low and trembling.

"What have you done?" she cries. "You've killed our father."

7

Keys To The Gate

ROBERT'S EYES SEEK mine in the crowd closing in on us like a circle of death. Someone pushes me away hard. I tremble and regain my balance. I reach out for his hand as his breath slows down. He is fighting for every single one. I clasp my hands over my mouth and swallow a scream. Frederick takes my arm and pushes me past the mob surrounding my dying dad. Grethe sits kneeling in front of him. She is in tears. A dark red colour is smudged on her face. I drop next to Robert and glare at him. Frederick crouches down by my side.

"It was the will of the gods," whispers Robert. "Now, among my children, I can die in peace." His hand grabs hold of Frederick's. For a while, he doesn't unclench his fist. He looks straight at me and knows that perhaps I've accepted the truth. But I haven't. I just have to learn to live with it. My mind wants to deny what he is to me. I don't have the courage to accept that it could be true. But it would be unfair and cruel for Frederick to lose the last moment with the father he never knew, if it is his father.

"Earl Robert Hunt..." A faint rasp leaves Frederick's lips.

"I…" He's out of words, and I know how he must feel, gaining and losing something all at once. Anger surges through me. How could Robert let this happen? The remorse and shame from killing my dad will leave me troubled for the rest of my life.

"You mustn't blame yourself, Nora," he says and looks at me. "The choice was not yours but mine. I had to save Grethe. She needs to carry the legacy of the Vikings and protect the city from our enemy and from invasion. She will let you pass through the gate that leads you to the City of Assassins. She must." He looks at her.

Grethe wipes the tears welling up in her eyes. An expression of sadness crosses her face, and I see her for the first time as more than a halfblooded sister. And I am afraid because I don't see a sister but a witch with trickery and spells. I sense the evil rising in her body and behind the golden shimmer in her eyes. Grethe will not grant us access. I did not defeat her.

"As you wish, Father," says Grethe and looks at me with lightning in her eyes. She stands and takes the sword out of my hands. The warm blood that ran through Robert's veins is now soaking the black cool earth. He looks at us and speaks in Norse, whispering a prayer I've heard before.

"May the gods of Asgard guide your steps toward their gates. May your journey be safe and filled with light. May you find strength from Thor in your darkest hours. May you find wisdom from Odin in times of confusion. May you find beauty and lasting bonds from Freya and Frey. May your web be spun tightly with that which makes you stronger, happy, and wise. And may the gods always look upon you with good grace."

I recognize the Viking prayer Robert recites. It's from the book I discovered in Eldor. These are his last words to us before he closes his eyes and ascends to Valhalla. And I condemn him for what he has done.

Frederick, Mina, and I are thrown into a dirty dark cellar. For a moment, I believed Grethe. I saw sadness in her eyes, grief in her heart. How could I be so stupid and think she could ever be a sister. The name evokes warmth and feelings. A strong and unbreakable bond. She is nothing of the sort. She is a witch with spells.

Not only is Robert dead, but also I killed him. Not because Magnus ordered me to do so, but because it was the will of the gods. Most of all, it was *his* will. Robert knew I was going to defeat Grethe, and he wanted her to live. He sacrificed his own life, and I can't even mourn him. I can't see his cold body and hold him one last time. I feel as if all this has no purpose. Nothing is worth losing a parent over. I've gained a sister, but it will not be long before she finds a cruel way to rid herself of us.

Grethe is undeniably unpredictable. I am convinced she was the one who sent Ulrik after me that night. Why would he otherwise attempt to kill me? He doesn't even know me. I try to gather my thoughts, but I can't. All I see is Robert Hunt dying, his blood seeping into the land he built, flowing like a stormy river.

"Frederick," I say. "She's going to kill us. We have to find a way to the City of Assassins."

"Grethe can't kill us," he says with little emotion and looks away like he doesn't want to know me. "The city is ruled by a council representing the nine races. The wizard was our..." He pauses and draws in a long breath. "The Earl's most trusted right-hand man. Grethe would be stupid if she tried to execute us. There are consequences, even for us, which could mean we're leaving without the weapons."

"We are—" I begin and glance at Mina, who is too scared to say anything. "We are here for the weapons, and I am not leaving without them. Robert wanted me to have them. He told me everything the other night."

"Nora, I never came for the weapons," Frederick says. "I may have at first before we were..." Another pause. His mind wanders, and I don't blame him. All the confusion and secrets are unraveling: The sudden announcement that Frederick is not who he thinks he is; The half-sister who wants us dead; Our Viking clans ready to slay each other to gain power over the Nine Worlds. We're still enemies in dynasty but perhaps no longer in blood, and for the first time, I wish to be Frederick's blood enemy.

If our blood is the same, then there's some comfort in that. Though I cannot live knowing that the one I love and always will love cannot be mine. Frederick feels the same tension; I know from the way he speaks. He is also afraid to learn the truth. I don't blame him. There's no one to blame but the late Earl Robert Hunt. Did he deceive our minds before he died? I never knew him, so why in the name of Odin should I trust him? The only string, we both hold onto is ignorance. It is a blessing in disguise.

"We've come this far, Frederick. It has to be worth something. Robert died to protect the City of Vikings for those willing to embrace life as a true Viking. I can't say what I am. I am not a true Viking and may never be. I am just *me*. Without those weapons, we have nothing to protect ourselves with. Soon the tree will wither. She will pass me the encrypted runes. Her purpose will be done. She will leave my body and soul. The Verans will be looking for me. Lord Nourusa's strength will have grown. The Goths would want me to kill for them. You will be caught between your dynasty, your clan, and your true blood. We must get to the weapons. They are our only hope."

"Do you actually know what you're asking for?" he says. "Have you any clue what hell we'll have to go through?"

"I'd rather go through this hell with you than living in one without you."

He says nothing. Our eyes meet, and the silence stretches. The ashes from the Earl are still warm, and we've hardly grieved him before planning our escape to a place I do not dare think of. If I did, I know I'd change my mind.

"Why are you so certain we're awaiting our death sentence?" he says.

"Grethe sees us as a threat, even though we have no intention to threaten or invade or ruin the City of Vikings. Why would we? It makes no sense. Our aim is to get the weapons and protect ourselves from everyone in the Triangle. Now that the truth is out, you cannot have any remorse for turning your back on the Verans. You and I belong together. We can make a difference. Midgard is ours to rule."

"Then what?" he says. "We find the weapons, and you just expect me to kill my own clan? Nora—"

"What are you saying? Frederick my life is in danger. *Your* life is in danger—"

"I know," he says. "And believe me, I will never let anything happen to you." His words are soft, reassuring. I trust Frederick. He turns around and peeks through the slit in the wall. "Just promise me when the time comes, you will trust me."

"What do you mean?" I say.

"You'll have to make choices."

"About what?" I say. "To pave the way for our enemy?" I shake my head. Frederick looks away like I've misunderstood him. I may have, but why would he suggest such a silly thing?

"Nora, all I am asking is that you trust me," he says. "We're in this together. Yggdrasil is soon to be awakened, and you have to give the Triangle what it waits for. Do you understand that?"

I shake my head. Why is he talking about trust? He's not thinking straight.

"Grethe wants us dead. She wants nothing to do with us," I say. "That's more important right now. Why are you asking me to trust you when I need you to help me break out of here?

"'Because," says Frederick. "She can't just kill us. The city follows rules and in the short time I knew the man claiming to be my father, I am sure he saw this coming."

"What do you know that I don't?" I say. "That we have some kind of protection?"

"You always had trust issues with me, Nora," says Frederick. "For once don't question me, okay?"

"You give me too much reason, Frederick."

"You just can't tell me that you trust me. Isn't that so?"

"Yes," I say firmly, but something inside me does not quite follow his urge to press on with his sudden need to be trusted. "No, I mean. I do, of course I trust you and I will continue to do so."

"Then remember that and when the time comes do not question me because I will never, ever betray you."

"I don't know what you're getting at but okay."

"Okay?"

"Yes, okay," I say. "I'll do my best."

"You always were special, Nora."

"What's that supposed to mean?"

"It means you still don't trust me, but I have to live with that."

"I trust you, Frederick. After all, we're on this journey together."

"I know a way into the Assassin's City," says Mina. "But no way out."

"How do you know?" I look into her big, black beetle eyes and realize this creature, whether Veran or half elf or troll, has more to her than meets the eye. She may have been a spy at first, but she's redeemed herself, risking her life to protect me.

"Ashes," says Mina. "Gate past Ashes. Key in Grethe's keep."

"Not another key," I say and hold my head, thinking of the trolls of Norumb and what Frederick did to them. He had killed them all in the blaze of dark tumbling clouds. "How do you know?" She smiles widely and stares at me then Frederick. "Never mind. I don't want to know. I wish there was a way we could leave in peace without having to steal the key or break our way out. Grethe, after all, is our sister and if Frederick is right, we might need her alliance to defeat both our clans."

"She's not exactly great sister material," says Frederick. "And I'm not quite sure what she wants from us, and why she's keeping us here, but I am hopeful whatever it is, she'll change her mind and see us as her own."

"What do you suggest we do now, Frederick?"

"We sit back and wait. What other choice do we have?"

"No escape?" says Mina with a look of disappointment.

"No," I say. "I agree with Frederick; it's not wise. And if we sit our time out, she might show us mercy and set us free. We need her to grant us permission to enter this damned place."

"Grethe no kill us?"

"Who knows what potion the witch is planning," I say. "In any case, she'd have trouble killing me."

"Why is that?" says Frederick and glares at me.

"Because of Yggdrasil. She still protects me."

"Not for much longer," says Frederick coldly. He looks away.

Part of me doesn't blame him. I've caused this to happen. I'm the reason we're held captive in the cellar. Only the gods know what will become of us. We may be deported from the City of Vikings, or we may face a death sentence. We may just be lucky and get what we came for.

Two days later the cell doors open. It's early in the morning. Balder stands firmly by the door, his stare like an evil snake's bite. At first, he says nothing, as if deciding what to do with us.

"Get up! The Duchess wishes to see you. Not you, and certainly not you." He lifts his hands to stop Frederick and Mina. "Nora Hunt, follow me."

I walk out, silent like a tomb, thinking of how to rid myself of Balder and return to the cell to get Fredrick and Mina out. Then I would find Grethe, snatch the key from her, and leave this place via the Ashes. It takes me a second to realize all this is not just impossible; it's also stupid and dangerous.

I follow Balder without any resistance.

"Where exactly are you taking me?"

"To the Duchess's chamber." He stops now and looks at me. "She has fallen critically ill and wishes to speak with you." He leads me into bright daylight, and we cross the main square reaching the front of a small house. A wooden door creaks opens. We enter a dark hallway. Underneath us are cobblestones and ahead are endless arches. As we pass through the archways we reach another door. Balder unlocks it, and we climb a spiral staircase, which takes us up to an attic. From there we step into a tower room. The space is narrow and the ceiling tall and vaulted. I hold my breath and control my nerves as we walk through.

He pushes the door in front of us open. When I look past his broad shoulders I see Grethe lying in a bed in the middle of the room. The wizard is by her side. She is pale as the winter snow. Her body could be mistaken for a corpse.

"What is wrong with her?" I say. "She looks like a ghost."

"She carries the death curse," says Balder. "You need to help her, please."

A thousand expressions on my face chase each other. I've been brought here so she can live. That's the only reason I am alive. Otherwise, I would be dead.

"Come, sit, Nora," she says, her voice raspy. The wizard shadows my every move.

"I did not do this to her, I swear." I say. "If you think—"

"I know," says the wizard. "Grethe carries a spell that was forged by the Earl before he died. The Earl knew his time had come. Just like he knew Grethe must take his place and rule the City of Vikings. He also knew you'd want what is yours. The only risk was Grethe denying you access to Arres."

"He made sure before he passed away that she would give me access to Arres?" I ask.

I think of Robert before he closed his eyes and said the Viking prayer. I wanted to hold his head in my lap, but I was too weak, too shocked. He never was a father to me. I thought about the love I never received because he gave it all to Grethe—the daughter he wanted—and not the daughter that was part of a scheme forged by his estranged wife.

Before I had hope that I might have a taste of fatherly love. Now, I know I never will. He's gone and has left a question darting in my mind. The pain stabs me. The Earl wanted to die and used me to kill him. I don't blame myself; in that moment, I had no other choice. Does Grethe not see that? She needs to realize I had nothing to do with the Robert's death.

"Child," says the Wizard softly. "The only way Grethe will survive is if you redeem her."

"How can I redeem her?" I say.

"Because…" she gasps for air. "Our father wanted you to have what is yours to claim, sister." Her head moves slowly, her eyes dim.

"The weapons?"

The wizard hands me the sword. "Nora, you must take the sword and leave with your companions immediately. Promise you will do all you can to protect the city your father built. Your father wanted peace. He trusted that you would use the weapons to preserve it and not embark on war. The Earl knew—"

"I promise," I say. "But I need to get to the gate, and the—"

"You will," says Grethe. "Sister." I don't know if it's the spell or the urge to do the right thing that speaks in Grethe, but maybe she finally sees me for who I am. By the gods, I am not her enemy. I never was, and I never wanted her dead. I dislike her because she had the love of Robert. But I'm not her enemy.

The wizard gives me a glass of blue water. "Drink with the intention of redeeming your sister and with the intention of leaving this city in peace, and to protecting it from harm." I take the glass and stare at the wizard, who switches to his female side. Her deep, dark forest eyes capture me and scream inside my head.

"LEAVE AND NEVER RETURN." Like some evil spell, the words spin inside my head over and over. I drink from the glass and feel it shoot into my veins like electricity. I toss the glass to the side. I hear it break. Grethe gets out of bed, her feet carefully avoiding the glass. The miniature suns in her eyes glow, growing like she's going to explode. She glares at me just for a moment and folds her arms around me.

Her pale skin peels off like a layer of onion. The warmth from her body expels, and I want her off of me. She takes one step away. I look at her. She appears renewed almost immediately. I kept my promise and redeemed her. The spell she was under has been lifted like a veil.

"Thank you," she says and breathes in and out heavily. I am afraid she will turn around and change her mind. But something in her eyes tells me she's not that calculating and evil.

"Now, get me and my companions the hell out of here." I stalk out, and I do not turn around to watch their faces. I am afraid if I do something might change.

Walking through the Ashes, I realize it is like no other place I've ever seen before. It is ghostly and grim and different from the rest of the city. I gaze at Frederick, wondering what he and Mina did here with Knud Forkbeard. Frederick didn't give away much, but whatever it was, was good enough to convince him that he is this other person, my brother, William. The father he never knew only gave him moments, if not seconds, of his time before passing away.

How must Frederick feel? Sad? Happy? Relieved? His face is blank. Mina looks terrified, and I don't blame her. This journey is not for the faint hearted. Mina pretends she isn't, but her silence gives her away. She is clever and has been a

84

good, trusted companion. Underestimated, which makes her even more valuable. But she is not as strong as she wants to be. She is frail, and I worry for her safety.

We walk past the Ashes and into a dark meadow with long grass seeded with black and gray wildflowers. We walk on dead leaves, forging our way deeper into the field as if entering a dragon's lair. Here and there I see bugs moving through the grass, spiders building webs, and odd looking gray foxes and other creatures slinking low to the ground. I feel the bite of an insect on my arm and lightly brush it away.

When I turn my gaze to the sky, I see dark clouds moving across the horizon like death spells. While this place has peace and serenity, it also has sinister darkness. I see mountains and hills in the distance and a mauve stream bubbling across the meadow. The air is sweet and warm. I smell moist berries and earth.

We walk deeper into the woods, and the trees sway across, forming endless green arches. Then the branches and twigs break, blowing apart. The green disappears, and we walk through a heath with low shrubby bushes, forming a long neat row as if planted there. The path stops at a large metal door. Nothing unusual, just a door. We hold back, and I look at Balder, and at the wizard who digs deep into his pocket.

"Our journey ends here," he says. "You're on your own now." He hands me a long golden key.

I glare at him, not knowing what to say. My mind is full of questions. I just don't know which one to pick. They're all important. Where will this door lead us? What makes the City of Assassins so special? Are we stepping out of time or back in time? Will we find what we seek? I need a hint or direction—anything from the all-knowing wizard.

Instead, I look at him and say, "Now what?"

I turn to Frederick and Mina; they look as confused as I do. Frederick knows a lot about the Vikings, but something tells me this is no longer about Vikings. It's about the time before the Goths and the Verans became two competing clans. Viking races tied into shrewd killings to claim the land they wanted. The Nine Worlds sealed in the form of a mysterious map on my back. Encrypted runes Yggdrasil will give me that open the door to these worlds.

"Be brave," says Alfrothul Gunnlaug and smiles. "Be courageous and strong. You are about to experience an ancient world. It's a world of smokeless fire, deadly spices, and wraith shadows in the darkness. In Arres the assassins of Justus Markus rule. They kill ruthlessly those that protest, and among the Rebels you must find solace. Only they can send you back to the Triangle safely."

"And the weapons?" I say. "How do we claim them from the assassins?"

"Your destiny will lead you to the weapons forged to protect Justus Markus. The assassins have their own foretelling and may be anticipating your arrival. But don't expect sympathy from cursed killers. To them you are not even their blood yet."

"How will we know?" says Frederick? "We can't just—"

"You'll know," says Åse, with her face of tragedy as she turns to stare at us. "You will have powers in Arres that will help you. You may forget who you are but will become what you must to survive."

"What?" says Mina. "I'm afraid something terrible might happen to us."

"Not if you try to stay in disguise for as long as possible," says the Wizard. "Hide and avoid being noticed."

"I don't understand," I say. "We'll clearly stand out if we're traveling back in time."

"The memory you have now may be lost temporarily, or it may be lost forever as you enter Arres. You are after all stepping five hundred years back in time. Such travel does things to the mind. Whatever it may be, trust your instincts, follow your heart, believe in battle and your inner strength when all hope seems lost, for you are Vikings."

My heart beats faster than usual. I snatch a breath as if it was my last. This may not be a good idea after all. Time travel? I can't get my mind to believe it. Am I entering this world to seek the weapons that will preserve peace or unleash war? What are we getting ourselves into? I hope by the gods this is the right thing. I need guidance from Yggdrasil, a sign or anything that will tell me this journey will lead me to the truth I seek. I wish Helena were here with me. I need her.

I turn to look at Frederick. His eyes are desperate. I sense the same questions poking his mind. We've come this far; we must continue our journey. There's no way back.

"Is there no other method we can use to get the weapons than traveling through time—"

"No," says the Wizard. "This journey is inevitable."

"There has to be another way to protect ourselves against our enemy. To travel back in time doesn't make sense."

"Did you think getting the most powerful weapons in the world would be easy?" the wizard says and locks his eyes with mine.

"No, of course not," I say.

"You will know what to do when in the City of Assassins."

"Alfrothul," I say. "What are our chances of returning?"

"This journey will be perilous," he says. "But Ohhh! The

beauty of the unknown, the unfamiliar taste of fear and anxiety. That's the life you've chosen, dear assassin—a life you must live by. There are no guarantees. All you have is yourself and your companions."

"But the seal to protect the weapons—"

"The seal will be broken as soon as you enter the gate. The only thing that will protect you is the sword. Don't lose it. It controls all the other weapons and without it, you will not be able to use of the shield, the spear, and the axe."

I drum my fingers against the pommel nervously. This doesn't feel right. It was a bad idea, and I cannot ask Frederick and Mina to follow me into this madness.

"Stay," I say, looking at both of them. "I'll go alone."

"Between the devil and the deep blue sea…" says the wizard and laughs. "Child, you will need companions. Arres is deadlier than any other place in the universe."

"The journey calls for me and me alone," I say. "I cannot risk their lives."

"You must be out of your mind," says Frederick. "There's no way, by Odin the almighty, you're going past that gate without me."

"And me," says Mina, straightening her spine. She looks an inch or two taller.

"Behind the gate, who knows what will happen?" I say. "What if we get separated or lost. We're—"

"You will always know me," says Frederick. "You hold my heart."

"About that," says the wizard rapidly. "I advise against such practice—"

"Practice?" I say and raise my voice.

He turns and walks into the meadow, returning with a mix

of herbs in his hand. He crumbles and blends them together, and says a spell in Norse.

"Here, take this and let it enter your bodies and as it does, lay your hand at each other's chests to awaken your hearts from the others' keep." We do as the wizard says knowing this may be the last time we'll see each other as ourselves. I feel the blood in my veins go cold, and my heartbeat fades. I catch myself from falling. When I pull back my hand, I look at Frederick. He is more beautiful than ever, and I treasure this memory of him. I realize I've let go of his heart, which was locked in my chest. Could he be William, my brother? Or perhaps he'll turn into someone else as soon as we walk past the gate. Someone I may not even remember.

"My heart—" I look at the wizard.

"Is where it should be." He smiles. "It's home."

Frederick, on the other hand, looks upset and confused. Could sadness be washing over him? I wish I'd never met him because the pain is unbearable. My heart has been ripped out of his chest as mine has from his. He does not belong to me. I am nothing more than a past memory to him.

"It is done," says the Wizard. "You're safer now."

"How can I be safe?" I say. "I've been in danger from the day I was born."

"Child," says the Wizard. "Some things are worth being in danger for, and some things worth being safe for. You asked me what are the chances of your return. It will be what you decide and in Arres, you will know your friends from foes. Do not be fooled by supernatural creatures. Some are stronger than they appear while others are weaker."

"Supernatural creatures?" I look at the Wizard.

"Evil spirits and the wizards and witches of Arres."

"Right, of course." I shrug like it's normal. Of course, it is. I am about to time travel to a new world. I have no idea what I am getting myself into.

In the distance a shadow emerges. It is Grethe. She's come to say her goodbyes. I am surprised to see her. I did not expect her to come after everything that happened between us.

Grethe confronts me and by the gods she looks glorious, like a true Duchess. She shines with the sun at her back, her health strong and her mind clear. The poison and resentment she carried in her heart for me seems gone, and I am relieved she hasn't judged me for what has happened. We both lost our father. Perhaps she feels as guilty as I for not being able to save him. He gave up his life, sacrificed himself, so we could both live. Not live as enemies—live as sisters. Maybe not now but perhaps someday.

"Nora," she says, raising her long neck. "I'm sorry we could not be sisters. I'm sorry our father chose to sacrifice his life to give you what you were meant to have, the freedom you're looking for. And to you, Frederick, my brother, I—"

"Don't," he says. "You owe me nothing."

She sighs, her long eyelashes flutter. She turns her head away and stares into nothing, then she gazes into my eyes, sharp as an ice pick.

"Very well," she says. "You leave in peace and must swear to protect us if our city faces danger. We want nothing but to keep this place sealed from the Triangle. We are the last true Vikings, and give you your freedom by keeping ours and letting you enter Arres willingly to search for the weapons. I, Duchess of the City of Vikings, Grethe Lise Hunt release this burden from my keep, and grant you access to the gate that leads to Arres, taking you to the heart of the City of Assassins.

By Odin and by Thor, may you find what you seek. May you use your powers to protect our world from evil, from darkness, and from corruption."

She looks at me again then shifts her stiff gaze toward Frederick and leaves without saying another word. Following her steps are the wizard and Balder, and just before disappearing, Åse gives me a dark stare.

"May the Norse gods turn in your favor." The wizard's whispers fade with the wind.

I unclench my fist, and the key in my hand shines in the dark daylight.

"Terrified?" says Frederick.

"Petrified," I say.

"We've been on deadly journeys together before."

"The past was different."

"Why?" he says.

"I didn't know."

"Does it change anything?"

"Everything. Frederick, I am in love with you. I will always—"

He steps toward me. But I pull back.

"Don't," I say. "We don't know what we are to one another."

"Why do you care?" he says. "You knew nothing until—"

"Frederick, stop," I say. "I always had a feeling I did not belong, and I knew the world around me was different. That I was different. I never cared. I still don't, but just in case—"

I take one step closer to the door. He grabs one of my hands and one of Mina's.

"There's still time, Mina," I say.

"Nothing to go back for," says Mina. "Where Nora go. Mina go."

"Wherever you go, I will follow, Nora—"

"Don't say it, Frederick. As long as you don't say anything, it won't hurt, and I can love you a little longer."

"You may love me for a little longer, but I will love you now and forever. Love has no label or demand. It's just love."

I put a finger to his lips. I don't want to hear him speak. It hurts. Why this has happened? I do not know. I only know that it changes everything if it is the truth, and that I have to let go of him. If only I could just forget I ever loved him.

A tear drops from my heart, and I let go of him and all my fear. Inside my head, I have the courage to roar and scream. What will become of me in Arres? Will I return? What about Frederick and Mina? By the gods, I am scared for what hides behind the door. It stands before me, like a big rock.

And Frederick, I wish there was a way I could forget the pain, and about the love I carry around for him like some stray cat, searching for purpose.

The wind whispers a strange name from the past in my ear, and I understand now what I must do. My hand shakes slightly as I place the key in the keyhole and unlock the door. I push it open and sharp light welcomes us as we thread past the ashes to enter the place of the past.

II

ARRES - FIVE HUNDRED YEARS AGO

8

NORA

THE AIR IS hot, unfamiliar, and strange. I don't know where I am, and I can't seem to remember how I came to be here. A storm, there was a horrible storm, and I was with someone. Now, I am not. I am alone, and the only sight at the crack of dawn is a magnificent castle far from my reach. I force my feet to carry me beyond the endless shifting sand dunes, stepping onto crumbling rock. The taste of tangy metal is on my tongue. I lick my lips and the taste gets stronger.

I spit out blood from my lips, cracked and bleeding. Panicked, I look around. I hear something—birds cawing? Screeching eagles? Or am I imagining all this? There's an odd, heavy silence, and then I hear something. The sand trickles down the hills behind me. *How did I get here? And where are my friends that came with me?* A boy and a girl. I am certain of that or maybe not. I don't know. I might be going insane. I remember nothing and my head hurts, and my back feels like it is on fire. Hot burning coals like the scorching desert sun.

My eyes pinch as the day breaks out of the night. I look around this deadly wasteland. I have to get to the castle. I reach out my hand as if my touching it would get me there. It will not. The castle is far away. How will I ever get there? And is that where I am meant to be going? My body slips from mental exhaustion and falls into hot sand. I lie flat for a while on my back. The thoughts I carry erupt into madness. My senses feel raw. Empty. The feeling of where I am going is terrifying. I might die out here. No one is with me. Not even a horse or a camel.

Maybe someone left me out here to die. Could it be the boy and the girl? Are they real or a part of my imagination? If I don't make it to the castle soon, I'll die out here. I am certain of it. I am thirsty. There's no water, no life, nothing. I get to my feet. My body feels weak, frail. How long could I have been out here? Maybe it's just a matter of time before I die. I drift in the direction of the towers of the castle. It seems so near, and yet it is so far from my reach. What hides behind those walls? People, food. I'm starving. I don't think I have eaten in days.

Suddenly, I hear the neighing of horses from a distance growing closer. I turn around, and see two men flying in my direction. The horses have large black wings and fiery red eyes. One of the men is wearing the finest silver armor and soft leather boots. The sword to his side is wrapped in blood. It doesn't smell of salt and iron but of something else. Rotten corpses. But how do I know this? And why do I know what a rotten corpse even smells like?

The man makes his presence known, dismounting a fine dark horse. A dry desert wind billows his cape. He says nothing just stares pointedly at me. His looks are severe, evil. His breathing is heavy, and still he says absolutely nothing. He stares, now more interested and curious than before. He tilts his head slightly to the side. He's thinking something unpleasant about me. Or maybe he's trying to figure out what I am doing out here. But that can't be it. There's something else on his mind. I can tell from the way his square jaw moves from side to side.

"Titus," the man calls. "Bring this slave to the city with you." He climbs back on the horse and waits. He looks over the dunes stretching as far as he can see. His eyes are sharp, deep, and raven black. They remind me of someone. A girl I know.

The other man, Titus, appears from behind. He is tall with dark, silken skin. He grabs hold of me, tossing me over his horse like I was no more than a dead log. *Wait! I am no slave, I am...* Who am I? What is my name? I lean on the horse uncomfortably. I feel weak, and vulnerable. I wonder how long I've been out in this desert. This hot climate seems to have clouded my memory. Why are my bones not among the sun-bleached carcasses hidden in the dunes?

I straighten my spine and sit up. The heat strikes me so unexpectedly. I fall, rolling into the gold colored powder. I sit on my side, spitting out pockets of sand. No one takes notice of me. It's like I don't exist. Or worse. It's like I am some object.

"Master, where shall I bring the new slave?" he says. "Straight to one of the whorehouses on the other side of the market?"

"Bring her to Vance and ask for the same price he gave us for Normandus," he says. "Brand her neck to mark her as a slave before she tries to escape."

"But Master, Vance never took in a woman before."

"Fool, she's no woman. She's a strong *girl*. She will serve well with the other legionnaires."

"As you wish, Master." The Master flies off on his horse in the direction of the castle. His red cape flares behind him, like a dragon's tail. His trail in the sand vanishes quickly as if erased by the wind.

Titus acts a little surprised. He looks after his Master long after he's gone, his wild eyes confused. He murmurs something under his breath. Sweat trickles down his forehead. With his arm, he makes one clean swipe. The sweat climbs on his dark skin. It sits there till he yanks down his cotton sleeve. Then he peers at me. He opens his mouth and closes it as if he doesn't know what to say. I wait. Nothing.

As I turn around to get up, I feel a burning metal sting my neck. I scream.

"Quiet, slave girl," hisses Titus. "A minute and you will feel better."

"What did you just? GRRR!" I roar.

"Silence," he shushes.

"Why are you whispering?" I say. "It's not like someone can hear us."

"Someone is always listening," he says.

It takes me a while to register what he's called me. *Slave girl.* He covers my wound with a cool, jelly like substance. The pain settles but doesn't disappear. I bite my knuckles to contain the frustration that surrounds me. *What the hell has he done to me?* Did he just brand me a slave? Is that what I am? Right this moment; I cannot remember who I am and what I am doing here. I am sure I do not belong in the desert, and I am certainly no slave. I may be weak, but an inner strength is gathering, flickering like a faint flame.

"Where are you taking me?" I say. His large black bug eyes consume me like I was some delicacy. "Answer me, where are you taking me?" He ignores my question. He must be used to getting it from all the slaves he captures and brands, but I don't give in. "Answer me!" I want to lunge at him, but I feel little strength in my arms.

He laughs. His teeth are shiny white against the dark tone of his skin. His wears a beige kandura that nearly touches his pointed leather shoes. The kandura sits loosely around his lean frame. On his head sits a dark red turban.

"Where are you from, slave girl? Did you travel from the North?" He glares at me with a familiar look and grins when I fail to hide my anger. "You're nothing like anyone I've seen before except for—"

"I am no slave," I say. "I am..." I don't remember. I remember a storm, or was it a hurricane, maybe? I was with a boy and a girl. Faceless. They were with me. Is it their bones sticking out of the sand? My fear ensnarls me. Fear of what is about to happen. "Where are we going?"

"Where all the slaves go," he says. "Into the city to the main trade tribesman." He points toward the castle. "I'll give you two days to survive in there if you go on like that." He raises the corner of his lips. "Bah! Maybe one, a girl of *your* kind."

"Please," I say. "I am not a slave." I roll off the horse and onto the hot sand. I realize I am wearing a strange black suit clinging tightly to my body. I feel sharp metal razing against my thigh.

His tall frame shadows me. He crouches down and strikes me hard. The heat rises to my cheeks. Titus looks at me with a dangerous edge, panting loudly.

"Wrong," he says. "You're a slave. I've just marked your neck, and you will belong to the trade tribesman as soon as I get a good price for you."

"Please, do not sell me to a tribe member." I tremble while getting up. My hand brushes against the weapon on my side hidden under my clothes. An urge rises inside me to draw it out and slice it against his neck, but I don't.

"You should be grateful. A pretty girl like you could easily fetch seventy-five dinars in the brothels inside the city for one night. Why the Master didn't order me to sell you to one of the whorehouses I cannot say. He might be in a good mood. He's never merciful. You must have done something right in your previous life to be this lucky. Vance is fair to his slaves and even feeds them occasionally. Bah! With your kind I'm not sure what he will say."

When he sees my horror, he just shakes his head and spits out the dry bark he's been chewing on while eyeing me carefully. He grabs a fistful of my hair and brings me close, sniffing me like a dog.

"But I—"

"Maybe even eighty dinars," he whispers. "That silver hair of yours–bah! The Master didn't see you properly. Why else would he send you straight to the tribesman? Quaint girl like you. Your looks alone are worth more than your dirty, curious mouth. Bah!" He goes on but after a while, I fail to register all the words he says. He talks fast about things that are unknown to me.

He tosses me back onto the horse. I feel my body weakening as I struggle to sit up straight. I feel a pull when the horse sets off toward the castle. I quickly grab hold of Titus's small waist. The horse races over the sand dunes, its wings beautifully spread out. The hot desert air burns my eyes and dry lips. The crumbs of sand scrub my skin.

What could have been hours of travel, we reach within

minutes. We are at the large port separating the deadly desert from the tall fortress walls. Nothing about this castle, the man called Titus, or the desert is familiar to me. It all feels new and alien. It doesn't help that my memory is weak. I don't even know if I've suffered from any injury, or battle. I have no wounds, except for the one on my neck. All I know is I am here for a reason, but what reason? I cannot remember. I try hard, but nothing comes up.

When the port opens, I see people moving. Men, women, and children. They wear long, colorful, cloaks, tunics, khaki trousers, and oversized cotton hats. Some wear turbans and others pointed leather hats. A tall man passes by me. He wears baggy pants caught in at the ankles, a short tunic, and velvet waistcoat with tiny mirrors. On his head sits a small round hat. His black long locks spills down his back like a curtain. In his right hand, he holds a long silver staff, with a bird head handle.

Everyone is in a rush, hobbling across cobblestones, with sacks of flour and spices hanging from donkeys, chariots, and other means of primitive transport, carrying jars of pickles, jam, and crates and barrels of drinks. Their skin is dark and leathery, their eyes beetle black.

I get off the horse and walk inside the main square with Titus by my side. I let my eyes wander. Nothing feels familiar. The air is warm and filled with zings, zests, and odd flavors: cinnamon, cardamom, citrus, coffee beans, and cocoa. We walk straight into a market with colorful oil lamps, leather goods, and silk fabric hanging from the market rails. Traces of golden sand trail behind us from the main courtyard, and Titus ties the neighing horse to a pillar and tells me to wait while he disappears behind curtains in the bazar.

On the other side of the market, thick smoke taints the air. Spirals of black rise into the sky and behind it I see something poking out. Something beautiful. A distantly familiar face of a boy smiles at me. He looks happy as if he knows me. He's tall and broad shouldered, his face pale underneath his hooded cloak. I think I do know him from somewhere, but I cannot make out from where. He keeps looking and smiling, his nose straight, cheeks high, and lips large and full. His deep gaze arrests me, and that's when I find myself gazing into the familiar blue ocean in his eyes. I know him; his name is—

"That's her. Fresh from the reef," says Titus.

He appears from the curtain, startling me and I look away. Slowly, I crane my neck, and the boy is no longer in sight. Titus stares at me, then at a short fat man at his side. That must be the trade tribesman, Vance. He's just tall enough to reach Titus's hip. He carries a dark look in his eyes. He zips his eyes up and down at me, driving his short round finger along my legs.

"How much?"

"Titus hands him a piece of paper." Vance tears it into pieces.

"Tell Xavi he's asking for too much for a slave girl of her kind. We can fetch plenty of other stronger men from the other side of the desert reef. We're not short of deserters. They don't have to be pretty. The Northern barbarians don't care much about looks."

"She's strong enough, Vance, and she's not missing any body parts. She's a bit too skinny maybe, but she's solid. Her hair alone is worth a fortune."

The short fat man can't reach my hair from where he stands, so he grabs a stool from the market, jumps up, and drives his little thick hands through my matted hair.

"Beautiful." He smells thick strands, and tosses it to the side.

"Don't touch me you filthy—" Another slap, this time harder. The blood runs from my nose. I feel a shot of anger rise. My fingers drum against the weapon I am hiding inside my clothes, but my courage lacks. Or is it my strength that's missing? I feel my hand fall limp. I am weak and unable to muster nerves to fight back and defend myself. I wasn't always this pathetic; I know because my mind tells me to do something, anything.

"Fiery too," he says and laughs. "She'll cause trouble I can tell. A fighter, huh?"

"Vance, you're not getting a slave like her again. She's one of a kind." Titus wipes the blood from his hand. "Sell her to the barbarians and let them sort her out."

"Nah!" he says. "I can make more money with her in the brothels."

"Brothels? Bah! Now I understand the Master," says Titus. "He said she's a strong girl and will serve the legionnaires. She's not brothel material."

"Why not?" says Vance hoarsely. "You'd like that wouldn't you, pretty slave girl?" He takes out a dagger and runs it against my other thigh where my sword is hidden. But I am not afraid. He can sense it. The anger in my eyes is visible.

"They need fighters. Soldiers in their army to control the growing rebel group of savage monsters. Hand her to them. The assassins will straighten her out."

"You want to be among the assassins, huh?" yells Vance. He glares at me.

"Assassins?" I murmur. An instinct buried deep inside me recognizes the word as if it's connected to me. "Who are they?"

"You may never know," he says. "I'll make sure you end up in the dirtiest little whorehouse—" Vance chortles. The saggy skin from his chin moves as if it was dough.

"Bah, you terrible man, Vance!" Titus says. "Sell her to who you like, just pay me my dinars so I can get out of your sight."

"Would you like to be sold to the assassins?" he says and circles around me like an annoying fly. "They'll carve you up and eat your insides raw if you go on like this. They're savages. Ha! Who would have thought the Emperor would make those thugs host of his land to fight off the Rebels?"

"Vance, do we have a deal?" says Titus impatiently.

I feel an urge to do something, defy him, or tell him off again. Something that will make him angry enough to take me to the assassins. But what should I do? Without thinking I squat and take a fistful of dirt and throw it onto Vance's face. He screams and swears, and I push my knee against his hard, round belly. My knee jolts back as if hitting a soft surface, but I keep my balance, like I've done this before. I am not afraid. I can fight. I am strong.

"That's enough!" Titus grabs me hard by the arm and throws me to the ground, kicking dirt in my eyes. I roll over and quickly scramble to my feet. "You are too much trouble." Just as he yanks me away, Vance motions for us to stop and whispers something into Titus's ear, nodding and smiling mischievously, like he's made a deal with the devil. Titus quickly snatches the small clinging sack from Vance's fist. He glares at me one last time.

"They'll sort you out, don't worry pretty slave girl." He leaves without turning around and for a moment, I feel relieved. He must have sold me for a good price.

From the shadows two small and burly women emerge and grab me by the arms, dragging me inside a dank chamber. One of them holds a large butcher knife covered in blood, and I cannot take my eyes off of it as the golden soil underneath her feet eagerly gulps in the dark shade. Vance steps into the room and looks at the women.

"Don't just stand there. Clean her up then tie her up. Make sure she doesn't escape. Tomorrow morning I'll bring her to the assassins' ground." He glares at me, his eyes tawny and small. "You've asked for it, dumb girl. By the Emperor Justus Markus, ruler of Arres, the holy city ruled by the ruthless and merciless assassins, you, slave girl with silver hair, shall be brought before them, and they shall give me a good price for your warm blood before turning it cold." He cackles, his belly bouncing as he walks out.

"Come here!" the woman pulls my arm. "Let's get the filth off." She takes a bucket and cloths.

"Take off your clothes." says the other woman.

I hear my heart drum in my ears. I keep my hands from using the weapon I carry. I need to get to the assassins and I hope I've made the right decision.

9

FREDERICK

SHE IS ALIVE. By the gods, Nora is alive. I pace the floor nervously, thinking how on earth I can free her from the tribesman's claws. He'll want to sell her. They always sell the slaves they get from the desert within hours so they don't have to feed them. Nora, a slave. I can't imagine what she must have gone through. She looked distracted, nervous. And she looked at me as if she didn't know me. But it is Nora. No mistake there.

"She's finally here," I say and look at Mina. She appears from the room, looking happy. One month in Arres and finally a sign of happiness on her face. "I just saw her entering the city."

"Nora, okay?" asks Mina desperately.

"I think so," I say. "She may not be herself coming from whatever time laps before ending up in the desert. She wasn't as lucky as we were, and I suspect she's lost her memory just like the old Wizard warned."

"We must get Nora." The concern in Mina's eyes is visible.

"It's not going to be easy. We need to think this through first. I will keep an eye on the tribesman. He is going to sell her in the morning."

"Nora, slave?"

"Yes." I sigh. "She might have suffered trauma. Her eyes were hollow and dark. Her body weak but not broken. She will be okay; she's strong and will know what to do."

"Why Nora no come to you?"

"She wasn't herself. She wasn't smiling or happy to see me. She was questioning who I was. If she'd recognized me, I'm sure she'd have found a way to cut lose and find us."

"Nora, no memory."

"Yes. That's the only explanation. I do believe she felt something when she saw me because she noticed me. She must be confused."

Mina and I have been hiding inside the city for nearly one month. We were lucky we didn't end up slaves. They must have caught Nora just outside the desert reef, the only point of life before entering the Sand Valley of Death.

"What we do, Frederick?" Mina is nervous and so am I. It's going to be more dangerous than I imagined to free her.

"I used my heightened senses and overheard the tribesman's wish to sell her to the assassins. He's no fool. He knows they pay a better price for strong slaves. The brothels and whorehouses are lucky. Nora would kill them in a matter of seconds if they were to take her there."

"Why tribesman take Nora to assassins? Kill them too. Assassins dead. Nora hold Sword. Frederick? Frederick" She yanks my cape hard like a desperate child.

"He has to if he wants to cover his cost for buying her," I say. "Mina, I need your help to keep a watch on the tribesman's house. We'll follow him when he brings Nora to the assassins."

Mina looks confused. "Tribesman dumb. Might change

mind. Sell Nora to housekeeping."

"He wouldn't. Nora doesn't look like a typical slave girl, ready to cook meals and keep a master's house clean."

"Nora fight with tribesman, kill him?"

"I am convinced she cannot remember anything. Maybe that's a good thing, as she will resist less. When we landed in that horse dung, I, too, had a minor memory loss but recovered swiftly. You remember that don't you, Mina? If Nora suffers memory loss, she will recover. She has to or else we might have a problem getting the weapons from the assassins."

Mina's eyes grow narrow. I can almost see what she's thinking. Nora is defiant. She always was. She has an edge about her that says, *"I'm not taking crap from anyone."* That's what drew me to her when I first saw her—her rawness. Her stubbornness and willingness no matter what the odds are. Mina sees that too, and I am sure so did the tribesman. They are fighters, strong men. Hardly ever any women are brought and bringing Nora will raise questions. I'm not sure if that's a good thing. We want to go unnoticed for as long as we can and find the Rebels to get out of Arres with the weapons.

"You no worry," says Mina and stares at me as if she understands what's going through my mind, She's bound to both me and to Nora, the wonderful creature that she is. She's shown her loyalty, which gives her purpose. She stares at me with her large beetle eyes. "We get to Nora. If not, Nora come to us."

"Don't do anything that will blow our cover, Mina. We've kept quiet and safe from the eyes of the curious crowds in the city."

"Nora must come."

"She will; she's smart," I say. "I've made eye contact with her, and she will come looking for me. I can feel it."

My body lies restless all night. I want to go to the tribesman's house to see Nora again. I could say that I want to buy her, but I don't have the money, and he will suspect something if I show up unannounced. It would do more harm than good. I wish I had the power of manipulation in Arres. I feel useless.

He is trying to get rid of Nora as quickly as possible to avoid caring for a deeply troubled slave girl. That's what she is in his eyes. He's the key trader of Arres, and all slaves that come from the desert pass through him, except for the ones that go straight to the infamous brothels.

For weeks, I've kept watch on people and events in the City of Assassins. I may not be the great Rognvald Viking with black magic, but I have other powers that allow me to hear, see, and smell things that go unnoticed by others.

The Emperor's bloodthirsty desert huntsmen leave the castle grounds freely while all other citizens need permission. How we shall ever return to the Triangle, I have no clue. We are relying on finding the Rebels to get us back. I hear people speak of them, but have not seen a sign of them.

It is our good fortune that Mina and I landed inside the city walls. The Triangle doesn't even exist in this world, but in Arres I have supernatural strength, and it is all we need to get by. I have powers and a strength I am getting to know, which is the only reason we have survived the past weeks. I hear danger lurking, people whispering, and scents and smells from miles away.

The moment we walked through that door leaving the City of Vikings a heavy storm swept me away. Nora was suddenly far from my reach. I became unconscious and when I opened my eyes, I was lying next to horse dung with Mina by my side.

Everything was different just as the wizard had predicted. The thick air is perfumed with deadly spices. The people are ruthless. Arrians kill without guilt, without hesitation. I've seen traders kill young children for stealing dry fruits from the market.

Who would have known an ancient world like Arres existed between time lapses? Who would ever have imagined the assassin weapons are kept in the past? Without a doubt, this mission will be difficult. Can we rely on the mysterious rebels? I don't want to be trapped here among these uncivilized people. They lack all morality, ethics, and manners and are no different to animals. We need the weapons fast. I pray to the gods the assassins accept the trade and take in Nora.

I've heard plenty rumors. The Arrians gossip about the assassins. They call them ruthless, merciless barbarians from the North. They kill people in the most unimaginable ways—carving up the bodies of those who dare resist against the rules of the Emperor. Beheaded bodies are hung on stakes and left to rot in the desert. Animals eat their raw flesh. Heads of men, women, and children are on spikes and countless dry skulls and bones decorate the tall walls of the castle grounds. I've seen the assassins from the deserted tower. Their watch and security is weak. They know anyone entering their territory will face a horrible death. No one dares or is foolish enough, except us.

It is hard to believe we descend from the assassins. For five hundred years, our line was unbroken, almost sacred. We've had to keep the one secret we are now ironically missioned to reveal—the weapons. They carry our legacy. We have to succeed. In the time I've been in Arres with Mina gathering information, I have not heard people speak or mention much about the weapons. That's a good sign. In a city like this, everyone gossips. They talk mainly about the Emperor and his apparent strength visible in the brutal army he keeps controlled by the barbarians from the North aka. The assassins.

According to legend the assassins forged four magnificent weapons to empower their greatness: The assassin sword, which Nora was given, slays anything by the power of magic, and a weapon that enlarges and reduces to combat any size and shape of enemy; A powerful shield, forged with a secret layer of protection against attacks. If faced with an army of thousands of men, if one has the shield one can walk unharmed through any battle; A spear that never misses its target, no matter how far the distance and how large or small the object aimed at; And an axe with a blade so sharp, it cuts through anything, just like Thor's hammer.

I've only read ancient tales about the weapons. After Ragnarok, the terrible war that destroyed the world of the past, the Triangle came together Peace was sworn among the clans. War was frowned upon. When the Verans took control, the transition led to a silent shift in power, and the Goths remained but only as a submissive entity, a threat. They've been trying to regain power ever since.

Should Nora fail, everything will be lost. Lord Nourusa will take the throne of Midgard, and the Verans will become stronger. They saw this coming. War will be a reality. The clan who holds supreme power will not want to give it up. They outsmarted everyone long before the weapons were in question. The summoning of the old Viking lord, Nourusa, who is powerful and cruel, makes me question my clan.

Soon Nourusa will be strong enough to wipe out those he

considers a threat. He will be hard to defeat, even with Magnus as leader. Rumor has it Magnus holds Odin's lost eye, and it sees everything. If that's true, then he has access to a great source of wisdom. Magnus strikes me as a reasonable man and not someone that wants war. He's also a man of ethics and rules. He'd prepare Jarls to chase us as soon as he gets news of our return. I have a feeling he's up to something. He'd know from Odin's eye what we plan to do.

Should Nourusa come to rule, the world will fall into darkness and eternal suffering. Life in the Triangle will become a horror. Everyone will be a slave to the dark lord. The East, where Nora grew up, will no longer exist. Everything will disappear, the green forests and meadows. The clear blue sky will bleed.

I am not sure how to feel about my own misfortune—my *crisis,* which I have suppressed. Ever since I learned that I might not be a Veran but of Goth descent, I've been living in a shadow. Suddenly, all I thought I was might no longer be. Am I someone's brother? Someone's son? Lord Wilhelm who raised me as his own, is he not my father? He taught me everything about our past as Vikings. Tommy was never cut out to do what he had in mind. I never questioned why I was different. Could Nora really be my sister? I don't want to believe it. But I may have to fake it, to get as far as I can on this journey.

I am not sure if I can stand up to the clan that raised me as their son and step away as leader from my dynasty. I can't deceive the ones that trust me the most. How can I stop loving the girl I cannot live without? The girl who reminds me of who I am—a Viking warrior. I'd rather run away than face the demons. Nora and I will become outlaws and fugitives when we return. We will not submit ourselves to the Triangle's cruel rulers.

I've traveled to the City of Assassins to take what belongs to us. I am learning new things about the assassins, and it is not pretty. Their grim past of killings, power, and greed is what lies hidden in the veins of our clans who strive to achieve absolute power.

I've heard the story countless times from the Arrians. It all began when the Emperor Justus Markus, took in three warriors that came from the North. He offered them everything they wanted in return for their sworn loyalty to protect his lands that faced the threat of the Rebels—a threat that has been growing. Arrians speak of them as if they were inhuman and odd creatures. With their fearless and mighty powers, the three warriors brutally killed some of the Rebels, those posing a threat to the Emperor and his kingdom. They forged the most powerful weapons and keep control of the City of Assassins, the thriving desert capital.

Despite the assassin's known brutality, inside and outside the castle walls the rebellion group is growing. They are becoming a greater threat to Arres every day. They call themselves Freedom Seekers. Justus Markus will have none of it. He makes all the rules in his desert kingdoms. There's a water supply from a large well on the rocky mountain peak, known as the Eternity Well. The water feeds the city. An eastern tribe brings animals and other trades into the castle from beyond the reef on flying horses. But that's not it; there's something more.

Something supernatural is looming. I can't explain it, but I sense it. It may not be obvious, and if the Emperor was a powerful magician or had a source of magic, then why raise and train an army to spellbind the assassins? Why not rule solely. Build his own army? He needs something from the assassins. They might be the source that feeds the city. Evil perhaps? Maybe the Emperor needs the assassins to fend off the Rebels.

They are breeding a legion of brutal soldiers, and the tribesman is taking Nora there to join them. The training is tough and has killed eight out of ten trainees. It's incredible what I've learned in one month while snooping around with Mina. People chatter. The women in corners of the bazaars whisper. The salesmen gossip with their customers. Even the children shout out things to one another. I've picked up everything with my raw new senses. Mina also keeps her eyes and ears open. Together, we've made it this far. Now that Nora is here, it's time we strike our target.

Whenever the desert wind blows, Mina knows. Nothing escapes her, and I've learned to follow her lead. The psychic strength I have gained in Arres has given us cover. Every time I sense someone approaching, I use my powers to escape quicker than the wind. From our appearances, we're obviously not locals and certainly not slaves. In any case, it has kept us safe. We've gotten by inside the city surviving without being questioned because we've kept hidden in a secret place, fallen and deserted behind the bazaars that no one cares much for.

Black magic cannot be used in Arres, as only some spells work in the ancient world. I've discovered that I have enormous strength in this world. I can walk and run faster than average. My ability to sense things is much stronger. The other day at the bazar, I picked up a ceramic pot with pickles and crushed it into dust. I escaped the scene before the trader could turn around. I didn't mean for it to happen. It just did.

In the Triangle, my powers were not as strong; I could barely lift off the ground or crush things with one hand. Nora, on the other hand, had something special, and I wonder what powers she is hiding in Arres. I fear for her. Yggdrasil will soon spread her roots to the Nine Worlds. Nora needs to be prepared for receiving the runes.

I remember when I first saw Nora at Dock Harbor, those bright green eyes. She hid her strengths and abilities. She was like a child growing up among lions to become a lioness. Stronger, better, faster than any of us. She was driven by her conviction and determination to find Robert Hunt, the man who failed her. She deserved better. And I've sworn to myself I will love her and protect her until I die.

Yet Nora is always a step ahead of me. She's saved me countless times. I feel for her and what she's been through and is still going through. Just like Nora, I feel my life was built on a lie, and it is devastating. I am Lord Wilhelm's most precious asset. I will seek justice when I return to the Triangle. Well, if I return from this cursed city.

The dry wind blows from the small window in the dark hole where Mina and I still hide, but the wind doesn't smell of rock or sand or even rotten corpses. It smells tangy and sharp. Familiar. Wild flowers. Just as I shift to my side, I feel the pointed edge of the steel against my neck, moving slowly and drawing a fine line of blood.

"If you move, I'll cut through the pulse in your throat."

There's no mistake, and even in the darkness, I see those beautiful green eyes glow. I knew she'd come seeking me; she is, after all, a Viking assassin.

10

NORA

THE HAIR AT the back of my neck rises when I hear them whisper of the creatures that haunt the desert outside the walls. They speak of rare breeds of creatures that carry a dead spirit and eat women, men, and children alive to gain possession of their mortal souls. I've never laid eyes on one as far as I can remember from the time I spent in the desert. But the stories they tell alone are enough to evoke nightmares. These creatures have claws, sharp fangs, and have the ability to talk. They are the reason the assassins are building an army. The creatures are known as Rebels.

From the curtain slit, Vance's enormous shadow appears. He moves heavily across the room. I see him take off his leather gloves, which he hands to one of the women that tied me up at the back chamber, where I've been sitting for hours trying to remember anything about who I am and how I came to be here. But I still remember nothing.

Vance cracks his fingers and sighs as their whispers dim with the fading candles on the table. His face is puffy and the demons are dancing in the darkness of his eyes. He looks worried, like he's witnessed some terrible crime. The woman puts a hand on his shoulder.

"What did they do to them?" She speaks in a low voice as I continue to listen in. I realize that I hear them speak as if they were standing right next to me. At this distance, I shouldn't be able to hear them at all. I sharpen my focus and hear Vance reply.

"They buried them, Petra. Buried all four of them alive in the desert." He wipes the sweat from his forehead. I see his bloodshot eyes.

"I helped dig their graves before closing the stone coffins to muffle their screams. They were all buried alive."

Cold shivers run down my spine. How can anyone be so heartless? I don't want to listen in, but I can't turn off the volume, which only seems to be amplifying inside my head. There's no door between us, only a thin, flimsy curtain with a slit long enough to see some of their expressions and movements. I realize I am not ordinary. But what is ordinary in a damned place like this?

The woman covers her mouth with her hands and steps back. She says nothing. Vance goes on, his gaze locked on to the dirt underneath him.

"The Emperor's will is the will of the sky god, Zohra, who chose him as ruler of this holy land and higher King of the kingdom of Arres. The god gave him a vision he still keeps secret from the Arrians. This vision must be the reason for his demonic acts. I saw him with my own eyes as he held his sword across the newborn necks of his daughters. He could not do it. We, the tribesmen know the desert. We were asked to bury his daughters, and so we did. I wish for no one to ever commit such a crime."

"You had no choice. Had you not done it—" The woman stops. She clasps her hands over her head and says in a muffled voice, "It might have been all of us in those stone coffins."

"Indeed!" says Vance. "Or it would have been my head on a silver plate. The Emperor is as merciless as the barbarians."

"But why bury them alive?" she says. "Why not—"

"Because they carry imperial blood, every single one of them. The Emperor wants no one to find out he has daughters. It will create an outrage. What if the Rebels find out?" He pauses, sucking in the air. "Should anyone find the girls they'd be as tempted as we were to keep them alive. They were not just newborns, they were angels. Beautiful souls. No one can kill such divine splendor. Burying them alive was the only choice."

"How long will the Emperor go on for?"

"Until he gets what he wants—a male heir. The Emperor killed his defiant milk-brother with his bare hands. For that he became Emperor of this holy land, and it is the only thing he cares about. Getting four daughters buried while there is still breath in their lungs is nothing to him." Vance sighs, his shoulders slump.

"A male heir is not written in the stars for the Emperor. When will he realize that this madness must end? The Rebels will not stop until he does."

"We must forget this ever happened." Vance looks up. "How's the slave girl?" he whispers. "Did you feed her anything? I don't want her to die."

"No, we've let the savage be. She scares me." Her eyes widen. "I never saw a slave possess what she does. She—"

"Speak woman, why?"

"We cleaned her, as we could. She refused to remove all of her clothes. Instead, we braided her wild hair and saw

118

something raised in black ink on her back, something strange, mythical." There's a long pause. "It moved beneath her skin like a lost animal carefully snaking its way through her body."

"What are you talking about? Are you hallucinating again? Did you smoke—"

The woman nudges her elbow at him "Obscene man! What are you accusing me for? I clean your home, look after the slaves you bring, tolerate your mistresses."

He catches his breath, and coughs out pockets of air. He straightens and stands pouring himself a glass of water from the ceramic jug. "No need to get angry, woman."

"Whatever that girl is, get rid of her!"

"Tomorrow, I will bring her to the assassins. They will decide her fate."

"That may be," says the woman. "I was surprised when you wanted to keep her in the house and not in the stables with the other slaves. I fear she's strong for a girl her age; strong enough to cut loose and slit our throats in our sleep. I see murder in her eyes. She's lethal, Vance, maybe even evil. She could be a witch. She looks nothing like us. Have you thought about it?"

"Don't overact, woman. She's is no sorceress or witch. The girl is special," he answers hastily. "I sense something in her. I believe the assassins will take a liking to her."

"That thing moved across her back like a snake. It was alive. I'm telling you the girl is a witch or cursed. Evil is lurking inside her, and it wants out."

"Petra, listen to me! The girl is branded slave. She's been in the desert. She's frail, broken, and starved. She couldn't even kill a desert deathstalker if she wanted to; that's how weak she is." He pauses. "She might eat it instead. When this girl is fed and strong, that's when I'd start to be afraid. I see determination in her eyes, and if I see it, the barbarians will too. They'll pay me any price I demand."

"Easy for you to say. You see her with dinars in mind. I see her as the devils do."

"After tomorrow we don't have to worry about her any more. She'll be gone."

He blows out the candle, and they leave the room. I close my eyes and try to remember what it is about the word assassin that calls to me. But my memories are empty. Then I recall the blue-eyed boy from the market this morning. Why did he look at me like he knows me? I have to find out. He can't be far from the other side of the market. If I get loose, I could track him easily with my heightened senses. He carries a sweet smell of vanilla and cinnamon.

At the back of the chair, my hands are tied but not very well. They underestimated me and speak in hushed voices as if I wasn't even here. Peasants. I may look a little pale and frail after surviving the desert, but I am still determined to get out of here and find out who that boy was. He must know something, the way he looked at me. He knows me. He has to. Is he the one that accompanied me on my journey? But if that's the truth, why didn't he come for me?

I continue to wiggle my hands. The rope burns against my wrists in the damp and clammy room. After a while, I feel the rope soften as the dripping sweat from my wrists loosens the knots. After several attempts, I untie the rope and pull my arms out from behind the chair and rise slowly without making a sound. I rub my burning mauve wrists. I notice a strange tattoo and plastic device plastered on my inner arm. It glows red and shows a message, which fades just as I look at it. What is this thing? It looks complicated.

The tattoo appears to be a symbol. I examine the shape and color. I am sure it's meaningful. A large eagle is marked on my arm. It's beautiful, powerful. I see the image of the woman who placed the plastic device on my wrist. The memory is weak. But I recall her sharp voice. The look in her eyes was unusual. Purple. There's something else. Inside my wrist a sharp metal is poking out. I received it from a dying woman. The image in my head appears and disappears so suddenly. No names and no clear faces. Not even a single clue what it all means. What tribe do I belong to? At least I know now I am no slave. I came here with someone. I need to get to the assassins.

I can't believe they were just going to leave me here in this small dark hole tied to a chair all night. I thought Titus said Vance was kind to his slaves. Doesn't seem a kind thing to do. He is also a child murderer. He just buried four babies in the desert. Maybe that's what is considered kind in this place.

Quickly, I slide against the wall and effortlessly carry my body across the red dusty ground in the room where Vance and the woman sit having their disturbing conversation. As I move, I realize I have done this before. I am good at this. A feeling inside me tells me to use the weapon I carry to slit Vance's throat and escape. But if I did that, where would I go? I have no purpose. I have to seek some answers, and I am sure the boy from the market can help me.

The Emperor of this kingdom sounds insane, murdering his own children just to get a male heir. And Vance did the dirty job for him. What a coward. How can he be an Emperor? I'd like to cut off his head. Bastard. If only I could. I believe Vance will show me no mercy if he's asked to do the same to me. I have to get out of here fast. Vance is a greedy bastard, but his wife, Petra, is smart and senses things. Not smart enough though. She left me in the room, loosely tied. But she picked up on the thing I've been feeling on my back, raising and burning. What is it?

I touch my shoulder blade. I feel something sticking out of my back. Could it be the branches of a tree making those creaking sounds? Twigs and a trunk. Is my body intertwined with a... living, breathing tree? What am I? What is that damned thing growing on me, and why has it latched itself to me? I have to find out.

I push the main door open, thinking it can't be this easy. There's nothing to hold me back from escaping, although I can't see myself getting far. The port that leads back out to the desert is a death wish and impossible to cross as it is filled with guards holding spears and arrows. Inside these walls, I can't hide or survive for long before they find me, a branded slave with silver hair. Still, I make my way out and realize I have to be fast and stay out of trouble and be wise enough to return before dawn.

The streets are empty and the market silent. I am in some strange quarter of the city. I walk, crossing a sandy road that leads me opposite the house in which I was kept. I wander from alley to alley. I have no idea where I am going. I follow my senses. In front of me, I see an empty building hidden behind some crumbling clay houses stacked up at the front of the dirt path. The air is cool and tainted with a spicy smell and other unfamiliar herbs. I try not to sneeze. I look up, holding my breath in the dead of the night. Not a single soul is visible except one. It is silent like a catacomb.

I see the shadow of a small creature move. Her large black

eyes poke me, as if saying, *"Follow me. This way."* She's tiny and looks peculiar, nothing like the natives. I follow her up a rundown stairwell that never seems to end. Her breath is loud and her steps clumsy. The dust falls from above like glitter. That's when I sneeze out loud. She stops and peeks through the many broken walls to find my eyes.

"Wait!" I say. "Who are you?" She runs up, stomping her feet. I don't move. This could be a trap. What do I know about this place? I recall nothing except that I may belong to a tribe. I once met a woman with purple eyes. A dying woman gave me a weapon. I was traveling with a boy and a girl. I don't even know my own name. Eagerly, I climb the stairs, believing this girl may have the answers to what I seek or just any answer.

Inside the crumbling wall, I see a small opening, a hiding place. It is raven black and eerie. But I force myself to climb in. I believe the girl went in there, though I cannot hear her steps anymore. The night is silent again.

I see nothing as I navigate my way further in. I feel the sword's blade tied against my thigh. It is illuminating. It touches my cold skin and feels sharp. I stretch out my hand, and the sword spins into my palm where it stays firmly. The sword knows me. It reacts to my calling. I clutch my fingers around the pommel. I remember holding this sword. I've killed someone with it and still smell the blood that washed its steel.

A shadow lies ahead of me. I step toward it and place the tip of my sword on the pulsing neck of a man. I can't see too well, and I draw the tip closer to his throat. When he turns, I recognize those blue eyes.

"If you move, I'll cut through the pulse in your throat," I say. He doesn't move at first and holds his breath. "Who are you?"

There is excitement in his eyes. At first I can't figure it out. Is he not afraid of dying? I know him from somewhere. He looks familiar. Among all the faces I've seen his feels different. I've touched him, felt the heat if his body, the kiss drawn from his lips.

"I knew you would come," he says. "Don't you remember? It's me, your brother, William." The sword drops from my hand and clacks to the floor. I see his features clearly now, resembling my own: a mop of blond hair, striking blue eyes, soft milky skin. In the dim room, I notice the tattoo on his wrist. It is like mine. A memory inside my head surfaces. I remember him, but his name is not William. He cannot be my brother. He is more than that to me.

"Don't lie to me," I say. "Tell me the truth, or I will not hesitate to kill you." I pick up my weapon and place it an inch from his face.

He stands up, the sharp blade pointing at him. "Do it!" he dares me. "Kill me, your own flesh and blood." I press the sword against his throat, drawing a thicker line.

"You are not my flesh and blood," I say. The sword sits tight in my hand, urging me to strike it against his beautiful throat, and just as I am about to, I hear a soft voice behind me speak.

"Please, no kill." It's the little creature I followed here. "Frederick..."

That's his name, Frederick. I remember it, although the memory is distant. Why don't I remember him clearly? I stare at the creature. Maybe she's that girl that came with me? She is also familiar. Could they be the two travelers that were with me? They must be or else I would have been dead.

"Frederick?" I say. "Is that your name?"

"Nora, I'll tell you everything," he says and leans in close. I lower my sword and peer at him.

"What did you call me?"

"Nora. That's your name." he says.

A part of me wants to fall into the shadows of the room and disappear for I am dreading what he is about to say next. When I hear him say my name I know he's right

"I hope you will remember what I am about to tell you."

After I leave the dwelling, I sneak back into Vance's home. My mind buzzes with everything that was said. I must to be a fool to believe what he told me: the assassin weapons, the death of Robert, two Viking clans hunting us. We've travelled five hundred years back in time? My mind can't even begin to conceive that.

Somewhere deep inside myself, I know he speaks the truth. I have no choice but to believe him. How else do I explain the plastic chip on my wrist, the sword clinging to my side, and the symbols on both of our wrists. Then there is the raised tattoo on my back. It is alive and moves across my spine spreading like a disease through my body.

He explains that I am the carrier of the map of the nine Viking worlds, and that I will receive the runes that unlock these realms. He knows so much. It can't be a story he's spinning. I admit some of the things he said, were familiar. But something is missing. He's not my brother. I don't see him in my memory that way. He is someone else. He is Frederick.

I swing my arm back to touch my back. I still feel whatever that woman Petra saw. It is still snaking around. It scared her. I scared her. She believes I am evil, a witch. Am I? Is that why Vance decided to bring me to the assassins? Xavi, Titus's Master saw something in me. He knew I was not a good fit for the brothels and whorehouses.

I feel trapped between events happening around me. Most of all I'm afraid of that growing tree on my back getting heavier. I'm carrying it for a reason. Or is it carrying me? I tiptoe back to the room in which I was kept. The rope lies on the floor where I left it. I tie it back on my hands, using my mouth to pull the twine tight together. I don't think they will suspect anything. As I sit on the chair, I get a feeling I've been in far more dangerous situations. I wish I could remember them.

I don't get any sleep. At dawn Vance comes to get me. He unties my hands and pulls me up. He hands me a glass of water. I thank him and show no resistance. He looks surprised but says nothing. Before we leave he ties my hands again. We pass the morning stillness of the markets, still sound asleep. We stride up a steep road and reach a large open space behind the walls with trees, wells, fountains, and green flower gardens. It's hard to imagine how this city, hidden behind castle walls, exists and flourishes in the middle of a desert.

All the things my assumed brother, William, said to me still flicker through my mind like an eternal burning candle. I play along hoping the answers I seek will come. Hoping the assassins will recognize something in me. I know I shouldn't expect much. So far I've not been terribly ill treated, except for the mark on my neck that's branded me a slave. When I touch my neck, the wound is no longer there. It has vanished, as if the branding never happened. Something strange is happening to me. I feel the knot in my stomach tighten. Should I be grateful for my situation? Could matters have been worse? I might have been sold to a whorehouse.

Slave. The word sounds so unfamiliar, and yet I feel as if it has relevance to how I used to feel about myself. I was no slave; *William* confirmed that. What he told me didn't surprise me much. I do carry a sword that has powers; it did light up the dark room where he was hiding with the little creature, Mina. She's not from this place. Everyone here is tall, dark skinned, dark haired. I am not. Nor is the boy that claims to be my flesh and blood. Could we be from that strange place called Triangle?

Vance brings me to a large and solid brick house. It is apart from the other narrow clay houses. He speaks to the guard in silver armor holding a spear. He scans me suspiciously and lets us enter, and just as we do, a guard crosses the courtyard walking briskly in our direction. He's clearly been expecting us. He carries fury and anger. His mantle moves lightly in the wind blowing in from the desert.

He stops when he sees me. There's a dangerous rage about this man that makes me feel that each breath I take I owe to him. Ember glows in his bright eyes. His skin is ashen like smoldered pieces of bark. I control my emotions and show no feelings. I keep my posture straight, holding my head up high. I dare not to speak unless spoken to. He holds so much contempt that I think if I were to speak, he'd just slaughter me on the spot.

"What filth have you brought me, Vance?" he says arrogantly and continues to eye me while I keep my gaze straight. His presence is like a cobra ready to attack.

"Commander," he says his voice low and pitiful. "You're looking for legionnaires in your court. This girl seems to possess the stamina of a fighter. She is strong, my lord."

"Is that so?" he says and moves in closer, examining me like I was a prize. "Let us see, shall we?" He cackles, his voice deep and dire.

I dare to look at his face. Gaunt bones poke out from his

high cheeks. Deep wrinkles carve around his eyes, and darker blotches cover his skin, stretching tightly across his face like dry leather. He places the tip of his sword on my tight braided crown. He pulls out a silver strand and holds onto it.

"The hair of a virgin," he says coldly. "You are still one, are you not?"

I say nothing. I smother my breath briefly. Then release the air, which flows through my lungs like a wire.

"Speak, slave girl," he barks into my face. I keep my eyes wide open. He does not scare me. In my mind, I begin to imagine how good I'll feel if I cut off his head with my sword.

"Yes, commander," I say, mimicking Vance. My gaze remains straight, the air in my lungs tighter. I hold back from saying anything that I know would not interest this beast of a man.

"Don't take me for a fool, girl." he whispers like the devil in my ear. "If you are one, you may no longer be, especially with that hair."

He motions for two large men. They walk briskly toward us. That's when I know it was a mistake to come here. I should never have trusted those strangers. I release the air from my lungs. Before I get a word out, the commander says, "Cut off her hair—all of it!"

11

FREDERICK

SHE IS OBLIVIOUS of who she is of who I am. Nora doesn't remember me. The murder in her eyes is vile, uncertain. It reminds me of when she first learned about herself in the West, just like now the irony of time is spinning her into a moment where she has to discover herself all over again. I tell her in a calm voice I am her brother. I use a simplified lie to convince her, as everything else is complicated. There's no easy way of telling her who I am. She looks at me in disbelief. Her mind is raging; I can tell. She is not prepared for this.

I wipe the line of blood she draws across my neck with my arm. She glares at me for a while, as if trying to work out if I am telling her the truth. I feel her deep gaze on me. She's trying to remember something. Anything. The anger in her eyes, the murder and contempt returns. She doesn't believe me and is threatening to kill me. I let her take the sword, illuminated in the darkness. She catches another glimpse of me.

I want to take her into my arms and hold her tight, but the love I feel for her is in a state of limbo. I cannot tell her how much she means to me. She wouldn't understand. She's different from other girls, stronger. Even when she should have been feeling vulnerable, she had the courage and strength to come out here seeking answers.

She doesn't seem to remember much. But my heart tells me she recognizes me. I stare at her as she tightens the grip around the sword's hilt. She's not sure if she should kill me. She is a coldblooded assassin, and the sword calls for killing. I see that clearly. She is fighting the urge, and if she continues, she'll cause trouble. In the darkness, Mina's shadow blends with the room. She draws in close and begs Nora not to kill me.

I take one step closer toward her. She stands, unfazed. Her eyes move between Mina and me. "I will tell you everything." I calm her palpitating nerves. The frustration she carries eases. She takes a deep breath and listen to what I have to tell her.

I try to figure out what part to begin with, hoping she will believe me. Half way through my story, she listens to the evidence of the tattoo on her back, and on her wrist. I think she believes me, but I am no fool.

As I listen to the words pour out of my mouth I realize what I am telling her is extraordinary. How do I expect her to believe any of it especially since she's suffering from memory loss? I wouldn't. Why should she? She's at her lowest ebb, feeling vulnerable, exposed, raw. I can tell from the way she sighs, moves, and stares at me. All she trusts are her emotions. I see it in her eyes. I know her better than she thinks I do—her feelings, her gestures. I observed her and was obsessed by her from the moment I met her.

That day at Dock Harbor, she looked like she didn't belong. Her provocative attitude was that of an untouched night.

In many ways, Nora is still a mystery to me. What is she thinking? How is she feeling? Sometimes, I am not sure she feels anything at all. Her emotions are guarded. Could I be her *brother*? I ask myself if it is true. The evidence is there. We look alike. We have the same drive, the same passions. We are on a journey to discover the truth about the world of the Vikings and about ourselves.

"You have to believe me. The sword in your hand is a family legacy. And your destiny as assassin has led you here to find the remaining three weapons."

"If you're telling the truth, and I'm not saying you are," she says, pausing and sucking in the humid air. "How will we ever succeed? I've been captured as a slave and will be sold to the assassins tomorrow. They may kill me or even worse, torture me, which seems like a common practice around here. The world you speak of, where is it? And how will we return if we can't remember how we got here in the first place?"

"You have to trust your instincts, Nora," I tell her. "This crossing is not going to be easy. If it were, we'd already have the weapons. But do understand, the weapons possess an immense power. I know what the sword in your hand is capable of slaying. The blade alone can kill men, giants, and dangerous creatures. I've seen you do it when we fought in the Forbidden Areas."

"What you say doesn't make any sense." The look on her face turns grave.

"Look, I can't begin to imagine how you must feel right now. It's not the first time you've been in a situation like this."

"Did I lose my memory in the past?"

I laugh a little. It's ironic the way Nora refers to the past.

"No, it's complicated. You have to trust me, and if you don't, trust your instincts."

"Trust my instincts?" Her mind is distant, confused. I can see it in the way she carries herself in the darkness, shades of her body moving restlessly. Arms swinging, hands twitching.

"I have to return before the tradesman finds me gone." She turns, but I tell her to wait. She lingers for a while. I reveal my plan.

"Tomorrow, I will shadow you into the assassins' ground. We need to get you in safely. Then you will wait for me." She detects the worry in my voice.

"What do you expect me to do once I am inside?" she says.

"Stay alive," I say. "And don't do anything irrational. Don't speak unless you need to give an answer. Try to mimic the tribesman's behavior. You do not want to make the assassins angry."

"What about the girl?" she peers at Mina. "What help will she be?"

"Mina is resourceful. Don't underestimate her. Her sense of detecting danger is strong. She foresees threatening situations before they arise."

"She's weak," says Nora. She sounds harsher than she ever was before, her voice a blend of judgment and prejudice. Mina looks at Nora without moving a muscle.

"You don't have to worry about that for now," I say. "There's more to Mina than you know." I touch Nora's shoulder, but she brushes my hand away swiftly. I wonder how she would react if I tell her we are in love. The truth suddenly seems beyond pathetic and yet believable. She came here for the truth. She feels something deep inside the cold chambers of her heart. I am sure of it.

"Very well. I don't have a choice. Tomorrow, I will follow

Vance to the assassins' ground. I don't know what to expect, except—"

"Expect the worst," I say. "Always expect the opposite of good in a place like this." She slinks away like a stray dog. Mina and I watch her leave.

"Nora no feel like Nora," says Mina. "She someone else."

"I know," I sigh and imagine what will happen tomorrow. The way I know her, she'll not want to do what I asked of her. "We have to keep a strict watch on the assassins' ground. There's a view from one of the abandoned towers into their courtyard."

"We no weapons. No magic, no—"

"Mina, in this world, we have to be without it and use our other *gifts*."

"How you want use gifts?"

"My physical strength in this world is still great. Should Nora be in danger, I will not hesitate to make use of my powers to save her. Even if it blows our cover. Her life is important. She might not even know, but tomorrow she turns seventeen. Did you know that?"

"No! What all means, Frederick?"

"It means the Verans will use the artifacts to awaken Yg-gdrasil." I stare at Mina. "It means Nora will finally receive the encrypted runes that unlock the door to the Nine Worlds."

"Nora knows," says Mina. "I see in her eyes. She no trust us. She no do what you say. What we do then?"

"She has no other choice Mina. We need to get those weapons. She's our only hope."

"Why you tell Nora your name William and no Frederick? Why not say you love—"

"Because I will have to ask her to make a choice she will not like. Telling her I am Frederick would complicate things. I can't take that risk. I need to make sure we succeed tomorrow. It's the only way out of here—the only way that will lead us to the Rebels. I think they've been watching us, following us. I feel an eerie presence, even now as we speak."

"No understand what you say, Frederick. Rebels?"

"I know all this doesn't make any sense, but I've seen things, Mina. Call it signs. I think I know what we have to do to get the weapons and get the hell out of here."

"Tomorrow," says Mina and waits by the edge of the room. She's as restless as I. Before dawn breaks, we sneak out and find a position that sets the tradesman's house in sharp view from our hiding place.

I see them departing from the narrow clay house. Nora's hands are folded and tied at the front. She walks behind Vance as they make their way toward the high walls beyond the main castle quarter. The air is cooler and lighter on this side of the city. Soon, they will get past the main guards at the entrance gates and walk inside the assassins' ground, which is a large mansion with high terracotta walls and brick towers. I've seen it before from the roofs across the city, and at night I've spied into their secret chambers without being noticed.

Mina and I cross the roof of the houses stacked shakily up against one another, soundless as the quickening of the wind. On the north facing side of the city, we avoid being seen by some early morning traders and tribesmen.

I notice the passing soldiers, some drunk and others sleepy with whores walking by their sides, casting lazy eyes. I cover my face in the cowl of my cape and pass them with ease to reach the deserted tower that looks straight into the assassins' main square. It's a long way up, and the air is filled with sweat and hot spices. Mina's feet are small but fast. She scurries to the top like the wind.

"Do you see her?" I ask while she stares into the open space. I reach the top and catch a faint glimpse of Nora in the main courtyard. It looks as if she's being questioned by one of the guards—a dangerous looking man with an ugly face. He looks Norse, from our world, but the sun has made his skin leathery and gaunt.

I wonder if he cares who she is. Doesn't look like it. He does not seem to recognize anything about her, not her unique features or the Viking symbols tattooed on her arm. Nora has the emblem of the eagle crest and it's visible even to me at this distance. The guard doesn't seem to notice much about Nora except for her hair.

Two large armed men take Nora away so suddenly. My heart stops. The air in my lungs evaporates. What are they going to do to her? The tribesman collects a small sack from the guard and leaves quickly.

"What we do?" Mina is anxious. "Frederick must help Nora now!" Mina senses the same danger I do.

"I need to think," I say. "But whatever happens, Mina, you must stay here. Do not follow me." She nods with a worried look on her face. I crane my neck to orientate myself. We're in the upmost north quarters of the city and as the day emerges, the sun's blazing rays burn my skin dry. I scratch my arms feeling frustrated. Why did they take her away and where to? I hope she doesn't do anything irrational.

This area is usually quieter but not at this hour of the morning. A group of drunken soldiers leave the whorehouses. If they spot us, we could be exposed. I lay low thinking this mission is suicide. I'd have to rescue her.

The tower we're in is higher than the dwellings overlooking the assassins' main square. It's too high to jump. I need to get to the lower houses and climb my way into the square, and I need to do it undetected.

The risk of being caught, chased, or killed in the main square is low. Not many guards are on duty in the morning. I have to put my powers to the test. It didn't look good the way they took her. If I don't blow our cover, Nora will.

Mina and I have done well getting by as foreigners. I've used my abilities to snatch fruit, nuts, jam, and jars of pickles from the bazaars and food markets without being seen. That's how fast I am. But can I move fast enough to pass without being seen on the deadliest grounds in the city?

My senses are heightened to that of an animal's. I spread my arms out like an eagle, ready to hover over the roofs of the city.

"You jump?" says Mina. "Do now, before late." She doesn't give me room to even think. She urges me to act. "Jump Frederick. No wait. GO!"

"Yes," I say. "I will." I take a leap of faith and walk to the edge of the tower, which is at least seventy feet high. I let my body plunge. It lifts off the ground, carrying me effortlessly across the rooftops. The breeze is warm and caresses my face. I land softly onto the roof. I climb down into the main courtyard. I made it without being seen. I'm inside the assassins' mansion.

12

NORA

HE YANKS MY arm and shoves me into a smelly old cell. It's dark and damp. I turn, my breath heavy, and my mind in eruption. In his hand, he holds sharp scissors. The other man blocks the exit to the cell, spreading his legs, arms folded on his chest. The sword calls for me. I crack my fingers, taking deep, steady breaths. My hands are still tied. Whatever William said to me is not going to work. I cannot let these men cut off my hair.

"Please," I say. "Don't make me hurt you." The man stops and turns around laughing. He looks at the guard at the door.

"Did you hear that, Gunnar?"

"I did indeed, Rune."

"The slave girl is threatening to hurt me." His voice is hoarse and dry like sandpaper.

"You're mistaken," I say. "I am no slave girl." I yank my hands lose from the thick twine. In one motion, I rip out the sword from my side and take off Rune's and Gunnar's heads. Their heavy bodies fall to the ground like timber, heads rolling out of the cell sprayed with blood. As I step out of the cell a memory flickers before my eyes.

I'm in a dank den. It's the criminal underworld. The atmosphere is dangerous. I stand facing a girl who wants me dead. I am an assassin, and I kill people for a living. That's why I carry this sword. I am here to kill someone. My thoughts are interrupted when I hear sounds of panic echo in the walls and corridors. The guards are chasing a tall shadow. Fast as the wind, a dark shade closes in on me, shouting.

"Nora! What have you done?" William reaches out for my hand. "Why did you kill these men?" He stops and looks down panicking.

"They were going to cut off my hair," I shout angrily.

"And you decided it was a better plan to cut off their heads?" He looks at the pool of blood and takes my hand. We run down the long hall of arches like wild animals chased by lions. Except the guards are not lions. They are sheep. I could easily kill them all with my sword.

We turn out toward the garden and into a maze made from low cut shrubs. When I look over my shoulders I don't see guards. We've shaken them off for now.

"We're done for," he says. "How could you be so stupid, Nora? Killing those two men will lead to our deaths. The assassins live to kill. Congratulations, you've just given them a greater reason to execute us. Not only that, you've made it harder to get access to the weapons and to find a route to the Rebels. Now what are we going to do? Death or the desert? There's no way out of this forsaken City of Assassins. Forget about the city. The damned kingdom of Arres. We're trapped; do you hear me? Trapped, and there's no way home."

William clenches his fists in the air. The expression in his eyes is severe. I try taking his hand into mine, but he jerks it away. He walks fast following the edge of the maze. I straddle behind. When we reach the other end, an army of guards greets us. I swing my blood-coated sword around. It feels familiar like I know every inch of its sharp blade. The men take a step back, the expression on their faces horrid.

"Be careful, Nora," he pulls me back while the guards close in on us. They have formed a tight circle. "Don't move a muscle until I tell you."

"I've got this," I tell him. "I can easily bring them all down."

"Oh, I know that," he says annoyed. "You've made that very clear."

"What are you saying?" I feel a pulse behind my eyes, a burning sensation.

"Just don't kill anyone," he shouts. "Okay?"

"We have no other choice," I say. "They will kill us if we don't kill them first." The guards are armed to the hilt with sharp swords, axes, and steady shields. Some wear glorious silver helmets. They swing their swords and axes into position.

"Drop your weapons," says a dark voice behind the circle of guards. The circle parts and a man pushes his way through. The guards all stand back and lower their weapons.

His long, light hair spills down his shoulders like a thick curtain. His eyes are dark gray, and skin pale. Ashen. His features look oddly familiar like I've seen him somewhere before. My heart tells me to drop my sword and reach out for him. To put my hand on his chest and feel his heart beat, but something stops me. I don't know what. Fear perhaps or maybe disgust.

"Lord Harald," says one of the guards and bows. The rest follow.

Harald tosses his black cape to the side and steps forward,

facing us. He is taller than average with broad shoulders and a narrow waist.

"Who are you? What are you doing inside my mansion?" His voice is deep and raspy, as if he speaks from the grave. He stares at my sword. He reaches out to touch the blade, but I step back, grunting like an animal. The boy who calls himself my brother pinches my arm. I say nothing while I feel Harald's eyes consume me.

"S- stay, away," I say, controlling my breath. "It-it is mine." I cannot get the words out. The air around me feels thin, and my head feels light. Everything around me begins to spin, and I feel like falling, but I hold the ground firmly with my feet. This man holds some kind of power over me. I hide the weapon in its sheath. Harald's stiff glare doesn't leave its sight.

"Yours? This sword belongs to us. Do you know how we punish thieves? How we punish slaves who kill guards that serve the Emperor?" I hear his deep voice echo, his head getting bigger and bigger as he comes toward me, but not close enough to touch his chest and feel his heart underneath the hard skin covering him. "Hand over the sword, slave girl." He takes a deep juddering breath.

"Try me!" I say. "And fail."

"How dare you?" he says. "Have you come from the North? Did my enemy send you here? Speak in the name of the Emperor, or I shall make your death memorable." I tear my eyes away from his and look at William, expecting an answer, but there's none. He's silent. "Where have you come from?" he demands.

"We're your blood, Lord Harald. We're not the enemy," says William. "We've traveled from the land we call the Triangle." William pulls down his hood and makes his face visible. His soft blond waves, striking blue eyes, and pale skin shine in the morning desert heat.

"Ohhh?" says Harald and presses his lips together. They form a straight bitter line. He walks closer and tosses back his long hair. He strikes William hard. A drop of blood colors the red soil. "What do you take me for? And why are you spinning up such preposterous lies? I've never heard of such a land."

"Lord Harald, I can explain," says William and wipes his nose clean. "I speak the truth." The pledge in William's voice is desperate but still convincing.

Puzzled, Harald stares grimly at us with contempt in his eyes.

"Explain how you got these markings, boy." He takes in William's tattoos, examining his arms. He mumbles something to himself. Then he notices the one on my arm.

"Are they from this land you claim you come from?" he says. "The Triangle?"

"You will want to hear what I have to say," says William. "But I will only tell you if you instruct your men to back down." Something is strange in the way William looks at Harald; he's pinned him down with his eyes, and it feels like he is manipulating him. Much to my surprise, Harald doesn't move or draw his sword out to kill us. He is under William's influence.

Harald motions for his men to back away. He leads the way through the garden back into the long hall. He stalks into a private chamber, and tells the guards to remain outside. The chamber is dark and cool and has a magnificent glass dome ceiling and an ocean blue ceramic floor. Above the dome a flock of desert birds caw. I hold the sword firmly in my hand. I fear something ugly is about to happen.

I'm surprised Harald let us into his private chamber, and trusts me with the sword he claims was stolen. I wouldn't trust me with a sword. I stare at William, and he seems absent, like all his focus is on controlling Harald's mind. How is he doing this?

I hear footsteps approaching from the back of the chamber. Three tall men with long, wavy, blond hair appear. Their ears are slightly pointed and their noses are small and round. Their sky-blue eyes are just like William's—clear and consuming.

"How I enjoy morning visits," says one of them. He drums the tips of his fingers against his forehead. I want to know what he is thinking. His presence is strong, intimidating. One of them glares at me familiar curiosity like they know me and have been expecting me.

"Henrik, Henning, and Holger, these slaves claim to come from another land."

"Another land?" says one of them. "Did Arres grow a new mass we do not know of?"

"They call this place the Triangle." says Harald. "The slave boy is eager to tell us something enlightening." He smiles, the corner of his lips curling.

"Did they just cause the death of Rune and Gunnar?"

"They did!"

"They were our best men." He lowers his brows.

"The slave girl killed them with the sword that was stolen from our keep eighteen years ago." says Harald. He joins the band of assassins. They stand facing me, their eyes stinging like needles.

"Are you telling me that girl killed them?" One of them points a sharp finger at me. I clutch harder onto the sword's pommel. The other reaches his hand out, calling for the weapon. It doesn't move. It stays in my hand. He grunts angrily. He is about to make a lunge at me, when Harald says, "Don't Holger." He drums the tips of his fingers against his taut mouth.

Holger stops.

"The boy has markings on his body. He is from our clan in the North." says Harald. "Look for yourself, Henning."

"Is that so?" says Henning, his voice shrill. "Show me your clan symbols, boy." William flashes all the tattoos he carries across his body. The deep dark ink sprawled onto his arms, his chest, and his knuckles. Henning pulls his wrist closer and examines the intertwined circles.

"Fascinating," he says. "I'd like to carve them out of your skin." Williams's eyes are steady. He's not afraid of Henning who regards him as if he wants to eat him for breakfast.

"What about the girl?" says Henning. "Why does she carry the same marks?" He shoots me a stiff glare.

"These are the tattoos from our dynasties," says William. "I belong to Rognvald and Nora to Jarl."

"Two slaves from different clans?" says Henrik and roams around us. "Nonsense." He touches Henning's shoulder. His eyes steady on the sword.

"Did the cunning witch from your clan steal our sword?" says Henrik. "She promised to break the spell."

"What? No!" says William.

"Do not lie to me boy, or I will cut out your tongue and make sure you never speak again." says Henning.

"We've nothing to do with the witch that promised you your freedom. We want to protect our world from war. That's why we're here." says William. "We ask that you give us the other weapons."

143

"Weapons don't prevent war, boy!" says Henning. "They inflict it."

"They're the most powerful weapons ever forged from the fire in Helheim." says Henrik, his body rising with the strength of his voice. "What makes you believe you can just walk in, and claim them?"

"Because," I say. "We descend from your Viking line. We carry your blood and your legacy just as my brother William said." The words flood out of my mouth from nowhere.

"I've never heard such idiocy. Not only is it impossible, it is also a lie that deserves the death sentence," says Henning. "Guards, slit their throats! Then rip out their hearts, their livers, and their brains and feed them to the desert wolves."

Soldiers march into the chamber, their spears pointing at us.

"But first" says Harald his face rigid. "You'll hand that sword to me before facing an ugly and miserable death." He raises his hand to strike me but stops, his face trembling with anger. His teeth are gritted. Harald is not merciful, still something stops him. He roars fiercely into my face. His breath smells like death, rotten. He senses something, a strong wind, and a hurricane. The earth beneath us trembles.

The living tree on my back moves, and a sharp pain embraces every bone in my body. I crouch down and see a clear image flicker in my mind—a long, dwindling pathway that leads to a portal buried in the forest. The way is dangerous and misty. I don't think I know where this portal is. It could be anywhere. I am used to the woods and forests.

The image dissolves from my mind so suddenly. I get up and draw my sword. I am ready to battle with my ancestors. Killers, murderers, assassins. That's what they are. That's what they will always be. I cannot expect compassion from them. They never had it. I should finish them off while I can.

Just as I am about to strike them, Yggdrasil thrashes her branches. I scream in agony. I realize she is trying to break free. My past, my present, and my future all appear before my eyes. I remember everything. I remember who I am. The images continue to run like a string of casual incidents. Images of what William said to me the day before. I know he is not William. He is Frederick. Everything is suddenly clear.

Yggdrasil has been awakened. She whispers to me, but I cannot understand what she says. Her purpose is to protect me, guide me, and make sure I unlock the Nine Worlds: She shows me Asgard, the divine home to the gods; Niflheim, the forsaken hole for dead souls, dangerous and daunting; Alfheim, where the powerful and wise elves live; Jotunheim, home of the giants; Midgard, where I must go with Frederick, the home of mankind; Svart Alfaheim, which belongs to the dwarves; Vanaheim, which will be claimed by the Verans; Muspelheim, where fire and the demons reside; and Helheim, which is where killers and dishonorable people are kept. This is where the weapons were forged.

These worlds are about to appear and as soon as they do, everything will be different.

Today is my seventeenth birthday. This is the day Yggdrasil has been waiting for. She's been part of me for as long as I can remember. The tree always was and always will be. Not even the gods have power over her. Her branches begin to release from my back. I scream louder. My bones rattle and my soul shakes. A million expressions chase each other across my face. I feel Yggdrasil turn and twist, her heavy branches lashing out, her roots writhing from years of enslavement. I feel a sharp pain bouncing through my body. The agony is unbearable.

"What in the name of Odin is happening to me?" I cry.

"Don't fight it, Nora; it is your destiny," says Frederick. "She is leaving you, but she is also giving you the key to open the door."

Harald's rage explodes. He roars like a wild beast and reaches out for the sword, his long thin fingers stretched. He calls for it, whispering mystic words.

"Get the sword!" he yells. Harald throws me a dirty look. Holger, Henning, and Henrik whisper spells to draw the weapon from me. But it doesn't work.

The tree breaks free and rises. She flounces forward looking like a giant raven that fills the room in plumes of black branches. It swirls faster than a tornado. Her leaves fall like feathers. From the corner of my eye I see a strong whirling wind sweeping away. A thick ashen smoke fills the chamber. There is no trace of Yggdrasil. She is gone to sow her roots into the Nine Worlds. I need to unlock the gate that leads to them. The vision... the door could be anywhere.

My body feels light, at ease. There is no more pain. My evil ancestors have stopped their spells and when I swing my hand around to feel the tattoo on my back, there is none. The palm of my hand feels hot like coal. When I stare at it, I see nine encrypted runes glittering on my palm, fading the minute daylight shines on my hand.

I take a deep breath and clench my fist tightly and pretend nothing is there.

"What are we going to do?" I say to Frederick.

"We either fight," he says in low voice. "Or we lure them."

"Be aware of the witch," barks Henning darkly. "She kept Yggdrasil captive with her witch powers." They step back as if afraid I might put a spell on them.

"I'm not a witch. The tree was my protector."

"Liar," growls Harald. "You say you're from a mysterious land and carry our blood. I say you lie. You're here to kill us and steal our weapons. What we witnessed was a spell. But the almighty Yggdrasil is strong. She broke free from your bewitchment."

"If you're not a witch or a slave then what are you?" says Henrik. His blue eyes are a shade darker. Twitching pulses stream across his angry face.

"I am an assassin," I say. "Just like you."

"Assassin?" They whisper among themselves. Horror draws across their stern faces.

"My esteemed lords," says Frederick firmly. "Nora Hunt descends from your bloodline. She alone has the power to set you free from your curse." He pauses. I want to interrupt him but he continues, "In return for the assassin weapons."

"Frederick, what are you doing?" I hiss. Anger surges through my body. "I had this."

A dark flicker passes across his face. I can't read his mind. I clench the handle of my sword and look at Henning, Holger, Harald and Henrik.

"The gods chose me to unlock the Nine Worlds," I say. "I—" My body goes rigid.

"You're both liars, con artists. We'll give you the death you deserve." The guards circle in on us. "I'll have your heads on stakes."

"Stand back." I hold my sword high. "Do not come near me." I breathe the moist air in and out, trying to calm my nerves.

Harald and Henning close in on me, whispering old Norse spells loud and clear. Harald's whispers are rough and angry, and I hear them inside my head now. I close my eyes. A memory breaks in—I'm in the East, in the meadows. The sky is blue, the earth beneath me red. I'm greeted by the familiar sound of crickets and dancing flowers. I hear someone calling my name. The voice is getting closer and a face becomes visible.

My eyes fly open. Frederick is shaking me. I jolt forward holding the hilt tighter to fight the enemy staring me in the face.

"What did she show you?" he says. "Where are the runes?" He looks around, frenetic.

"Why did you tell them I can set them free?" I take a step back "I can't."

"Maybe you can. You are after all a witch with powers," says Henning. "You set the tree of life free. Maybe you can set us free from the Emperor's spell?"

"The ancient runic symbols." Frederick stares at me. "Where are they, Nora?"

"Do you really think I'm going to tell you now after the mess we're in?" I hiss angrily. "Frederick Dhal, your timing could not be worse."

"Did you just say my name?" He smiles. "You have your memory back."

"It makes no difference what I remember," I say. "Doesn't change a thing about the situation we're in. I'm not a witch or a slave girl. I don't have special powers to set anyone free."

"You do, and you will break our curse." shouts Henning. "If not, you'll face punishment for lying, and for stealing the sword."

"Nora, trust in me," says Frederick. "You alone—"

"Are you really playing your 'trust me' game, Frederick?

148

After all we've been through? You held my heart! In the name of Thor, I will not tell you where the runes are."

"What runes?" says Henrik. "What is she talking about?"

"Runes that I received from Yggdrasil," I say. I point the tip of my sword sharply at the assassin lords; their eyes hungry, their minds wide open with questions. They consume me with their eyes, their evil thoughts.

"Hand me the weapons, and I will spare your life." I say.

"Nora, why don't you do as I say? It's the only way out of here alive with the weapons," says Frederick. "Soon the worlds will show. Yggdrasil is awake. You've turned seventeen. It's time you use your—"

"Enough!" barks Harald. He drums his fingers in anticipation, his patience slowly diminishing. Henrik growls, his eyes are thunder and his face creased into a hard ball.

"You will break the curse," says Harald. "For too long we've lived this hollow life under the Emperor Justus Markus. Killing to protect him, thousands upon thousands. The rising Rebels will not stop, and we do not care anymore."

"Witch from the Triangle," says Henning. "Set us free from the spell."

"What will you do to me if I don't?" I say and play my next move carefully. "Will you kill me? You are killers and have no morals or sense of regret. You'll kill me no matter what. Even if I wanted to, I cannot set you free."

"If the tree of life gave you the runes, I will not kill you," says Harald. "You will have a choice, though, slave girl."

"My name is Nora."

"We had our own prophecy. Only I did not believe it, not until now." says Henning.

"Don't waste your breath," says Holger. The slits in his eyes appear vertical. He curls his lip and growls. "We can't be sure that the foretelling—"

"What Prophecy or foretelling are you talking about?" I say.

"A descendant from your bloodline shall come from another world. She holds secrets from the future that will lead into the present. She will be the one to set you free from your curse to kill." says Henning.

"You knew?" I say.

"Knowing is not believing," says Henning.

"What makes you believe the prophecy?" I say. I suck in a deep breath, slowing my mind before it wanders off. My heartbeat slows as if sinking to a rough halt. How do I tell the assassins that their prophecy is untrue? They've been lied to.

"But you cannot leave Arres," I say. "You belong here."

Terror strikes me. If the assassins were to leave Arres and enter the Triangle, murder would unleash like an epidemic. Everything would turn into chaos. They cannot leave Arres. They need to remain here. I have to figure out a way to get out of this and return to the Triangle with the weapons, even if it means killing them.

"We're trapped by the Emperor. All he wants is a male heir to continue his doomed legacy and protection from the rising Rebels who demand this land. This world of dust and sand means nothing when compared to where our souls must be."

"And where's that?" I say.

"Among our own kind," says Harald. "Midgard. We've been trapped here ever since we came. There's an evil spell hovering over us. Break it. Set us free."

"We are assassins from a bleak and barren land in the North. We serve the gods and live to battle. The curse we carry is bound to us like air to all human life. You are our blood sent

150

to free us," says Henrik. "Now show us the way to break the curse to kill that haunts us."

I dust myself off and look at Frederick. I know what I have to do.

"First, hand over the weapons," I say.

"Nora," says Frederick. "Let me handle this." But before Frederick gets to say another word, Henrik takes out the axe, Henning the shield, and Holger the spear. They look like mad beasts from the Forbidden Areas. They have been carrying the weapons all this time. If I had only known—

"You condemn us to hell," roars Harald.

"Nora!" I hear the panic in Frederick's voice. "RUN!" The assassins swing their weapons and circle around Frederick and me. We cannot escape. Holger snatches away the sword from me in a flip of his hand. His howl spreads like thunder.

"Frederick and Nora from the Triangle," whispers Harald. His evil cackle echoes in my ears. "You're under our authority. Either you do as we demand or you face death." Something sharp and heavy hits my head. I lose consciousness instantly.

When I wake, I find myself in a dirty, dark cell. It's warm and smells like death. In the corridors I hear people screaming, as if tortured. When I dive into my feelings, I feel lost, useless. I have nothing special inside me now that Yggdrasil left. No real powers, no abilities that makes me who I am. I don't even have the sword.

All I am left with is the encrypted runes. What will become of us? They won't kill me, because they want me to free them. My power hungry, evil assassin ancestors had a foretelling. But I cannot set anyone free. I possess no such powers.

My head feels sore and is aching. How did I let this happen to me? All seems lost, even Frederick. The assassins outplayed us; we didn't have a chance. They must have seen right through our weaknesses. I wonder what they've done to Frederick. Is he still alive? My senses are numb, and I feel inept. Without the sword, my powers, and the tree to protect me, and without Frederick, my life is hollow.

Why do I always have to do things my way? I failed to listen to Frederick most of the time and now because of me, he is in danger or could already be dead.

The door to my cell creaks open. I see the chestnut brown eyes of a guard looking at me.

"Oy! Get up!" he says. "It's time for battle."

"You can't make me," I say. "I'm not going into anymore battles, so piss off."

"Silly slave girl," he says. "If you don't, we will kill your companion."

13

FREDERICK

THE ASSASSINS left me in the gutters. In this black hole of emptiness that stretches endlessly for miles, marked by nothing but shadows of the dead rambling restlessly underneath the city.

There's no sunlight, a thick fume coats the air, and I feel forgotten among the dead down here. I have no memory of how I was dragged and dumped. I only recall Harald's face laughing, his eyes full of hatred and misery.

The moaning from the countless, soulless wraiths does not scare me. They walk through me like I, too, was a shadow, and it makes me wonder, am I dead or alive? I escape the shadows and pull out a small dagger from the side of my boot.

I stole it from one of the bazaars the other day. I suspect the assassins don't care if I live or die. They have no interest in me. But when Harald left, he said I needed to survive for the test ahead of me. But what test is he talking about? What does he want to see?

The gutter is cool and moist, and the stink in the air tells me I have to head west, where the blend of spices and charcoal soaks the dry air above me. It could take me a day to get out.

I think back at the disappointment in Nora's eyes when she thought I was deceiving her. Sooner or later she'll realize what she is capable of. The ancient runes are powerful forces. Not only will they unlock the door to the Nine Worlds, they also give Nora temporary powers to defeat her enemy. She is unaware of this gift. Does she even care about the mission she's been given?

She can't possibly care about the Goths. I cannot believe she cares for anyone right now except herself.

The smell is unbearable. I tear a strip of cloth from my shirt and wrap it around my mouth and nose. I have only my heightened senses and the ten-dinar dagger I stole from the market to rely on.

After walking for what seems like an eternity, I see rays of light and a glimpse of the sun lowering in the clear sky. I feel the warm, dense air haunted by chili and lemon flavors from the endless souks, so sharp and tangy it burns my nostrils. I lick my dry lips. They are parched with thirst, and my legs are in agony. My powers are passive now, like someone flicked off the switch. I am unable to connect to my emotions, my abilities—the things I was relying so heavily on to get me the hell out of here.

My escape route is nowhere near. As I leave the darkness of the gutters, I come out to an odd part of the desert. Everything is red: the mountains, the wind worn rock formations, and the silky sand. But there's life in this place. To my left I see acacia trees and tumbleweeds rolling. I shift around when I hear the fluttering of feasting birds and set out at a steady jog.

My fatigued body blends with the blue hazy atmosphere, and my eyes struggle to stay open. I want to collapse after a mile of running through thorny shrubs, but then I smell something, and it's not spices or even pickles or apricot jam. I smell smoke and death.

The day disappears and turns into a velvety night with no stars glinting, just a glowing moon. The smell fades and is replaced with my own scent. I taste the salt from my sweat and collapse suddenly on the dry baked earth. My clothes chafe my skin from the sweat and the gutter dirt still coating me.

The gritty sand sticks to the corners of my eyes. I do not drag my body across the hot sand; I just lie flat, dizzy, dehydrated, and numb from hours of walking. All I see is her face, and she has the most beautiful face I've ever seen. It feels so real, and I reach out my hand to touch her.

"Nora? Nora?" But it's not her; it's something else. It's a large mass of black. I curl my fingers to feel my dagger. My strength fails me, and it slips out of my palm. I pick it up and tuck it into my belt. I turn my face in horror, knowing that this hideous black creature might kill me. But instead it opens its slimy mouth and gulps me in like I was no more than a little crumb. Everything turns dark and my senses go numb.

14

NORA

THE CREATURE'S SAGGY purple face is livid. Through the seeping flesh, the ancient bones protrude, black and gray. Its fingers are long and sharp, its arms and legs, thin sticks, and its body an overwhelming mass of brown flesh. When I move my eyes to see the face it holds, there's none. Just a skull with carved hollow eyes and a nose.

The creature touches the ground. Its breath smells like death and rot. My neck cranes anxiously to meet the eyes of my ancestors, who observe me with great pleasure from one of the towers.

I've been placed in the middle of an empty arena, with no weapons. I rely on my inner strength and raise my fists to protect myself against the odd creature ready to lunge at me.

"Soon, I will eat you, slave girl," it says in a hoarse voice like scraping sandpaper. "Don't resist; it's less painful if you let me swallow you." I try not to panic and remember battling with bigger and uglier creatures like Noddabah in the Forbidden Areas. But back then, I had Frederick and Mina and my sword.

I turn my eyes to the assassins with their stern and cold faces.

Is this meant to entertain them? Or do they want me dead?

"Is this some kind of joke?" I shout. "Do you really find this scenario amusing? To watch me battle against this ugly creature."

"It's your test, slave girl," says Henrik. "No one has defeated the monster, Djangal. He serves us and in return we feed him living things. We haven't fed Djangal in weeks. He's starving, I assure you." Henning and Henrik's laughter echo in the air.

"There's not a lot meat on my body," I say. "I don't think Djangal will be happy chewing on a witch's bones."

"You admit your defeat then?" says Henning looking surprised.

"There's no way Djangal is having me for dinner tonight."

"Prove it," he says. "Your strength should be more powerful than ever if we are to believe the prophecy. If we are to believe who you say you are."

"Of course," I say. "I've traveled five hundred years to lie about who I am."

"You'll face battle or die." says Henrik. His voice echoes in the arena.

Why are Vikings so hungry for battle? Hundreds of years, past or future, we still choose to savagely kill one another to prove a point. If that's what they want, I'll give them a show to remember.

"By the gods," I say, looking at the creature. "I've defeated uglier and smellier looking monsters than you."

Djangal opens his mouth and hisses at me, his teeth sharper than shards of broken glass. He leaps at me. I sink my fist into Djangal's abdomen. He howls and strikes me, knocking me to the side like a fly. I roll and get to my feet, but my leg is hurt. I can barely stand straight. Djangal moves fast toward me like he wants to crush me. His empty eyes fixate on my every move.

The monster strikes with his sharp fang. I stagger back, unharmed. Something comes between me and Djangal—a small, black shadow with gleaming daggers in its hands. Mina. The creature screams, and the blood tainted ground beneath me shakes. Mina's daggers go through Djangal's skin. The snarling creature strikes again but misses me.

But the monster doesn't miss Mina. A fatal blow and Mina flies against the far wall, her spine crushed with a hard crunch, her body sliding to the floor. I scream, my hands reaching for her. The echo of my voice is captured in the empty arena. My tears blend with the sweat dripping from my body. If only I had my sword to give me the strength. I need to finish this monster off. Because of it, Mina is dead.

I tear my eyes away from Mina's lifeless body. I pull out the daggers from the monster's gooey flesh. I roar like a wild beast and leap at the vile creature. I raise the daggers high, and stab the sharp blade into his skin. But something doesn't feel right. The monster's shape and size is beginning to change. It takes human form. I fall and stagger back, almost trembling. It's not a monster; it is a shape-shifting creature transfiguring. The form it has taken turns into Frederick. I rub the itching sand away from my eyes. It can't be. This must be an illusion or a spell. I'm being tricked.

"Frederick?"

"Nora," he says in his deepest and darkest voice.

It doesn't sound like Frederick. It's an illusion, some kind of Viking spell.

"How do I know it's really you?" I hesitate to kill him. What if it is Frederick?

"It's me; the creature swallowed me," he says and leaves the vessel that carried him behind. A slimy dark substance coats his body. The bits of skin that covered him crumble away like paper in flames.

"I was trying to break free. I tore its flesh with my knife from the inside and pulled myself out. You nearly killed me with those daggers." The look on his face is relieved. He lives, but he will not be happy when he discovers what the monster did.

I look to the other side. Frederick's eyes follow mine. That's when he notices Mina's lifeless body crushed against the wall. He stares at the assassins who look down at us. They stand like tall pillars. Evil is smeared across their faces. Holger cackles, his chest bouncing. Henrik clenches his fists into hard balls. Harald's nose is blazing fire. The anger in his eyes is poisonous. They make no move and watch us like hawks, following our every move, our every fear.

"What happened?" he says. "Is she alive?"

"The creature you were possessed by killed her." I say my voice breaking. I fall to the ground. My heart sinks to the pit of my stomach wrenching. Mina is gone. I couldn't save her. I did nothing.

"What?" Frederick's voice echoes in my ears like a thousand screams. I know it is him. He is back to normal. He quivers. There's a deep hurt in his eyes. "She can't be dead!" He runs across the ground. He takes Mina's lifeless head into his lap. I am certain it is the normal Frederick and not some evil monster in disguise. I follow him, my numb legs carrying me to her. I crouch down and see that Mina is still breathing heavily as if counting the last she has left.

"Promise you stay together," she says. "Together, you

conquer all." Her eyes are shutting, her lips quivering. The blood drains from her face, tainting her skin in a deep dark red.

"I swear it, Mina," Frederick and I say at the same time. He looks at me. The pain in his eyes is grave. Mina smiles one last time before her eyes shut forever. I hear voices echo and the same ugly laughter. Min is gone. The pain I feel inside my heart twists and writhes like a knife. The feeling is unfamiliar, devastating and different to when Robert died.

"What are we going to do?"

"Stay together," he says. "Keep our promise to Mina."

Anger shoots through my body. I slap Frederick hard. He glares at me, his teeth gritted. He grunts like a wild animal.

"What the hell was that for?"

"For betraying me and lying to me," I say. "And for giving me the wrong answer. Tell me what are we going to do now that all hope is gone? Mina is dead, and it's all our fault."

He cools his red-marked cheek with his hand, and tilts his chin to meet the assassins' eyes that glare at us in silence, feeding on our misery, taking pleasure in our loss.

"If only you'd listened to me," he says. "Stubborn girl."

"Is this all my fault now?" I say. "I gave you the choice to stay behind. Now, look what's happened. We don't have the weapons. We lost the sword and now face an ugly death. The evil assassins will steal the runes from me and rule Midgard. Hell, they might even join forces with Lord Nourusa. The world will be in eternal darkness because we failed."

I open the palm of my hand to show him the runes. "You see that?"

"What are you trying to show me?" he says, bewildered.

"You don't see it?"

He shakes his head. "See what?"

I remember the Wizard's words of wisdom before we left the City of Vikings. I know what we need to do next.

The assassins come down to the arena with burly looking guards who carry Mina's body. I watch her head slip away from Frederick's lap. My hand is a tight fist. I feel tempted to pounce at the assassin lords. Their faces are maps of misery and contempt. Shame washes over me. I am related to these monsters. I carry the same urge they do, to kill.

"Leave her," I yell. I control the tears in my eyes. I feel the burning in my eyes as they narrow.

"Why morn death when it's just the beginning of your unprecedented journey," says Henrik and cackles. "More is still to come, delightful slaves."

"What was that monster that killed Mina?" Frederick growls. He charges, as if he wants to leap at Henrik, but I hold him back.

"Djangal is a shape shifting creature that feeds on others fear to gather his strength in battle. You gave in the second it saw you. He took your strength to kill what you care about. But I must admit, I did not expect you to defeat Djangal carving your way out of his skin. Have you passed the test we set before you? I'd like to think you did. But you also failed."

"You're evil to the core!" I say. I may belong to their kind, but I will never be like them. I take no pride in what I might become after this day, but I will take the pleasure in killing the nasty heads that stare me in the face. They can't change their destiny, and lucky for them they do not know about it. Whatever prophecy they believe in, is false. I see myself in their image. How do I cut loose from the curse? I cannot fight the urge to kill. It runs through my blood like poison.

"It is not we who seek something. It is you who must give us what belongs to our kind," says Harald. "Without it, you're not leaving Arres."

"You don't care about killing your own blood?" I say.

"There's no such thing," says Harald. "In our time, you are not even born yet." His face hardens.

"Are you prepared to sacrifice more lives of those you care about?" Henrik says. He places the sharp blade of the sword on Frederick's throat.

"No," I say. "I will not have you kill my *brother*." The words leave my mouth so suddenly, like some spontaneous declaration.

"Brother?" laughs Henning. "Even if I believe that a slave girl is from our bloodline, I can tell you there's no male bloodline after ours to carry the legacy of the assassins. Women carry the cursed blood, after us. Not men."

"Frederick is my brother; his name is William Janus Hunt." All three lords laugh out loud. "We're under Justus Markus' curse. Because of him our line is corrupted to female carriers of our legacy."

"We can smell our own blood." Harald says. "You, William Janus Hunt are not a descendant of the Viking assassins."

He digs the sharp blade harder against Frederick's throat.

Frederick and I share a moment of hope where all seems possible again. Deep inside myself I didn't want to believe what Robert told me. Why did he lie to me? He believed in peace among the Viking clans and set the example in his council. What made him spin up a lie that would separate me from Frederick?

"The witch of a mother who bore you is seeking the fortune of the gods for herself," Henning says. "She stole it from us, the sword is mighty and powerful. It rules all the other weapons. She also refused to set us free."

"What do you mean?" Thoughts flicker rapidly through my mind. Karen has deceived her husband, her daughter, and her ancestors. She's a dangerous woman, but she's also my mother.

"Nora! This is your final warning," says Henrik. "Either you set the curse free—" His sharp blade presses against Frederick's neck, drawing a line of blood. "—or you watch your friend die." The sword doesn't stop; it continues to cut into Frederick's flesh.

15

FREDERICK

THE BURN OF the steel bites into my throat. I can't help thinking is this what happens when you're about to die? Excruciating pain and eternal darkness. I fall to the ground, my vision blurry and my senses dim. Nora's screams fill my ears. Her despair is uncontrollable. She lunges at the assassins and through the dust and heat, I see her as if in a dream. She's battling against the three vicious killers; her only weapon is inner strength.

The old wizard's words echo in my mind.

Trust your instincts, follow your heart, and believe in battle and your inner strength when all hope seems lost. Nora is up against her ancestors with nothing except her own unique abilities, fighting against powerful, evil forces. She gets hold of the sword and the other weapons land at her feet. She turns slowly to look at me. The air is dry and breathing feels like swallowing fire. I hold her gaze, but not for long.

"Frederick!" she cries. "Hold on, you hear me?" But I can't. My hand travels to my throat and comes away dark with blood. My senses are shutting down. Life is leaving my body. Nora's green eyes lock onto mine as she roars at the assassins who powerlessly step back. Nora's abilities have come out. She's stronger than ever and is crushing the guard's skulls with bare hands and smashing their weapons into pieces as if they were glass. Her cries are loud, angry. The assassins run away.

Her face is covered in blood, her inner animal, and savage. But there's a glow around her, and I reach out my hand to touch the light that surrounds her. She's a true Viking warrior. Her blade is sharp and her moves fast and smooth. There are more guards now, and bloodcurdling screams fill the air, heads rolling and blood splashing.

"Nora," I hiss and cough. She comes running.

"Frederick!" she catches her breath and pulls me up to her chest. "You can't die; do you hear me? I need you to live, to survive this. I can't do this without you. All this means nothing without you. Nothing."

The oxygen in my lungs thins out, and that's when I realize I may be breathing my last drop of air. I close my eyes and feel myself slip from her arms. She's whispering my name over and over again.

Frederick, Frederick, Frederick. The softness of her lips touches mine and fills me with life. My heart beats next to hers. I am not dead, but I am not alive either. I'm caught somewhere in time and space where my body is floating in the night sky. I see stars twinkling, the blackness of the universe consuming me.

This sensation is strange, unfamiliar. Is this where souls travels to before dying? I want to give in. The pain has eased. I cannot be here. It feels wrong. I am not ready. I can't get out. I am trapped. Darkness consumes me, and I hear the wraiths closing in on me. The air is cold and dry. I'm falling into a

165

bottomless pit. The silence is deadly.

"FREDERICK!" I hear Nora call for me. She is shouting. In the black hole that's swallowed me, there's no light. "Open your eyes."

I open mine abruptly and bring back my body and mind to Arres. Nora is not by my side. She's battling with giant monsters, released from behind bars in the arena. She's standing in the center, her arms to her side. Her clothes are torn, but she has the weapons. One of the gates crash down and out comes a giant beast, running toward Nora.

She ducks and spins just as the beast leaps at her, teeth bared, quick as a cobra. Its fangs catch Nora's trousers and tear away the fabric, leaving her leg bare as she staggers.

"Nora?" I shout her name, but my voice is lost in the melee. Nora is howling as she uses the weapons to take out the beast. Another beast attacks her from the back, and she struggles to yank herself away. She swings the axe and cuts off its head. It rolls and lands at my feet, screams still emitting from its large open mouth. I kick the head and sit upright, unable to stand.

Other creatures surge forward and surround her, ugly and misshapen representations of crocodiles and snakes. One by one she finishes them off, using the axe, the sword, and the spear, and hides behind the shield to protect herself from being attacked.

The air is torn apart by an explosion. Broken glass and bricks fly. Henning, Henrik and Harald, ride in on black horses with wings. Their eyes are blood red. Behind them extraordinary animals crouch low and snarl. Their eyes target Nora and me. I hold my ground for a little longer before I muster the courage to get up. My hand clutches my throat. My vest is a smeared mess of sweat, desert dirt, and blood. Nora runs to me, offering me protection behind the shield.

"Stay with me, Frederick. We're going to get out of this."

"I hope we do," I croak and add pressure to the wound on my neck.

The gang of blood hungry beasts and the assassins move in closer. Cruelty, a ruthless desire to kill, is visible on their faces. The broken bricks and shattered glass glitter in the merciless heat. One of the beasts, a large crocodilian animal with fiery eyes, lets out a low growl from its throat. If heaven and earth were crashing, I'd think we still have a chance to survive. But this army of killers and deadly beasts appear undefeatable, even with the powerful weapons that Nora holds.

"By the gods!" shrieks Nora.

The army surround us fully now. Nora and I stand back to back facing them. We're trapped; there's no way out except to kill.

"We've seen worse, don't you think?" I say and force a faint smile.

"This is a war," she whispers. "And we're all alone."

"We have each other," I say and tear a piece of cloth from my shirt and tie it around my neck to keep it from bleeding.

"The weapons," says Nora. "Take the axe and spear." I grab them and feel a tremendous power pulsing through my veins. This is a test of our courage and bravery. In one month, I turn eighteen. I may not even live to see the day. All I wanted was a motorbike and race it against Nora, riding over the Guldborg Bridge in the West. How far that place seems from my memory. It's as if it never existed. I thought I knew what we were getting ourselves into coming to Arres. I was wrong.

A loud drumbeat follows, and two massive elephants crush the ground of the arena, along with dozens of guards armed with arrows and bows on their backs.

"Did you really think you would escape with our weapons?" screams Harald, his face furious and suffused with stains of black blood.

A larger creature, a dark green monster with sharp fangs, moves closer. As it moves, bit-by-bit, its shape and form changes like curling waves. Harald climbs on top of his horse and raises his hand to the creature crawling in our direction.

"Kill them," he says.

"Are you sure, my lord?" says the creature. "I smell something suspicious."

"You smell meat," says Henrik and snickers. "You shall taste human flesh soon enough."

"My lord," says the creature desperately. "Something doesn't feel right with these humans. I dare not eat them."

"No need to worry," says Harald mockingly. "They are only children." Henrik and Henning join him. They stand facing Nora and me, fearless with an army of creatures at their back, ready to tear us apart. Nora and I can't possibly be fast enough to kill them all, even with the assassin weapons. There are too many of them. We don't know what we're dealing with. But there may be one way to defeat them, and I will need Nora's full attention. Is she thinking what I am thinking?

Her breathing slows down. She tightens the grip around the sword with one hand and takes my hand into hers with the other hand.

"You will break the curse or die a pitiless death with your companion, slave girl," says Harald.

"My name," Nora shouts, with her hand tight around mine. "Is Nora Hunt."

I swing her up in the air. Her sword moves fast. In one flash, she buries it inside Harald's heart. She lands back on her feet, squatting, and swings around to place the blade into Henrik's chest. Henning steps back.

"Not so fast," I say and drill the spear into his stomach. "I thought you were assassins and not cowards." Henning's mouth is bathed in blood, and he joins his brothers in death.

"Real assassins fight," says Nora. "They don't need a killer army."

Heat raises from underneath my feet and my body collapses. Nora takes me in and covers us under the shield while the army of creatures wash over us like a catastrophic tide. I see and hear nothing. All is black.

16

NORA

I SHAKE HIS lifeless body, but he's not moving. His breath is still, his heart asleep. I lift the blood-soaked cloth from his neck; the wound is deep. He has lost a lot of blood. *What am I going to do?* When I look around I see the blackened corpses of evil creatures and among them my ancestors. I don't know what happened. When I took shelter under the shield, I heard the growls and attacks and snarling of the monsters. Nothing touched us. The shield protected us. When the clashing storm was over, in the dust and dirt all I could see was death.

I get to my feet and walk over to my ancestors and draw my sword. The expression on their faces will haunt me forever. But I had to do this. I don't feel guilty for saving Frederick and myself.

Frederick's body makes subtle movements. I look down at his face, serene and calm.

"Frederick?" I shake him hard. "Wake up." He's not dead; he's taking a snooze. Small bubbles of air leave his lips. I break out laughing while tears wash down my cheeks. By the gods, he's asleep. I give him another kiss and taste iron and metal on my tongue. He opens his eyes slowly.

"I knew you couldn't just leave me like that, Frederick Dahl."

"What happened?" he says and looks around. "Where's everyone?"

"I've killed them."

"The assassins?"

"I assassinated them," I say, satisfied, and point at the beheaded bodies. "I went over and took off their heads just to make sure they stay dead."

"They could come back and haunt us as wraiths."

"Let them," I say. "They don't stand a chance."

"What I saw back there was—"

"Real," I say. "I felt an electricity inside me unleash."

"It's part of you, Nora. *You* are unstoppable."

"How's your wound?" I say.

"I'll live," he says. "For now."

"It looks bad, not like an ordinary wound," I say. "You need to be treated."

"In Arres?" says Frederick. "Forget about it."

"Then let's leave this damn place," I say, looking around at the flood of dead bodies encircling us. "And find those Rebels and bring home the weapons."

"The shield did all this?" Frederick asks.

"It's more powerful that you can imagine," I say. "The shield must have released a force, an electricity that fried the men and burned the army to ashes."

"If it can do this in Arres, what will it do in the Triangle?"

"Maybe nothing," I say. "Who knows what spell works where? The assassins forged these weapons to protect Arres. Who says they'll protect our world?"

"What do you mean?"

"I have a feeling something is wrong," I say. "Like we were lured into Arres to serve another purpose. Who are the Rebels and why must we get to them to return?"

"I don't know," says Frederick. "But let's find out."

We leave the assassins' mansion at dusk and end up in the city's dirty backstreets filled with sewage. Thick smoke curls up from the corners and melts with the hot night sky. The streets in this part of the city are filled with rats, thieves, and possibly the Rebels watching us slink away.

"Do you really think the Rebels will help us return?" I say. I turn my head and peer into the dark ally behind me. I have a feeling we're being followed.

"They're our only way out," says Frederick. "They have to help us."

"Where do you suppose we should look for them?"

"I don't know, Nora. Maybe they will look for us." He grabs my arm and turns me around to face him. His elegance, grace, and beauty are covered under thick filth and blood. His eyes sparkle, alive. I'd thought I lost him.

"Something is bothering you," I say. "What is it?"

"I don't know," he says, irritated, and walks ahead of me. "I can't help think why you didn't just release the assassins from their damn curse. If you had, maybe we could have avoided all this—"

"What?" I say. "How was I going to do that? I'm no witch and I don't have the faintest idea about breaking curses—"

"You saved the Duchess, didn't you?" he says.

"What I did have nothing to do with my capabilities. The wizard took care of breaking Grethe's death curse. I am an assassin—"

"Slaughtering people," he says. "You're a killer, and I think part of you—"

"Ha!" I cry out. "Do you think I enjoy killing living beings? I grew up in the East. Killing is frowned upon."

"Didn't stop you," says Frederick. "You are no longer in the East."

"What's that supposed to mean?"

"You kill because—"

"I'm cursed like my ancestors." I say. "Get used to it because it's who I am."

"What? Where does that leave us?" His voice is loud, angry.

"In limbo that's where," I say. "I must have killed hundreds back there."

Frederick stops and pulls me back when I walk past him. "Are you telling me you're going to become what your ancestors were?"

"Maybe," I say. "The Earl told me—"

"That's where this is coming from," he says. "You can't possibly believe what *he* told you after lying to you about us, can you?"

"It's not what I believe; it's what is true."

"And this entire assassin killer curse is true?"

"Maybe," I say again and avoid looking into his blue eyes. I continue to walk. I don't know what to think anymore. I feel a constant urge to kill, to slaughter anything that breathes or threatens me. I have no guilt and no shame. When I walked back to the assassins to take off their heads, nothing stopped me. No fear or compassion. It almost came naturally, even instinctively.

The change that is inside me I feel to my blood and to my bone. Something is happening. Maybe I've grown up a little, or maybe my emotions live in isolation. I don't feel things as deep as I used to. It doesn't help that something seems off about Frederick, too; he's nervous, agitated, and snappy. One minute I kiss him back to life, and the next he's dying again. As my strength grows, he falls weaker. *Why?*

The backstreets are endless and snake between shaken clay houses and abandoned homes. We continue going unnoticed for miles. We have to find the rebels. If we don't, we may never return to the Triangle. The very thought of being caught in Arres terrifies me. Ruled by darkness and evil, the fate of the Viking worlds will change if Lord Nourusa conquers Midgard.

By now I am certain the Emperor of Arres has sent his own army to look for us. It won't be long before they find us. The City of Assassins has spies, gossips, and eyes of mystical creatures hidden in dust, dirt, and trickling desert dunes. I constantly feel as if someone is watching us.

The silence of the streets is as vast as a moonless evening, and something unnerving is in the air. Ghosts or other creatures haunt this city. We slow down our pace when shadows in the distance move about on the roofs of the deserted houses.

My limbs are still in the warm night, and beads of sweat coat my skin. Frederick continues to walk ahead and when he notices I have stopped, he turns around. His eyes widen. I feel a cold blow against my neck, but it is not the wind.

"Do not move a muscle," a voice says. By now I am sure Frederick has detected the panic in my face. A creature jumps down from one of the tiled roofs and pushes Frederick onto the ground. The heat bubbles over me like a soup about to boil over. I don't want to kill more creatures. But this is no ordinary being. I have seen one of its kinds before. Slowly, I drop my hands against my sides and crouch down, lowering my weapons. The beast's eyes follow my movements carefully as if I were something precious that would disappear in the blink of an eye.

The animal has dirty, long feet and thick, sharp claws protrude from its four black toes. It slowly approaches me on two legs, moving its body like a dark shadow and baring its long fangs. Drool spills from the creature, and the corner of its mouth twitches like it's trying to say something. It gazes into my eyes without any fear, without any threat.

I communicate with Frederick without moving my lips. I hope he hears me.

Frederick, stand still if you hear me.

Can you hear me?

He stands still, but he's not reacting.

Frederick?

Is that your voice inside my head?

Yes!

How did you—By Odin, what are we dealing with? Wait, don't tell me. It's something ugly again, right? Another vile and dreadful monster. How nasty is it?

It's a Mulhog.

How's that possible?

It has its eyes on me.

Mulhogs cannot be trusted. Remember they belong to a lower order. They are flesh-eating creatures that love to feast on humans. That's all they care about.

We are not in a position to be picky about our allies, Frederick. It's either the Mulhog or wandering the filthy backstreets of Arres.

Nora, wait...

"Why are you following us?" I say. "And what are you doing in Arres?" The Mulhog tucks its tail between its legs, scratches its long, flat ears, and flashes me a dry glare before it opens its mouth.

"You seek the Rebels?" it says in Norse. "Follow me and I will bring you to them."

"How do you know?" I reply back in Norse.

"I heard you chatting miles away."

"I don't trust you," I say. "I've met you before, have I not, Mulhog?"

"Your memory serves you well, Nora Hunt," he says. "My name is Gautam."

"You wanted to eat me back then," I say. "Changed your diet, *Gautam*?"

"I still want to eat you; you'd be a juicy delicious meal," he says, licking his dry mouth. "But I mustn't." He looks away, worried.

"You've said that before," I say. "What's the matter, not enough meat on my body for you to grab onto?" I want to tempt him enough to tell me what is keeping him from eating me. What's stopping him? Did he take a vow? My suspicion is growing. Why have we come here? What is a Mulhog doing in Arres, and why will he lead us to the Rebels?

"Nora?" says Frederick. "What's going on?" He jumps to his feet and sets out to attack the Mulhog.

"Frederick, no," I say. "I've got this, okay?"

"Have you lost your mind?" says Frederick. "Do you really think after escaping war and death that we need this creature to help us?"

"We don't have any other choice. It's our only chance if we want to return to the Triangle before the emperor sends his killer army after us."

"How about using your instinct?" he says. "We have the weapons. Why worry?"

"I'm sick of everything. The killing, the unknown," I scream, and my voice echoes down the long, dark streets. "I want to go back to the Triangle, but we are not even safe there."

"I know," says Frederick. "Me too."

"Follow me," says the Mulhog, his voice croaky. He takes off in the dark. Frederick and I look at each other.

He sighs heavily. "After you."

"Now you want to go?"

"I'm not afraid of Garm Klan scum," he says.

"These scums are our only hope," I say. "They were promised this wasteland. We have to trust him."

"Arres is not a place for people with morals," says Frederick. "It's a place of blood, deadly spices, lust, and murder. A place where the Emperor kills his own children to get what he wants."

"You know about that?"

"Everyone in Arres knows about it," says Frederick. "He's built an empire in the ashes, and these ashes can choke you to death in a heartbeat."

"You spent far more time here than I did," I say. "Has the desert syndrome started to get to you?"

"Be quiet, humans," says Gautam. "And follow me."

Gautam takes us underground to some sort of vault through dark passages. He could kill Frederick and me. We must be desperate to trust a flesh-eating creature, and stupid to follow him into the dank tunnels. I don't get why he'd want to help us. Like hunted, craven animals, we slink along into the darkness.

Odd noises and screams emerge from the shafts, whispers in the dark. Panic begins to strike me with all sorts of crazy questions. What if he's leading us into a trap? Is he planning to feast on us? How did he make his way into Arres? What does he really want? He wants something and will tell us when he knows we're at our lowest point.

Gautam is unusually quiet as we wade through dirty black water. The smell is awful, sour, and acidy. I turn to discover Frederick's gone pale, his breath still. Something is happening to him. He's stopped responding. I shake him and try to get an answer out of him. But he's not reacting. The boil on his neck is spreading like an epidemic.

"Do something," I cry. "He's turning blue."

Gautam turns, his eyes popping.

"Stand back." As he is about to feed on Frederick's wound, I block him. Another move and I will kill him using my sword.

"What do you think you're doing?"

"He's been poisoned."

"That's not possible," I say. "Poisoned with what?"

"With whatever cut his neck," says Gautam. "Assassins poison their blades, and if their victims don't die on impact and escape, the poison will kill them."

"How do you know this?"

"That's irrelevant," he says. "Do you want me to rescue him?"

I nod, and my arm goes limp. "Yes," I whisper. "Can you save him?"

"I'll try not to eat him."

"What's that supposed to mean?" I shout. "Either you help him or else."

"We're meat eaters," says Gautam. "Blood is a temptation. I won't deny it. But I will do my best not to eat Veran meat."

"Well, resist," I say, "or lose your life." I place my sword on his chest. Gautam opens his mouth and bites into Frederick's neck, sucking out the venom. Slowly, Frederick's color returns, his chest moves, and the flow of oxygen returns to his lungs.

When the Mulhog is done, it spits out a thick silver substance into the gutters.

"What the hell was that?" says Frederick. His wound begins to heal rapidly.

"You're lucky I didn't turn you into my dinner," says the Mulhog and walks ahead.

"Do you want to tell me what that was about?" repeats Frederick.

"The gods must have given you ten lives," I say, relieved knowing that he lives. I give him a firm hug, but his arms hang lifelessly to his side. He is worried and so am I, but I try not to show it. I try to be strong. What's happening to Frederick? How long will he go on? I'm terrified that his luck will run out.

17

FREDERICK

A PART OF me does not want this. The unknown, the danger of getting Nora and myself killed with each step we take into darkness. I'm shaken from defeating death over an over. I can't go on. The Mulhog resisted the temptation between my rescue and my death this once. Maybe it will not hesitate next time.

Nora glares at me, questioning my condition. I know what she's thinking. Why am I not grateful she took a chance and let the beast suck out the poison? She puts her hand on my back and rubs it gently. What do I tell her? That I am angry with her?

"Breathe, Frederick." But I don't. I hold onto my breath as if I was under water and breathing would kill me. She tries to knock the air out of me, her fingers curled into a hard ball hitting my spine. "Breathe, by the gods, breathe." Her voice is alarming.

I toss my head between my legs and do as I am told. I breathe. But she doesn't know that breathing is my enemy. The air feels toxic, enriched with poisonous fumes that are infesting my lungs. I feel vulnerable and exposed. Why don't I feel grateful for being saved?

When I was much younger, I'd laugh so hard that I couldn't breathe. These days I rarely laugh and when I hold my breath now, it's because I am either under attack or surviving whatever it is that's trying to kill me.

As I begin to breathe again, I see the ease on Nora's face. She's trying to break into my mind, questions always questions. I want to take a leap of faith and fall. I want to shout that I don't want to do this anymore. I'm tired of risking our lives. Tired of putting us into dangerous situations. It will not stop when we return to the Triangle. The Verans and the Goths will want our heads.

I wish we could run away and never return, not to Arres, not to the Triangle, and certainly never to the City of Vikings. Like Nora's dad, I seek comfort in starting over, perhaps in Midgard, if we get that far. As I keep my inner thoughts sealed and my breath steady, I fool the girl I love into believing I am okay. But how do I tell her I am not? My anger is partly to do with the constant danger I sense. Anytime now something terrible is going to happen. The Mulhog will deceive us. When did a flesh-eating creature from the Garm Klan ever help humans? He might have helped me now, but only because he needs something from us in return. Nora carries all the weapons strapped around her body. The Mulhog knows what he's up against. He'd be mad to challenge us to battle.

Hunger strikes me, and I feel tired and dizzy. Thirst burns my throat. I remain strong and follow Nora and the Mulhog into the dark underworld of Arres. The tunnels appear smaller at this end, like the walls are closing in on us. I never was fond of small spaces. I grew up in mansions, tall towers. The Dahl residence was prestigious and glorious. My entire future was planned for me. I knew what I wanted to be and where I was going, until I met Nora. I think of my past: my father, my brother, Tommy, and my dynasty. What will they all do when I tell them?

She changed my life, and I will never know my expected future. Instead, I will know more of the unforeseen dangers ahead of us. Forbidden love, wars between our clans, our dynasties. Lord Nourusa's evil forces wait to click the switch to darkness, and the shadow worlds are prepared to unfold. Nourusa's followers stand ready to battle, murder, and to take what Nora and I would die to protect–Midgard.

How do I fit into all this? With more than our lives at risk, the Viking worlds are waiting, and the battle for Midgard is about to begin. How will Nora forge ahead? She needs me. I know she does, and there's no point in being angry about the fate we chose for ourselves. It will only lead to a quicker death. I need to gather my strength, and shut down my inner voice. I don't want to alert Nora. But by the gods, it will affect her. She keeps strong for both of us, and I sense her growing fear. Sooner or later she, too, has to break, but if she does, she won't tell me. She's too tough.

It's in her nature to contradict, be impulsive, change her mind, and show bravery, determination, and stubbornness. She's one of a kind, and I see why the gods handpicked her to lead the way to the Nine Worlds. Only a character like Nora can carry that burden. She carries fire in her belly. Fearless, she forges ahead to claim what she believes is her right.

"What's happening to you?" Nora says. "You're blocking me from your thoughts. Why?" Her face shows anger and frustration.

"I'm having second thoughts about the Mulhog." I pause. Her face tightens; she's confused. "He may have sucked out the poison from my body, but there's something bigger at play—"

"What are you saying?" she whispers. "The Mulhog wants to cook us up for dinner?"

"What does he gain from helping us?" I say. "Ever thought about that?"

"I do know if he wanted us dead, he'd have attacked us and let you die."

"Mulhogs are smart creatures," I say. "They like to lure their prey first."

"You've read too much Norse mythology, Frederick."

"That day in the Forbidden Area, the only reason he didn't eat you was because the damned creature was alone."

She furrows her brows. "He didn't eat me because he knew I was a Goth. He's hiding something."

"The Garm Klan feast on their prey in groups," I say. "It's part of their—"

We stop, and I hear something in the distance, heavy footsteps closing in on us. I smell burning torches and spot fire flickering ahead. The flames get closer, and the warmth touches my skin. I make out a small crowd of shadows that are not humans, Mulhogs with loaded bows aiming at us. I catch a glimpse of their hungry jaws. I knew it. We're going to die.

18

NORA

SOMETHING STRANGE IS happening to Frederick. He's quiet. Something's bothering him. Could it have been what I said or did before? Whatever it is, he needs to wait it out until we find the Rebels. We can't slow down. Not now that we are closer to a way out.

I think Frederick is vexed at me for not listening to him, but I couldn't help myself. Lately I feel changed, like I am wearing someone else's skin—a thicker skin than I wore in the East. The skin of an assassin: someone that kills without guilt, without conscience. That doesn't mean I have no emotions. It just means I suppress a lot. But I need to embrace who I am becoming if we are to get out of Arres.

My palm I keep closed, hiding what I think someone might see. Perhaps it was just Frederick who could not see the runes. One by one I release my fingers and open my hand. In the darkness they shine beautifully, like miniature suns. The runes glow, all nine of them. The force that's hidden in these symbols is powerful and strong. It will open the gate to the Nine Worlds.

We're up against the Triangle in the battle for Midgard, which belongs to us, and together we must create a new order. Much like my dad, I, too, have a need to form a world that is built on the pillars of justice and integrity. It is what I want, what I need. But first I want to understand what's happening with Frederick. He's blocked me from his thoughts and is not speaking with me the way he usually does. If the splinter in his mind grows, it could cause problems, and I am already feeling guilty for blaming him and never showing him the trust he deserved when it mattered.

When I ask him what's the reason, he's silent as a lamb. He says he's afraid that the Mulhog is leading us into our death. I think the Mulhog has other intentions; he wants something from us. If he wanted to murder us, he would have attempted it when we were at our lowest point. Mulhogs are animals after all and like any animal, they are driven by their instincts.

My knowledge about Vikings and mystical creatures is not as good as Frederick's. His background is refined and sophisticated, as he grew up in fine mansions.

My heart twitches. I miss Helena's rationale, logic, and reason. I need her. She'd never believe what I've gotten myself into. Or maybe she knows and watches over me with Magnus who holds Odin's eye. Does he see me? And does he watch over us as we follow the Mulhog, Gautam, into further darkness?

Frederick's arm stretches out in front of me. I suck in the dense air and hold my breath and release it slowly like a dying balloon. Maybe Frederick was right. We shouldn't trust Gautam. But I'd rather take a risk with this creature than being hunted by the mad emperor and his killer army. What will he do if he finds us? We've killed his assassins and legionnaires in the capital city. What other forces does he hold in the other lands of Arres? And will he use them to indict us?

The air burns, and darkness brings forth a glowing shade of light. Smoke dances like snakes. Several flickering torches become visible held by an angry looking mob of Mulhogs. A sharp arrow set against one of the Mulhog's bows touches my skin. The pain is not what I fear, but what would happen to me should he release it.

"Why are you not taking us to meet the Rebels?" I ask. The question feels redundant because we've been fooled. I hope playing a little stupid will get me an answer that will turn in our favor. What if this is all a misunderstanding?

"We are the Rebels," says the Mulhog, lowering the arrow set against my heart.

Frederick and I stare at each other in disbelief. "I'm Anid, the leader of the Garm Klan. You must be Nora Hunt and Frederick Dahl."

"You're the Rebels?" says Frederick.

I look around and there's about five of them. "Where are your other Klan members?"

"We hide in a secret den deep underneath the ground, where it's cool and safe from the Emperor and his legion of killers."

"What are you doing in Arres? You belong in the Forbidden Areas," says Frederick.

"Most of the Forbidden Areas are barren. Nothing lives for long there. This land belonged to *our* ancestors," says Anid. "We've been trying to claim it back since the agreement made between the Garms and the Goths."

"What agreement?" I say. "And why?"

"This is not the time to talk about the agreement; you will know more when you need to," says Anid. "There are many other ways to enter Arres, but we've found a way out. You already know that Arres is indestructible. It's the only world that will remain when everything else falls."

"You want it back and want to overthrow the Emperor?" says Frederick.

"Help us, and we'll help you," says Anid. "You hold powerful weapons—"

"Forget about it," I shout. My voice echoes in the empty tunnels. "I've already shed enough blood as it is."

"You're an assassin. Killing for justice should not matter," says Anid. "But when you kill for lust, for desire—"

"That comes from you?" Frederick says. "You eat humans. You've killed women and children of Arres. The people here are frightened of you. They want you dead."

"We cannot escape what lies in our nature, but we will take what belongs to us, and nothing is going to stop us," says Anid. He looks at Gautam sharply. "Bring them to the underground. Nezma, the queen of the Garm Klan, wants to meet the two famous raiders from Jarl and Rognvald."

Deep underneath Arres, the Mulhogs have created a secret underworld. We're miles away from the whispering dunes moving like ocean waves in the warm wind. Here nothing moves; it stands still with time. We walk into a dank hole with a low entrance and ragged drapes that fail to serve as a door. Inside, light flickers from torches.

Anid places his hand on my back and nudges me further into a room. My grip around the weapons is tight, my palm burning and itching. *What is this forsaken place?*

It's an eerie cavern, and rats skitter across the floor. Gautam opens a scraping door and guides Frederick and me forward. The cool air washes over me, sweeping away the clamminess of the desert heat. The rich smells of wood and smoke curl up into my nose, and it makes me think of the East. The face of the woman who raised me appears before my eyes. I stopped thinking about her. Her feelings toward me were not exactly motherly. I can't say the same thing about Karen. She did show feelings when she saw me and embraced me as her daughter, but she also caused the mess to start with.

"Where's your queen?" says Frederick impatiently. I look around. The room is dark. It's hard to see anything. Red lanterns are glowing among the torches. It reminds me of the assembly in the Tower of Swords on the day Magnus announced that I was to lead the Jarls. "Well?"

A stocky, dark-haired woman walks in, looking at me carefully. Behind her a group of Mulhogs follow, growling. I should feel afraid, but I am not. I am more curious than anything else. Why is the queen of the Garm Klan not a Mulhog? What conditions will she line up before we are allowed to return to the Triangle? I'm tempted to use the weapons to solve matters if I have to.

My battle is my own. I am not ready to win a battle that's not mine. Justus Markus controls the vicious Goths that belong to the Mulhogs, but that is not my concern. Frederick and I are wanted in the Triangle; we'll be outlaws. We have no alliance. The senate and the opposition I have reason to believe are all corrupt. Even if Arres is eternal, my interest is to open the gate to the Nine Worlds and pass into Midgard where I can live with Frederick. I have to gather strength, rest, and then face Magnus. It will not be easy. I already carry labels of betrayal and disloyalty.

Queen Nezma doesn't say anything; she just glares as if assessing what our next move will be. She knows I have the weapons. Will she still demand we fight for her, or will she allow us to go home? Her eyes are pleading.

"Before you leave Arres, we will need your help," says Queen Nezma.

"We could not help you," I say. "Even if we wanted to."

"We have to return to the Triangle," says Frederick. "Time is running out."

"From one battlefield to another," says the queen. "What difference does Arres make?"

"We were not prepared to battle on behalf of anyone," I say. "We have our own fight to win against forces much stronger than Arres."

"We cannot hold you back," says the queen. "But when the time comes, Nora Hunt and Frederick Dhal, the Mulhogs will not help you. Our alliance will be broken."

"Why would we depend on your help?" I say. "You don't owe us anything."

"Garm and Goth made an alliance," says Nezma.

"What alliance?" I say. That day in the Forbidden Areas when the Mulhog saw me, it didn't eat me. It said, "must not eat Goth." Could that have something to do with the alliance Nezma is talking about?

"We would take the land of eternity that was forged hundreds of years ago by our ancestors and lost in battle. Arres is a portal to the past and where the assassins lived an afterlife in exchange for our loyalty. We took an oath never to harm the Goths. We've kept our side of the bargain. Frederick is no Goth. Yet we let him live with that creature in one of the fallen houses behind the markets. Oh yes, we knew about your arrival. How do you think you survived the desert all alone, Nora? Have you forgotten the mercy we showed you?"

"Your oath has nothing to do with me." I say. "I have my

own battles to win."

"Let me remind you, Nora Hunt, you are an assassin by blood and by descent. We've kept our part of the deal, whereas your ancestors have suppressed us and driven us underground. Now, they are dead and all that stands between Arres and us is the Emperor. He's a cruel and heartless man; you shouldn't feel guilty killing him. His blood is cold, his soul black. He belongs in Helheim now and in all eternity."

"If we help you, will you keep your end of the bargain and help us when we need you?" I say looking into her eyes. "Will you get us out of here, and send us back to the Triangle?"

"You still being alive is a sign that the Garms are not just a low ranked Klan but loyal and stick to their promise."

"So have the Goths," I say. "You were given Arres."

"Arres came with baggage," says Nezma. "The assassins were cursed to stay. Now that they're dead the Emperor is weak and must be defeated. We will not trouble you about Midgard. We've waited long enough for Arres."

"What do you want me to do to the Emperor?" I say. "Should I murder him in his sleep, cut his throat in front of the very people that fear and worship him, or do you want a war?"

"Nora," whispers Frederick. "What are you doing? We should just leave. Like now!"

"Wait," I say. "We might need their help. We have no one else to rely on. The Garm Klan is better than nothing. If I help them they'll get us straight into the Triangle."

"We don't need them; we have the weapons."

"What if that's not enough?" I say. "What if they don't work in the Triangle?"

"The sword does, so why not the remaining weapons?" he says. "Nora, please listen to me. We need to leave Arres; we're putting far too much at risk for low-ranked creatures."

"Frederick, trust me. I'll make it a swift kill, and then we're out of here."

"While you're at it, why not kill his entire army? It seems to me you enjoy killing. While you happen to be in Arres, why not collect the Emperor's head for a souvenir? You'd like that, wouldn't you? You have a thing for collecting human heads."

"You sound ridiculous," I hiss. "What's the matter with you? I need you to trust me."

"And I need you to listen to me," says Frederick loudly. "But you never do. You're just too stubborn, and now you're becoming a stubborn killer. An assassin."

"Don't go all soft on me," I say. "You knew what you signed up for. Did you think any of this would be easy?"

"No, I know it's not," says Frederick. "It's not about easy. It's about being fair. Where's that girl from the East? The one who wouldn't kill animals or other living creatures?"

"That coming from you?" I say. "You use black magic, is that better?"

"You don't know what you're getting us into," says Frederick. Nezma is looking at me, her eyes wide and intense like she's showed up to an uninvited party. "To hell with everything," shouts Frederick, and I don't think I've seen him angrier than he is now.

19

FREDERICK

I'M FURIOUS. STEAMING. It makes no sense to form an alliance. We have the assassin weapons; it's what we came for. Not the assassination of Justus Markus, his army, or any other political crap that Nora is getting us into. I still don't trust the Garm Klan. Why haven't we heard anything about the alliance before?

Some part of me just wants to grab Nora's hand and get us the hell out of here, and another wants to leave her behind. I feel as if she never listens.

As we gear up to journey to the Emperor's palace, I can't help thinking that we may not get out of Arres alive. It will take us days to reach the southern tip. To gain time, we have to travel by air, and may risk being seen.

Queen Nezma is half human with Mulhog blood. Although she looks nothing like an animal, her instincts are animalistic and she kills ruthlessly. She handles all the affairs of the Klan, but was unable to strike a deal with the assassins who refused to let them inhabit the holy land. That's when they rose as Rebels and began killing the people of Arres, and the believers of the sky god, Zohra. According to their own legend, the Emperor was chosen by Zohra to rule Arres, and the rule cannot be given to savage animals.

The Emperor rules as the higher King of the kingdom of Arres, and Zohra gave him a secret vision that no one knows the details of. Some say it's the reason he kills every baby girl that's born among his several wives, concubines, and mistresses who desperately want to give him a boy. No boy has been born for the past decade. Rumor has it he will die without an heir, and his kingdom will fall.

The Garm Klan is not sitting around and waiting. Their Rebel group has been growing, but not as fast as the Emperor's army. With the assassins dead, the barrier to take over City of Assassins is broken. I am not sure why the Garms don't move their troops in. Are they afraid that the Emperor will defeat them? The assassins were his strength, and their loyalty was bought in return for power over the city they viciously ruled. The assassins killed many members of the Garm Klan and broke the trust that was established. The Garms are no fools. They knew of Nora and what she's capable of. They need her to claim what is theirs. Without her and the weapons, the Emperor may not be defeated.

We're out of the City of Assassins, and the air is damp. The desert heat feels dry and cold. We head south, through isolated streets and abandoned houses. Nora has tried to hold my hand, but each time I break loose and walk ahead of her. We're actually doing this– assassinating the Emperor. Is it a good thing? I don't know. Whatever gets us back to the Triangle.

We have to get past the main gateway and travel across the desert for days to make it south to the Emperor's ruling land, Trinzantine. I'm assured there are means in place to get us there faster, but the Garms don't reveal much. They are secretive, unpredictable. They are animals, I remind myself. We pass the gateway unusually fast, through a secret backdoor in one of the houses closer to the portal between the castle and the desert.

The heat of the sand dunes and the cawing of the predatory birds are all I see and hear. For hours, we wander across the deadly rocky valleys. To begin with all we can see is red dust, and then in the distance we see caves and hollow canyons that stare at us like death. We walk into the mouth of this deadly gorge and continue our journey. We have little food and water and can't go on for much longer.

"What is this place?" I say. "Where are we going?"

"The port of time is hidden here," says Queen Nezma. "It will take us straight to Trinzantine."

"How about the Triangle?" I say. "Can this port transport us home?"

She's quiet, but her silence speaks volumes.

"It can take you anywhere," she says. "But there are consequences."

"What consequences?" says Nora and leans in closer.

"Your mind," she says, "will be affected."

"You expect us to walk through the port and suffer brain damage," I say.

"It's temporary," she says. "In the worst case, you get out of touch with some of your emotions."

"What if I don't want to," I say.

"Wait!" says Nora. "Why did you not tell us this before? You expect us to walk into Trinzantine and murder the Emperor, and we may not even know who we are or what we feel for one another?"

"You have a choice," says Queen Nezma. "Leave Arres now and return to the Triangle with the same consequences or—"

"Or what?" I say.

"Or help us release Arres from an evil Emperor who will not stop until he gets what he wants."

"What's that?" says Nora. She holds her breath, her eyes wide. "By the gods, I know now... I know what he wants. You tricked us, you dirty animals." She draws her sword, but the Garms have surrounded us and take away the weapons from Nora. We're trapped and have no choice but to surrender.

20

NORA

FREDERICK IS ANGRY with me, and I can feel his fury radiate like a burning torch. I want to hold his hand and tell him I am sorry for risking our lives. I cannot walk away from Arres knowing we could have done something to prevent the Emperor from killing innocent girls. The very thought makes me feel ill, and I need to know his reason for taking the lives of his own daughters. I want to look into his eyes before I slit his throat and ask *why?* I can't explain the emotions I carry, but I feel the need to put things right. I feel responsible.

An alliance with the Mulhogs could benefit Frederick and me. We don't know what to expect when we return to the Triangle. We will not be met with a warm welcome after serving time away. I need this alliance. Besides I am accountable for keeping the promise that was made by the Goths, am I not? My ancestors viciously murdered Garm Klan members and threw them out of their own land. They've done *us* no harm. I understand Frederick's troubled mind. We have the weapons. It's the only thing we came for, why risk everything now? Frederick doesn't trust the Mulhogs. He thinks they are hiding something, but they've not made an attempt to eat us yet. Should I be worried something bigger is at play? Is Frederick right and will the Mulhogs corner us? I doubt it. I don't think that's what they're after. Animals don't have that kind of intelligence. If they did they'd be ruling the world.

We walk into a deep ghostly gorge leaving the hot spell of the desert dunes behind. The shade gives the air a subtle chill and my thirst and hunger disappears. After walking a great distance Frederick stops and demands that Queen Nezma tell us why we're heading into the rocky mountain terrain. She says to get to Trinzantine quicker we'll have to walk through the portal of time hidden inside the canyons.

Frederick's expression changes, and I sense danger as he persists in asking about returning to the Triangle via the portal. I can see why. We could walk through the door and forget about the Emperor, Arres, the assassins, and the Mulhogs. We need to go home and leave this eternal land. Anything else is madness, isn't it?

"Speak in the name of Odin," he shouts. The sound of his voice echoes in the deadly valley. "Can we go back to the Triangle through that portal?"

"You can go anywhere, if you know where you're heading and have the right spells, but be aware of the consequences." she says.

I walk up close and look her straight in her golden eyes bright like miniature suns. I sense suppressed animal instincts, secrets and lies. She's hiding something, but I don't get a clear sense of what.

"Consequences?" I say and tighten the grip around the hilt of my sword. The other weapons are fastened in a belt against my back. "You didn't mention anything about that."

"I'm sorry. I should have, but I was afraid what it would mean if I did. Travel between time lapses has an effect on the mind," she says. "You could lose your memory for a longer period, and the impact could also change certain feelings, simply because they get erased or replaced. Nothing is certain, and we try not to use the portal of time unless we absolutely have to."

Frederick is furious. He fears we'll suffer permanent damage, but Queen Nezma assures us it's only temporary. I have other worries. Why didn't she tell us this before? What is she up to? Killing the Emperor to stop his insanity is one thing, but it's another to suffer unknown consequences. I've already lost my memory once. What will happen the second time I walk past the time portal?

"Why did you keep it a secret?" I say keeping my voice controlled.

"You are here because you want to be," says Queen Nezma. "Leave Arres or—"

"Or what?" I say.

"Someone has to stop Justus Markus from getting what he wants," she says. "Nora, you're the last Viking assassin. It is your *responsibility* to set this right."

"What does he want?" I say. I thought he wanted a male heir. Why is he killing his own newborn daughters? Then it all becomes clear like rays of morning light. I hold my breath so I don't explode. *You fool, Nora!* How could I have been so blind? Before I get to take out my sword the Mulhogs surround us and take away my weapons.

"I never forced you," says Queen Nezma, "I wanted the choice to be yours. You feel it now, don't you? The urge to kill the Emperor, for he will not stop until he finds you."

"Nora, what's going on?" says Frederick. "Why does he want to find *you?*"

"You know what you need to do," says Queen Nezma. "You're the chosen assassin after your ancestors, the last of your kind. We're just *animals.* We use our instincts, which is why you have to enter Trinzantine and do what your heart tells you to. If you don't the risk remains and he *will* come after you. It's only a matter of time till he finds out what you did to the assassins, to your own blood."

"Will someone tell me what I've missed?" Frederick's voice is shrill.

"The Emperor's secret vision from the sky god Zohra, no one knows it, but there are rumors," says Queen Nezma. "According to their own myth and legends Justus Markus was chosen to rule this holy land, but all great leaders fall one day, and the Emperor's rule is threatened. We think the vision showed him his future murder committed by his own flesh and blood. A girl. That's the only explanation we have for his ruthless killings. Other gossip suggests a girl of Viking assassin descent will bear him a son from divine light. The Emperor is rumored to be behind some secret killings of the newborn girls in Arres. The assassins were his army of protection against us, against the Arrians. He will never see it coming."

"See what coming?" says Frederick.

"Nora Hunt," she says. "Even if he does, she will only trick him."

"You sound too certain," I say. "I am not going in there to seduce or carry some divine light to life. The deal is off."

"When the Emperor first set out to kill his newborn daughters to favor a male heir he hesitated, but only until the vision became clear in his mind. We cannot be sure of what he saw, but everything suggests he's protecting himself from being assassinated."

"He kills the girls before they become a threat." I say.

"Do you want this madness to go on?" says Queen Nezma. "Nora, you can't leave Arres without killing the Emperor first."

"Why did you not tell me sooner?" I say. "This changes everything."

"Nothing is purer, more impeccable than free will," says Queen Nezma. "Had I forced you or mentioned this earlier your motives would have been driven by guilt and responsibility. Belief is driven by willpower and gives better results."

"You were afraid I'd bail on you like the Goths?"

"You were going to as soon as you learned about the portal of time, were you not?"

"Maybe," I say. "But I am not going to now."

"Nora," Frederick holds my hand. "Think carefully what you're getting yourself into. Who knows what he saw in this vision of his. Don't do this. Think about the time lapses. They can cause more than just memory loss."

"That is true," says Queen Nezma. "Hallucinations can occur in rare cases. An open and vulnerable mind is prone to them."

"All this has a connection to me. Besides, I refuse to live with the guilt that I could have done something to stop him. Where does that leave the Triangle or Midgard? We don't want to blend the past with the future. The Emperor has to die."

"Then do it," says Frederick. "I'll be by your side." I look into his deep blue eyes and see hope, fear, and love. Most of all I see a reflection of my own determination.

"Frederick must return to the Triangle," says Queen Nezma. "The two of you will attract far too much attention and curiosity in Trinzantine. Nora's advantage is her feminine charm which will serve well there to seduce the enemy if she has to."

"What do you mean?" I say.

"You'll see when you get there." says Queen Nezma.

"I'm going to Trinzantine with Nora no matter what." says Frederick his voice firm.

"Frederick, I think Queen Nezma is right. I need to do this on my own."

"Are you sure?" he says. "I can't just let you do this alone."

I nod and look away so I don't lose courage.

"It's time I put an end to the evil," I say. "But we cannot lose the weapons. You have to bring them back. I'll kill the evil monster somehow."

"If that's what you want," says Frederick. "But don't let your bravery control your emotions. You don't have to do this. You don't owe the Garms or the people of Trinzantine anything. You are not responsible for your ancestor's doings. They promised the land to The Garms. No one predicted the Emperor's rule. His curse. We deserve to be returned home and be free. The Rebels made a promise to bring us there safely."

"I need to do this." I say "We both know it's the right thing to do."

"I do, but I don't favor the right thing over your life," says Frederick.

"I will return, I promise you," I say. "Do you believe me?"

"I do." says Frederick. "If that's what you want then I will meet you in the City of Skies." He stands tall looking strong, but I know deep inside he feels weak and afraid, just like me.

"Get me to Trinzantine." I say and stalk away, before I regret my decision.

The Mulhogs lead us to the portal of time – a black hole buried inside the canyons. Queen Nezma gives me a spell that will take me straight to the Emperor's palace and another one to return to the City of Skies. I have nothing to protect myself from. The weapons I've trusted Frederick with. I don't want to risk losing them at any cost.

Once I recite the spell the Mulhogs have given me, it will take me to the desert of Trinzantine. *A swift kill, that's all this is.* I tell myself. That's all this will be and I will be back in the Triangle united with Frederick before I know it.

"This is it," says Queen Nezma. "Remember who you are and what you have to do. Don't lose the trail of your thoughts. Repeat them to strengthen your memory for no one knows the state of your mind and how fragile it is except yourself."

When the portal of time opens, a furious wind begins to pull me in. I stand with one foot in Trinzantine and the other in Arres. Frederick seals my lips with a warm kiss and I wish he was coming with me, but I cannot risk his life. I need him to return the weapons.

"I'll be waiting for you when you return." Frederick's eyes are beautiful and deep like the ocean. His face hides anxiety, and it is the last thing I see and hope will be the first to greet me when I'm home.

"I know." I smile and take off the pressure from my foot holds. I feel nervous, my heart pounding. Gravity releases me and I float into the deep dark hole, my hair drifting like algae in the sea. My fingers stretch out, reaching for Frederick's hands, but they become smaller and smaller as the darkness consumes me. The vacuum is vast, fearless. Thoughts I want to release are kept hostage. Emotions I want to dig up are buried. I lose myself and I lose my senses. I see and hear nothing.

It feels like I'm inside someone's dream. My vision is blurry and white like I am behind a light cotton veil. Underneath the padding is soft, comfortable. The bed I am in has silk sheets, and the wind traveling through the window is warm, infused with sweet scents. My skin is prickled with goosebumps, and to my horror I discover my skin is coated with dry blood—someone else's blood. I toss aside the sheets and scramble out of the bed.

I need to find something to remove the blood stains. I look around the room and find a cloth and attempt to rub myself clean. I take off my outfit and slip into the black cotton dress hanging on a chair. It fits snugly around my figure like it was tailor made. I know where I am, but cannot remember how I got to be here. I know I've been here a while. The room is familiar, so is the bed. There are large white pillars, a marble floor, and a water fountain in the middle of the room. The sound of water should feel soothing and calm, but it doesn't. It sounds deadly and makes me feel fretful.

Something isn't right. The water in the fountain is deep red. When I look under the surface I see a stern face strangled, no longer breathing. I know who it belongs to the Emperor, Justus Markus. I assassinated him. A cold blackness fills my mind and the past hours are missing from my memory like someone wiped it clean.

What happened to me? I have to get back to the City of Skies, but how? I hear footsteps and whispers outside the room and hide behind one the many pillars separating the mezzanine bedroom from the main area where the fountain is.

I pull out the gray soaked corpse and run my fingers over the Emperor's horrid face. His black eyes move and stare right into my soul. He opens his mouth.

"BRING ME TO LIFE!" His scream pierces the air. I step back, my chest heavy, my breath uneasy. Am I inside a dream or is this all an illusion? This isn't real. It can't be. Voices gather and form unfamiliar faces in the dark, all staring at me. The Emperor rises, his face poisonous and resentful. I look back. The wind is pulling me toward the open window. My hands try to reach for something but hold only air. I swirl around like a fluttering bird trapped in a cage.

In the mirror, I see my own reflection staring back at me. It's not *me*. Or at least I think it's not me. I look different. My face looks mature like I've aged. I am a woman stuck in this place and in this body. What happened to me? Frederick, I have to get back to him, back to the Triangle, before I lose my mind. I'm delirious, that must be it. I'm having hallucinations. My mind was always open, fragile to what it does not know, and it still is. *What is happening to me?*

My movements carry me out of the bedroom and into the hot open air. My body floats above the sandy and rocky landscape. The wind is a silent grave. My grave. I could be dead. I could be fantasizing. I spread out my arms and they turn into large wings. I caw like an eagle, Jarl's eagle—strong, fearless, and powerful. My eyes see miles ahead over the deadly desert dunes searching a way out. The memories flood back like a black screaming tide.

The time lapse spat me into Trinzantine, but I somehow ended up in the Emperor's future vision, which became a reality for he is dead. I killed him. My memory is in a haze. Everything happened so fast, and I only have glimpses of flickering images. I held his face between my hands. I licked off the bitterness from his lips, a poisonous kiss, his tongue stuck down my throat. I had to push him away, I couldn't breathe. The feeling of anger and disgust, controlled, but not well enough.

Just as he lay down in his bed I ripped open his throat and dragged his body into the fountain where his filthy blood poisoned the water black. I wanted to muffle his screams because even in his own death he kept shouting, *bring me to life*. I have taken his life, like he has taken the lives of others. If I didn't, he would have taken mine, and more to come.

In disguise, I seduced him looking older than what I am and killed him. It's no ancient secret, the art of seduction. A man like him has an obvious weakness. The picture is still vaguely inside my mind of the harem where the Emperor keeps hundreds of his slave girls, concubines, and mistresses. I made sure to stick out among his many women; enough to catch his interest and it wasn't hard. He fell like a thirsty beggar drowns in a well and I don't feel guilty, I feel free.

The black tide hidden in the desert is the portal of time calling for me. My emotions are beginning to disappear. I don't know who I am anymore. I'm losing my ability to connect to myself and to my mind. My powers are giving in and fading. I roll onto the sand and face the swirling pool of black, as it gets smaller. *This is it.* If I don't jump I'll stay in Trinzantine, in this body of an older woman, shape shifting forever. Eventually the Emperor's army will catch me and decapitate me. His screams are still amplifying inside my head. *Bring me to life.* Even if I could, I'd never want evil of his kind to ever live again. He reminds me of Hildebrand, when I first met him in the City of Skies. Perhaps even of my own mother and Frederick's father. That evil lives in so many shapes and forms and it is my duty to finish the things that threaten the

Viking worlds.

I turn around and let myself fall into the black hole of time while whispering the spell the Mulhogs gave me. I imagine all the things that are waiting for me in the City of Skies. I imagine Helena, but she's troubled. I spin endlessly and faster into darkness, into the shadows.

Slowly I step out of the skin I wear, the skin of a powerful and seductive woman who always gets what she wants. Her only weapon is beauty, before she turns into a beast. Is she a vision of what I will become? It's not who I am and not who I want to become. But I know who I am. I am the deadliest Viking assassin.

I travelled in time to get the weapons and to murder the evil that would free the Garms and restore Arres. It was an obligation I felt committed to, to redeem myself from my ancestor's barbaric rule. They are cursed and will dwell in Arres forever as dead spirits. I know why the Emperor killed his own children. It gave him life, made him stronger. He was seeking life by taking life and would continue to do so until he got what he wanted—a male heir to reincarnate his spirit.

The taste of his blood still stings my tongue. I knew I shouldn't have, but I did. I tried his blood and it runs in my veins and I cannot rid myself of what I carry. Something sinister, something living inside of me and I dare not think of it. The feeling may stay with me all the way back to the Triangle of Peace or it may die out. I hope it does.

The darkness devours me as if I belonged to it. I feel the blackness around me and for a moment I am afraid. I am neither my old self nor a new person. I let the shadow consume me and move me beyond the desert heat all the way into the Triangle of Peace.

III

THE NEW WORLDS

21

The Return

SNOW FALLS FROM the open sky. Everything is covered in crystal ice—the pointed skyscrapers, the cars zooming on the roads, and the people wandering like soulless drones. It takes me a while to figure out where I am, and then it hits me, I'm back in the West. Everything is different and yet the same. I realize I must have been away for quite some time. The City of Skies has fallen under a weather spell. Warm once, now it has become a place covered in layers of snow. I crack my fingers feeling the cold seep under my pale, almost blue skin. I'm unable to remember how I ended up here in the city's most deprived area.

The smell of poverty embraces me. I remember when I came here last. It was destiny that brought me here on a mission to kill Maja Gustafson. A rush of adrenalin sweeps through my body when I think of that fateful night in the underworld of Zenghis. The deformed beings that rule it know me.

I seek familiarity among the faces flashing by. I seek Frederick. But my mind is absent and I feel numb. I remember everything now. The East, Blossom Heights, Gustav, the woman who pretended to be my biological mother, the recruitment. The painful memories flood through my mind. My anxiety is electric. I remember the time served at Dock Harbor and when I saw Frederick for the first time. He was like a dream, a mysterious shadow teasing me. A dangerous fire of love. I can't wait to see him, but I have to be careful and smart how I go about my return. Magnus and the raiders that serve our dynasty want me.

"Watch it!" says someone, as he storms into me pushing me so hard that I land in the corner of a dark alley. Thick leather covers my body. Black creaking trousers and a jacket. This part I do not remember and discover the blank spot in my memory. How did I come to be in the City of Skies wearing my old raider outfit? What happened in Trinzantine and when did I leave? I realize I carry several holes in my memory. Things are not as clear as I thought they were. My recent past is blurry.

I dust off the snowflakes layering around my hair and my clothes and walk into the narrow alley. A stink of death and rot hits me. Undernourished cats wander around the overspill of trash covered in white. I need to get in touch with Frederick. What happened after I left Arres? Did he make it back all right? Does he still have the weapons? I hope the Garms didn't hurt him. I hope for their own sake that they stuck to their end of the bargain. I turn to look at the chip flattened against my inner wrist. There's a vague signal coming through and a fading blinking light of red as if it's about to die. I tap it and transmit a message to Frederick. Will Magnus be able to detect me? Of course, he will.

When Tanya installed the chip, she made sure I would be traceable as long as there was a signal. Sending Frederick a message, I am running the risk of revealing my return, and it could compromise both our lives, but I don't have a choice. I need to speak to him.

Wading through the street restlessly I take a left turn and the alley connects me to another busy road. Across from it I see the Common Grounds. I met Frederick there after we'd become enemies in the dynasty. I will meet him there again, but this time as allies, friends, and lovers. Or maybe as nothing at all. I push the thought out of my mind. I need to see him.

As I walk toward the Common Grounds, the view becomes unpleasant. The water is icy and the harbor covered in a thick layer of frost. I wonder what happened to the weather while I was gone. How can the sun shy away from this place? Just as I am about to cross the road a sleek black car pulls up next to the curb. Beneath the shiny silver tires thick gray icy slush splashes onto me. The door opens sideways and I see a familiar face framed in a soft golden light.

"It is you. I thought it was, but I wasn't sure." His voice is soft and eyes bright. He looks ecstatic as if he has been looking for me for years and has finally found me.

"Andreas?" I say. "You look different." I offer a warm smile. I saved Andreas' life that day in the North on our mission, and I am glad I did. He's exactly what I need – a discrete and wealthy friend I can rely on.

"So do you. Now, get in," he says. "What are you doing out here in the cold?"

"I—" I'm not sure what to say. He's wearing a sharp wool suit and blue shirt. He looks polished, clean, and much older. "Can you bring me to Chelsea?" What place could be better right now than Karen's? Would my own mother turn against me? I'd have to find out.

"I'll bring you anywhere you want." He slides over and pats his hand on the empty seat. I hop in and sit next to him. The car takes off. "Should I think it's normal to find you in the most dangerous part of town?"

"I could say the same thing about you," I say and lean against the soft leather seat, my breath forming a cloud. "How are you, my friend?"

"I'm great." He gives me a wolfish smile. "Not being a raider is wonderful."

"You expect me to believe you?" The numbness in my body is disappearing. My hands wiggle, the color shifting from blue to red.

"I might be missing out on some action, but I am well and alive." He snaps his fingers at the driver. "Take a U-turn, Karl; we're heading to Chelsea."

"As you wish, Master Andreas," says the driver. Through the rearview mirror, he tosses me a hard glare. I know what he's thinking. In the West, I am an elite raider. I belong to my dynasty. Why is the driver then dropping me off in Chelsea, where officials from the opposition reside? I should be heading to the Towers. I don't feel safe going there. I have no means of protection.

"I need a favor, Andreas." I say before I lose my nerve. I hold back a while twisting my hands. Andreas puts his hand on mine, and it calms me.

"Anything you need." Andreas has been a good friend. He's always been generous and didn't hold back the times I needed him. I trust him, and I feel safe with him.

"You know that my life may be in danger."

"I know," he says. "I've followed the whole thing from the day you left the West."

"How did you know?" I say.

"I have my sources," he says. "In high places."

"Were you looking for me?" I say. "Why were you here?"

"I happened to be passing through when I saw you." he says in such a way that I believe him. I can't be suspicious, not now.

"Andreas—" I stop myself from saying anything that could create any further tension.

"This route is not my preferred one, but it's faster than passing the Guldborg Bridge gridlock," he says.

"Where are you heading?" I say.

"Home, of course," he says. "After Dock Harbor, I started working for my dad. I know—"

"I wasn't going to say anything." I stare at him and sense the failure he hides.

"It's not great, but I didn't have what it takes to become what you are," he says. "Very few do."

I look out the tinted glass window. The snow falls heavily. It doesn't stop. Before I only noticed the snow, but now I see it for what it truly is—a sign of change.

"What happened here?" I say and swiftly change the subject. "Why is it suddenly snowing?"

"You've been away awhile haven't you?" he smiles and looks at me. "The snow started falling some months ago. It didn't stop. We're getting used to the cold, aren't we, Karl." The driver, who is a great deal older, nods and agrees with Andreas, but the look in his eyes is wary.

"Snowing for months? How long was I—" I pause. Can I really trust Andreas? I feel changed, different. "—away for?"

"What do you mean?" says Andreas. "Nora you've been away nearly a year. I was starting to believe you'd never return."

"A year?" How could I have been away that long? I know

he speaks the truth, but it is hard to hear him say it. I turned seventeen in Arres. It *has* been a year. "So what caused the snowfall?"

"It is believed to be caused by the awakening," says Andreas. "She brought it with her when she planted roots into the Nine Worlds."

"The awakening?" Of course. I should have known.

"Karl, can you take us to one of the city's viewpoints? I want to show Nora *the view*." Andreas curls his lip. I don't like being played with and I feel a sudden urge to scream, *just tell me what the hell is going on!* But I don't. I control my curiosity and anger. What has she done? What in the name of Odin has happened?

Karl glares at us from the rearview mirror, shifting his eyes nervously as if he wants to say something but can't quite muster the words.

"Master Andreas, it may not be possible to see anything from the vantage point. The snow is coming down too heavy right now." he says.

"Just do it," Andreas says his voice clipped. "Nora should be able to catch a small glimpse." I try to relax, but I can't. My nerves are jumpy, and the black leather begins to feel too tight against my skin.

"Andreas, what is going on?" I say. "What do you have to show me?"

"You'll soon see," he says. "She's here."

"She?"

"Yggdrasil," his words leave a bad taste in my mouth. "We've all been waiting for her since the official awakening, except no one knows how the heck to actually reach her. If anyone should know, it's you, Nora."

I lean forward closing my fist tightly. It has happened. She's made herself visible to the world waiting to give us what she carries in her branches. I remember Yggdrasil leaving my body. The pain she caused me and the encrypted runes still burning in my palm. I tend to forget my Viking duties. There's much more at stake than the battle for Midgard. The decision, I realize, is mine. What am I to do now? Should I burn it all to the ground? The hope and dreams of the return of the Viking worlds.

A feeling of despair washes over me. I remember most of what I had forgotten, except the vision Yggdrasil gave me. The gate to the Nine Worlds, I don't know where to find it. I remember that I once knew the location. There has to be a way to recover from the lost memory. But what if I am unable to? How will I convince the Goths that the vision she gave me is unfamiliar. They'll never believe me. The runes stinging my hand will be of no use. The snow will continue to fall, and the city will be buried in cold and ice. Yggdrasil will wither and her branches drop the worlds she's been carrying into darkness.

The car stops at a pointed edge overlooking the harbor. Andreas steps out and opens the other side of the door. Slowly I pull myself out into the cold air and look at the white sky turning bleak. Among the falling snowflakes black shadows hang above the city. Stretched like burning thunder across the sky are the branches of Yggdrasil and in them she carries our precious worlds.

"I don't believe it," I say and throw my hands over my mouth. Through squinted eyes the view becomes clearer. I let my hands fall to the side. "She's causing chaos, the snow—"

"It is getting worse," says Andreas. "If it continues, we're going to die."

"Die?"

"What are you going to do?" He expects an answer, as if I am holding the key to all this. I am, but how does he know? Andreas is from a wealthy family, and I am not surprised he can buy any information he wants. He must have spoken to Hildebrand. I rush back into the car, my hands are shaking. I look at the chip. The signal is still weak, and the message I tried sending to Frederick didn't go through. Andreas gets in on the other side.

"Are you okay?" he says. "What's wrong?"

"Andreas, I need you to get in touch with Frederick and tell him to come to Lady Hunt's house." He looks at me for a while analyzing my obvious panic.

"Sure, I'll do it straight away."

"Wait," I say. "Be careful what you tell him. Do not mention meeting me. I don't want him followed."

"Would you like Karl to drive you to Chelsea now or?"

"Now," I say. "Do you know a safe way to get in touch with Frederick?"

"I guess I could contact Tommy."

"What are you going to tell him?"

"That Frederick is invited to a reception in Chelsea," says Andreas. "Chelsea is famous for hosting all kind of high society diplomatic events. If he's smart enough, which I believe he is—"

"You've made your point," I say relieved. "Let's hope all goes according to plan."

Karl turns the car and drives in the direction of Chelsea. When it pulls into the main square the atmosphere is dark, silent. There are no guards on duty, and the black iron gate that protects the old red brick houses is wide open. When the car stops, I step out and look around. The place is deserted, a ghost town.

"Are you sure I should leave you here?" Andreas steps out. "It looks rather spooky."

"I'm sure," I say. "Thank you."

"If you need me or anything else—"

"There is one more thing, Andreas. The motorcycle—"

"Considered it delivered this evening. Someone will somehow bring it."

"I owe you." I say.

"You saved my life that day in the mountains, Nora. I am the one who is forever in debt to you."

"I did what was right, Andreas," I say. "I'd do it again if I had to."

"I know," he says and stares right into my eyes. I place a soft kiss on his cheek and watch him step back into the car. "You know how to reach me, Nora." I nod and make my way toward Karen's house. The cobblestones are icy, white. My black attire shines in the bright evening light. When I turn, Andreas is already gone.

I grab the door handle and step into the house. Everything looks exactly the way I remember it. The red rug, the dark wooden furniture. Except the walls in the hallway are empty. The large oil paintings are missing. The marks from the frames dust the vacant walls. I place my hand where Harald's painting used to hang. His face is vividly printed in my mind. His vicious face. The rot from his head makes me want to throw up.

A deep juddering intake of breath reach my ears, and I turn around.

"Home so soon?" says Solvej. Her face is stern, and looking straight at me. There's a faint humming in my ears, like an ocean breeze shrieking through a dark storm.

"Home?" I glare at Solvej and something doesn't feel right. Her eyes are stone cold. Empty. "It has been a year."

"Yes, it has." she stands firmly rooted to the ground. Her shoulders are wide and her face is stiffer than before. "She's expecting you." Solvej's severe face lights up a little, and she takes my hands into hers. The runes hidden in my palm warm my hand. Solvej doesn't seem to notice anything, and even if she did I wouldn't know what to say. I can't trust her. The way she looks at me, something is off. But I play along and hope she doesn't notice my suspicion.

"Karen—"

"Is waiting for you. She has been expecting your return," says Solvej as if she has been sedated by a spell. "Come this way." She pulls me along eagerly and walks up the stairs. I look around as we cross a corridor on the way up. I notice a sharp object, an animal tusk from a wild boar perhaps, decorating the wall. My hand slides out of Solvej's. She doesn't stop to look at me as I grab hold of the tusk. I hide it behind my back. My heart is pounding wildly in my ears. Sweat coats my hands.

I sense an unpleasant surprise, an ugly danger lurking. What does she have up her sleeve? Solvej cannot be trusted, and I know what I need to do to protect myself if it comes down to a battle. She's the kind of woman that would feed me to the wolves and watch me become their dinner with a broad smile plastered over her face.

"We need to hurry. She has little time." She stops and turns. I halt at the split landing, my hand resting on the rail.

"What do you mean?"

"Your mother is dying."

"What?" The urge to kill rises inside me. It feels like Solvej is to blame, and I have to stop my hands from closing around her neck. I have to speak to Karen. She can't die before I speak to her. "What happened?"

"There's no time to explain," she reaches out her hand. "Come now, before—"

"Not until you tell me what's going on." I pin my feet to the floor.

"What did you expect," she says. "We're in war. The enemy got to her when they came searching for you. She no longer has the strength to fight the death spell."

The light from the landing darkens, like a black cloud closing in. I see a shadow breaking through the window. Glass shatters across the landing. I hear Solvej scream as dark blood pours out like a stream of water from her neck. A man, dressed in black from top to bottom, holds a knife in his hand. He turns toward me. I step down, my fingers twisted around the tusk.

He towers over me like a big crow filling the white light with plumes of black feathers. I bury the tusk into his throat. He gasps for air, his eyes wide. He drops like timber landing between my feet. With the tip of my shoe I push him, and he tumbles down. A pool of red soaks the floor. I rush down to tear the mask from his face.

"Who are you?" I say and yank him up, holding his collar. He sputters out blood, and I let go of him. His face is unfamiliar, but the tattoo creeping around his neck is not. He's a Rognvald. "Were you sent by Lord William?" I shout.

A dim whisper leaves his lips. "Orkeney." he says.

"You are a liar." I scream. But it's too late. He's dead.

219

I rush back to Solvej. She is trying to slow the flow of the blood pouring from her neck. But it's no use. The thick dark blood keeps spilling. Air bubbles leave her mouth as she says. "Hurry, before they come for you."

Her hands drop to her side, her head still. Silence fills the air as I stare at her dead body realizing what has happened. I stand over her rubbing my eyes. I can't believe she's gone. A ray of colorless light creeps in from the broken window. The wind seeps like a whining child. The smell of iron fills the corridor.

They are coming for me? Did she mean Magnus? He'd want the weapons. Only I don't have them, Frederick does. I peer down the stairs where another dead body is sprawled across the floor. Why would Orkeney send Rognvald to kill Solvej and me? I am unable to move and struggle to gather my thoughts when I hear a voice. It's not just any voice. It's the sound of an old woman. It's the sound of Karen.

22

Last Encounter

SOLVEJ'S BLOOD STAINS my hands when I bend over her body to take the shawl from her shoulders. I use it to cover her face. *Calamity.* What just happened? I try not to let fear poison my mind. Solvej is dead, so is the man who killed her. Karen's voice calls for me. I skip over Solvej's corpse and walk up the stairs. I try one door after the other in the corridor. Every single room is empty. The house feels ghostly, eerie. I don't have much time. Karen must be in one of the rooms. I need to see her, the deceitful mother who used me as a pawn in her game of power. Did she ever care about me? Or does she only care about one thing. I want to see her face when I tell her what I intend to do, before she dies.

"Nora?" I hear a faint whisper. It's from the room on the top floor. Hidden behind a tapered door is a narrow staircase. I hurry up the steps. I swing open the door. I find Karen in bed, battling between life and death. Her face is grey, ghostly. She notices my blood-coated hands.

"So you finally decided to kill her." she says leaning forward.

"I didn't kill Solvej." My voice is clipped. I don't feel much when I see Karen. No emotions, no sorrow or love. Perhaps I feel too much anger and regret.

"The blood on your hands. Whom does it belong to?"

"To a Rognvald raider. He must have been watching the house."

"They're coming for you, Nora. You took a risk coming to see me." She lowers her eyes, as if unable look at me.

"I've not come to see you, Karen. I hope you die as soon I as I tell you—"

"My own daughter wishes me dead." Tears seep from her eyes.

"What did you think? That you could hide a truth like that from me?" I sit on the bed next to her. Her face is in hopeless despair, like she knows she's lost me. But of course she never had me to begin with. She gave me up the moment she decided to use me to execute her plan.

"It's no use telling you anything. You're stubborn like your father." Her voice is trembling, the air that expels from her lungs dry.

"He's dead." I say.

She sinks into the bed. Her face turned.

"Is Robert gone?" The little glow left in her eyes, dies.

"He sacrificed himself so that his other daughter could live."

"Grethe."

"You knew about her."

"I didn't tell you because some things are better left unsaid."

"How about everything!" Anger boils in my veins. "How could you do this to me? Create my life to fulfill your own purpose? I've been through Helheim. Those scoundrels you call my ancestors, my blood. They're all dead. I cut off their heads with their own sword."

"You did what? You fool of a girl. They were your only hope to—"

"They were evil to the core, seeking release from the Emperor's curse, and a return to Midgard. What would have happened to our world if I—"

"I only have few breaths left. You must hurry away. They're coming for you. Magnus's men. They know you're back, and that you have betrayed them. How could you side with the enemy? He's a Veran."

"You know about betrayal. You caused all this, and I hate you for it. Do you hear me?" I yank her up. She is light as a feather.

"Nora, the weapons. Where are they?" she croaks.

"Why should I tell you?" I grit my teeth. "I'll use them to defend us from the enemy."

"You have to be careful when you use the weapons."

"What are you talking about?" I bring her closer. I can smell her, a wilted flower.

Her eyes shut so suddenly. "Karen?" I shake her, but she's not breathing. Her skin is sallow, her hair white. Karen's skin looks aged, like she turned ninety over the span of one year.

I stare at her for a while. Her body is cold, frozen. Her death doesn't affect me. I feel happy, like I should celebrate. My only remorse is that I never told her how I truly feel about the web of lies she pulled me into. I needed to tell her about the decision I have made. Now she will never know. As I walk away I stop to turn around. I stare at her one final time. Her soul is not in Valhalla. It's in Helheim burning in all eternity. That's not what I wished for her. That's not what I would wish for my enemy.

I hear the front door creak open downstairs. Heavy boots

make slow even steps. I walk to the edge of the stairs and see a shadow. It's not the army of men I expected to barge in, but someone else.

"Frederick?"

The shadow unwinds, and in the darkness I see his blue eyes sparkle.

"Nora." He smiles, but it fades as quickly as it appeared. "Hurry, we have to get out of here," says Frederick. "I have a tail following me. They'll be here any minute."

"How did you—" I pause and catch my breath. "Did Andreas—"

"In the name of Thor, move!" he hisses. He doesn't seem happy to see me. I hurry down the stairs and reach for him. He takes my face into his cold hands and kisses me. The warmth from his lips and the softness of his skin feels familiar, and it eases me. There's something on his mind, and he's too tense to tell me. I can sense it from his body language. Stiff and locked.

"Did you get Andreas' message?"

"I did" he says. "Nora, listen, we're in danger and need to leave Chelsea this minute."

"What is going on?" I say. "Tell me."

"Raiders from both dynasties are looking for us," says Frederick and drags me out. I stop and draw back. "What are you waiting for?"

"What else aren't you telling me?" Frederick feels different, the way he was when we were enemies. His mind is distant, far away.

"There's no time to discuss this here." He looks at my hands, the red color dark and dry. "Why is there blood on your hands?"

"A raider from Rognvald killed Solvej. I was sure she was trying to trick me. Except she wasn't; She was bringing me to see Karen."

"Who the hell is Solvej?" he says. "Why would a raider be here?"

"She is— was Karen's housekeeper. The raiders have been watching the house."

"Did you speak to your mother? Did she tell you about the weapons?"

"She's dead." I say coldly.

"What?" His face creases, and a shadow surrounds him.

"Don't worry. I didn't kill her. The last thing I wanted is Karen's blood on my hands, not after what happened with Robert."

"We don't have time. Come on!" He motions with his hand and turns his back on me. "If we don't leave now…"

"Frederick, where are the weapons?"

"They're in a safe place."

I trust Frederick. He's going to bring me to the weapons. He needs to or else I don't know what I might do. I feel this urge to react madly; as if I was guilty of something terrible I cannot explain. Something that will only go away in an act of rage and murder. Is my curse taking over my reason?

Outside is the motorcycle Andreas sent. Frederick must have brought it. I am reminded of the silly promise I made him. We'd race over Guldborg Bridge. Instead we race as one, together, fleeing from the eyes of those that want us for treason.

Frederick hops onto the majestic ride. I sit tight behind him, my arms clutched around his waist. We drive off at high speed. The slushy roads are dangerous and frosty. Just as we leave the gate of Chelsea, Karen's house and all the other houses explode. I watch through the rearview mirror the flames rise like a dragon's rage. Thunder shakes the earth beneath us. Black smoke and red fire curl into the air. The smell of petroleum and gas blends with ice and frost.

I tighten my grip around Frederick's waist. The snow doesn't stop him from speeding through the traffic. Frederick drives smooth and fast around the gridlock, cutting corners in the heavy congestion of cars. Lines after lines, jammed up chaotically. In the central part of the city, there are pools of fire. Towers are burning, people screaming. BOOM. BOOM. There are explosions. Buildings are crumbling, and the large pillars holding monuments and sculptures fall into the harbor. People run in panic through the streets and avenues. We cross Guldborg Bridge. The images of horror are strangely familiar. I had this vision when I was in Dock Harbor outside Frederick's apartment. The city is quickly turning into dust, and black smoke surrounds us. Balls of fire shoot over our heads and thunder continues to strike across the sky. It is our doom. The war has begun.

On the other side of the bridge, across the frozen water, the Dome, in which the Viking lords rule is in flames. The magnificent pride of the West is burning away and is quickly turning into gray ashes. I hear screams echo in the streets as we flash by. There are hundreds of distressed faces flickering by. I can only look away to hide my own fear

The weather is turning vile and the ice underneath the bridge is breaking. As I watch the City of Skies turn into nothing but dust guilt surrounds me. Why is this happening? Could I have done something to prevent it? The black twin towers where raiders reside and the surrounding skyscrapers are also in flames. Everything is falling apart. Everything.

The black smoke and white snow together dance a deadly dance. My neck cranes to capture all the terror striking in lifeless colors. Bombs and missiles shoot, ships burn in the harbor. Frederick doesn't stop, not for a moment. I feel his heart beat faster. He takes a sharp swing on a curved road and the noise settles, muffles as if it was never really there but part of my imagination.

We reach the border outside the city and I catch a glimpse of Slotsplads. The turrets and towers are collapsing to the ground. A thick white cloud rises. It curls its way into the gray sky. She's out there, Yggdrasil. If I don't feed her the runes she entrusted me with she'll wither. The Nine Worlds will fall into darkness. We'll be left with motes of dust smudging our minds. The decision will not be easy.

We've been speeding on the road for a while, and I am beginning to feel tired. The City of Skies is long behind us. Part of me doesn't know what to believe. The glory of the West has turned into ruins. Is Lord Nourusa causing all of this? Has our world fallen into the hands of evil? After Arres I understand what evil is and it terrifies me. The ashen souls of my ancestors. The murder in the Emperor's eyes as he ordered the killing of his children so that he could live. I snatch in the cold air, and it freezes my lungs. Ahead of us the road through the forest is becoming narrower as the trees are arching in on us.

Where are we? Frederick tells me it's a hideout, away from the city. But is it safe? I fear what's going to happen when I'm faced with Magnus. I didn't betray him intentionally. Yes, I formed an alliance with Frederick, trusted him with the weapons instead of returning to the towers or reporting anything back. I have no intention of fulfilling my purpose as assassin. Sure, that makes me a traitor. But I'd rather be an outlaw on the run than succumb to the rule Robert never wanted to be part of. He knew power and greed is all the Goths care about. Magnus is no different. He has his duties to carry out, and I have mine.

Frederick slows down and turns left down a long and winding road by the side of the forest. It leads us deep into private property. We stop at a silver gate of a large yellow mansion. Frederick dismounts from the motorcycle and opens a small silver box next to the gate and presses in a long digit number that pops up in a bright red color. Seconds later, the iron gate creaks open. We drive into the main square. He stops a hundred meters from the main entrance and kills the engine.

The bright full moon is bathing in the cold starless night sky. The large trees around the manor look as if they're pale shades of ghosts. The water in the majestic fountain in front of the house is frozen. A deadly silence surrounds us. As we trail up to the front door he takes off his helmet and glares at me.

"We should be safe here," he says. "The estate has been deserted for at least a decade."

"What is this place?" I say. "Why have we come here?"

"This manor belonged to my grandfather," says Frederick. "I spent some of my childhood here, and it's the only place I could think of as a hideout for us. It's far from the city on the outskirts of the woods. No one will come looking for us here."

"No one lives inside the house?"

"The caretakers used to," says Frederick. "But they've left."

"How do you know?"

"I came to the estate after leaving Arres and found the place empty."

"Is this where you are keeping the weapons hidden?" I ask impatiently.

"Yes." He's silent. I sense a trail of thought stinging his mind. I decide to say nothing. We glare at one another.

Frederick takes my hand, and we continue to walk up to the main entrance of the grand mansion. Our feet crunch the snow covered gravel. I step carefully onto the steps. Two huge lion sculptures are majestically resting on each side. He pulls out a key to unlock the large wooden door. We step inside, and it's as dark and cold as a tomb.

"Hello?" says Frederick. Only his own echo calls back. "Is anyone here?" He peers at me. I shrug.

"Let's go inside." He tightens his grip around my hand, and we walk into a grand entrance with a swirling marble staircase in the middle. Dirt and red brown leaves lay scattered around. Hanging above our heads is a large crystal chandelier, which decorates the vaulted ceiling. Frederick flicks the switch and the light sparks to life devouring the gloom.

The walls hold old portraits and paintings of lords and ladies. Their expressions are stern and cold just like the house. In the mirrored walls, two shadows appear that I don't recognize. One belongs to me, and the other is Frederick's reflection. Sweat soaks underneath my black leather attire as I walk closer to the mirror examining myself. My hair is matted and lifeless, my face pale. Dark circles are visible underneath my eyes. *How can this be me*? I stare at Frederick's image. His hair is raven black. Mystery is drawn on his unshaven face. The circles under his eyes are a dark purple. We look aged and ugly.

"Who are we?" I say touching my face. "This is not us." When

I glance at Frederick, he doesn't look like the reflection in the mirror. He shoots me a peculiar glance as if afraid to say what I need to hear. "Why do we appear different than what we are?"

"You don't know, do you?" he says softly.

"Know what?"

"What I am about to tell you is going to shock you."

"Nothing you can say will shock me." As the words leave my mouth I feel my heart sink into the pit of my stomach. "Maybe just a little."

"Arres has partly aged us. But the signs are not entirely visible. They are from the past, and we are in the future. And that's not all."

"What do you mean?"

"I went to see someone, when I saw what you see now in the mirror."

"Who did you see?"

"That doesn't matter," he says. "I've discovered that time travel is dangerous. What we did could have killed us, even trapped us. We have been lucky."

"I don't understand. What do you mean partly aged? What else is causing this illusion?"

"Follow me." he says.

I walk behind him into the living room. There's a sofa in front of a wood burning fireplace with a limestone mantel. He set's fire to the logs. The wind seeps through the windows, howling like a midnight wolf. The storm rattles the window-panes. Thunder strikes. The cracking burning fire from the hearth fills the empty vacuum between us. I sit down and stretch my fingers feeling the warmth from the flames. I gaze at him. There is a disappointment in his eyes and a fear that I don't recognize.

"While you were in Trinzantine killing the Emperor" Frederick pulls out a blanket. "I came out here in hiding." He unfolds the blanket and reveals the weapons. The sword, the spear, the axe, the shield.

"You kept the weapons safe." I say relieved to see them. I tilt my head. There's more on his mind. I get a feeling I won't like what he's about to tell me.

"You were right." he says.

"About what?"

"The weapons are—"

I clasp my hands over my mouth. "Please don't." I take a deep breath as if it was my last. "Karen, she tried to tell me just before she died—"

"Nora! The weapons have to be destroyed. They are cruel, and desire only to kill. They don't manifest good or bad. We'll have no use of them, unless we see ourselves as dark monsters, killing ruthlessly to win over our enemy. They'll corrupt our soul. The more we use them, the more evil will spread in our veins like venom. The change in our appearance is not just from the time travel. It is also from the weapons. If we hold onto them, use their power; we will become those images we saw, or something worse. Faceless shadows. We need to destroy them before they destroy us."

"No!" I say. "Do you know what we—"

"Yes! I was there with you. It's not an easy decision, but we have to destroy the weapons. Do you understand? We must!"

I swallow hard. My eyes don't leave his sight.

"How are we going to do that?"

"The fires of Helheim, where they were forged. They can only be destroyed there."

"You're asking me to use the runes." I say.

"What seems to be the trouble with that?"

"Nothing..."

"Don't lie to me," he grabs hold of my shoulders. "What did you have in mind?"

"I made a decision," I say. "To let Yggdrasil wither. See her roots rot and die."

"Why?" he shouts. "Have you lost your mind?"

"It's the only way we can stop all the evil from spreading. Without the Nine Worlds there will be no war to fight, no battle to win. This is just the beginning."

"You have gone splitting mad. Is this some revenge against your mother?" says Frederick. "Because war is upon us. Nothing will stop Nourusa or our dynasties from hunting us down. We cannot use the weapons as a means of defense. Only if we desire to become the evil we set out to fight. So we should destroy them and use our alliances to win this war."

"Then what?"

"The Nine Worlds await where every outcast, every race, and every creature has its place. Together, we can create a new world, in Midgard."

"Try to understand, Frederick, the only way to win is using the weapons—"

"I don't believe you!" he yells. "I trusted you. If I'd known you would make such an asinine decision, I wouldn't have let Mina give her life for you. Your parents are dead. You're wanted by Magnus. My father has put all his forces in place to find you. Nora, I can no longer protect you if you go on."

"The weapons were meant to protect us," I say. "Did you forget why we set out on this journey, Frederick? We'll destroy them in Helheim soon after defeating our enemy."

I hold him close and feel his heart beat next to mine. He pulls away, but I follow him. His face is an unreadable map. His body, a quiet storm.

"They might help us defeat them," he says. "But be aware of the curse they carry. Evil comes from using them. Don't tell me you don't feel it running through your veins. What happened at the City of Assassins? Did you not ruthlessly kill your ancestors and their army? Did it not make you feel invincible? Does your blood not crave for more? You can make a choice and break free from the assassin's spell. Don't let it do to you what it did to your ancestors. You'll wake up one day begging someone to set you free. But it will be too late. You will have to live with all the lives you've taken."

"I'll live," I say.

Frederick walks to the window. The black night is cold and windy. I hear the trees swaying. But it's not because of the wind. It's something else. A loud familiar sound, hovering over the roof.

"What is that?" I say.

Frederick turns. He grabs me, folds the weapons together and yanks me out of the room. We run through the corridor and tumble down the stairs entering a dark cellar. He holds a torch in his hand, and guides me through a long tunnel.

"They're here. They've found us."

"Frederick, is Helena with them?"

"She's with Magnus."

"No." I stop and bend over. My hands spread across my knees. "How could she?"

"Orkeney has agreed to help Jarl to hunt us down."

"How do you know all this?" I say.

"Andreas."

"What else did he say?"

"Hildebrand was found dead in his secret library. His corpse was rotten like he'd been there for months. Neck slit from ear to ear."

"And the books? He had all sort of spell books, ancient secrets."

"All burned to the grounds. Every map, every clue."

"Who would do that?"

"My father," says Frederick. "He takes orders from Nourusa now."

"Have you seen your dad since getting back here?"

"He figured out I was back and had me tailed. But I have my ways around him. "

"Frederick." I stop and he turns around. "We can't keep running. We need to use the weapons. The sooner we do. The safer we'll be."

"Do you know what you're asking? Do you want to become the queen of darkness?"

"No, together we will make sure Midgard is peaceful."

"You're suggesting I should kill my own father, destroy my dynasty."

"If you don't, they will not hesitate. Would you rather that?"

"Let's get out of here first then decide." He pulls me along.

We reach the end of the tunnel. Frederick pushes the door at the end open. We pass through to the backyard. I can still hear the helicopter. Sharp light sheds across the mansion's roof. He beckons for me to follow. We hide in the shadows.

Frederick slips into the garage. He motions for me to follow. At least a dozen odd cars are in sight. He pulls out the keys and presses a button. We sneak into a small silver car, with beige leather seats. He starts the soundless engine and drives the car out. At the main gate, armed men seal the entrance. There's no mistake. It's Rognvald raiders.

"Hold on tight," says Frederick as he puts the car into gear. The blood drains from my face when I see the tall, lanky shadow standing at the gate. Under a black cowl red blazing eyes shoot at me. There's no mistaking who that is. My heart twitches. Pain paralyzes my limbs. I hold my breath as Frederick drives the car at full speed in their direction. There's a loud crash, and my head bounces against the side of the car. I lose consciousness.

23

Home

DAYLIGHT PINCHES MY eyes. When I peer out of the window I notice the car is floating on water next to a gray deserted beach. Seagulls cackle loudly, and one lands on the hood of the car. It crawls forward and starts poking the mirror with its beak. Then it flies away fanning the sky with its white wings. A mist circles above the water. It continues past the bay like ghostly smoke curling into the forest. This place looks familiar. I've been here before.

I look over my shoulder and find Frederick fast asleep as if he has no worries. I shake him gently. He opens his eyes just a little and catches a glimpse of me.

"You are awake," he says.

"How did you get us here?"

"I thought you'd be happy." He opens his eyes fully. There's a determined twinkle in them. "The car brought us here. It's fast, and it floats."

"So I see. But why did you bring us *here*?"

"Because of the gathering." I give him a pensive stare. "Andreas works as my spy and keeps me informed." He smiles. "Welcome, Nora Hunt, to the only safe place left in the Triangle."

I am not happy. I am fuming. His irony irritates me to the core.

"What are you talking about? What gathering?"

"The alliance," he says. "We need to gather forces to gain peace among the dynasties. They're coming. All except the seven Veran Viking lords."

"Don't tell me." I pause. "Are they?"

"Dead," he says. "Every one of them."

"By the gods—"

"No," says Frederick. "By Magnus. He ordered an attacked on the Dome and destroyed an old legacy of the Vikings. One big evil is down. They never wanted peace. Their ethos throughout time has been battle. How they survived under the peace treaty this long is amazing."

"I don't understand. Weapons are not allowed in Triangle, and we swore never to go into war after Ragnarok. Now, everything is lost. This war has been brought to the shores of the East. I can't watch as my home gets destroyed. We need to find another place for the gathering. We'll hide in the Forbidden Areas. The border is not far from here—"

Frederick is in deep thought. He is quiet for a while.

"Tanya, the leader of the Talent Allocation Institute has formed an alliance with Magnus. They don't want the war to continue. They want peace. I believe we can reason with them. Find a solution. Magnus knows about the weapons. He wants to destroy them as much as we do."

"I betrayed Magnus's trust," I say. "He'd not want to cut deals with me."

"He has to. After all, you're the chosen one. You hold the

key to the gate. If you can reason with Magnus, I will speak to my father." There's a formal tone in Frederick's voice. I feel as if I am in an official meeting with him.

"They are on their way here, aren't they?" I say.

He nods. "Expect them by nightfall."

"The only way for this war to end is to learn to live together in peace like we used to. But with Nourusa in charge that's not going to happen. He's after Midgard, and I cannot let him have it. I'll use the weapons against him if I have to. Or I will let Yggdrasil wither."

"You can't, Nora. The consequences of that are dire."

"The decision is mine Frederick."

"How can you say that? Twice the gods chose your Viking clan. You cannot make a decision against them and every living being in the Triangle."

I take a deep breath. I feel lost. Frederick has a point. Maybe we need to speak at the gathering to reach peace. There's still hope. Helena, Niels, and Magnus will be there. They know me. I can try to reason with them and hope that Magnus decides to forgive me for deserting him and for betraying his trust. He must have known the minute I went into the City of Vikings. He sees everything with Odin's eye. That's why he sent me that message. He was testing me.

"First, we need to get to Blossom Heights," I say. "I have to speak to Gustav. He's an old friend of mine. He'll help us."

We drive through the forest. There's no road, just a mud trail, and hidden swamps and bogs. The fields are dangerous with strange creatures lurking. I spot a Nøkken in the water, and black crows in the trees whispering of our arrival. In the shadows, I see the dead spirits of Draugars. Their swollen and blackened bodies hang like skeletons among the fallen trees.

The road is bumpy, uneven. We jolt from side to side. I see more of the Draugars. They are out of their graves and are waiting for the gate to open that leads to the Nine Worlds. Something feels eerie. The creatures appear battered and frightened, as if they've been in a war.

The morning light streams through the tall branches. In places the blue sky shows the black roots of Yggdrasil getting smaller. She wants to descend and spread her roots before it's too late. I can hear her screams in my ears. She's calling for me, urging me to the pathway. My back stings, as if full of needles. I miss the tattoo of her sprawled against my skin, tugging me close to the secrets she carried. Instead I carry the runes glowing in my palm. They don't speak to me, nor do they give me visions. A faint image flickers in my mind. It's a vision of the long, dwindling pathway. It snakes its way through the forest. It looks more familiar now. It's the only way to the gate.

The car gains speed and lush green forests and silver-peaked mountains come into sight. The wild blue river streams next to free running horses. I was here with Gustav when I let him win the Chasing Game. It feels like just yesterday when I was with him, hunting and exploring the woods. Frederick slows down and takes a sharp turn. We're only a few more miles from the village now.

"We just crossed the southern route. If you drive through the gorge next to the river, it will lead us into Blossom Heights." My heart is slamming hard against my chest when Frederick sets the course uphill. The soil beneath us is no longer black and muddy. It's red and dusty. Just as I remember it. My eyes are desperate to see the serene village I was torn away from. How I long to feel the wild flowers tickle my fingers. The straws of green brushing against my face as I lie in the fields listening to the chirping of the crickets.

"By the gods!" His deep slow voice rolls over me like big barrels of water. We both stare at each other. The sky in the East is dark. Streaks of gray, shadow the burning lines of the sun. Blossom Heights is burned to the ground. Blood-spattered bodies color the soil. I turn my face away. I know these people. All of them. Lisa, Sasha, Agatha, and the woman I called mother. There are more whose names prickle my tongue.

"Take me away from here." I hold my breath. A burning twists inside my stomach. I release my breath. "Why would anyone do this?"

Frederick pulls the car away from the village. He drives down the hill to where Peace Point used to be. Caravans and shaky built houses were once here. Now there's nothing except birds, cawing and scraping the remains from hollow carcasses.

Frederick's mouth twists in despair of the memories he never knew. He stops the car. We get out. The smell of blood and coal reaches my nostrils. I turn my eyes to the sky. The hallowing darkness of Yggdrasil is still there. I turn sullenly to Frederick.

"The attack on your village must have been by creatures from the Forbidden Areas. There's no one else out here," he says.

"It makes no sense for them to attack so suddenly," I cry. "We've lived in peace for years. It could only have been that evil Veran lord from your clan."

"I don't know what to say. I had no idea, Nora. I'm so sorry."

I fall to the ground and let the earth carry me. Then I close my eyes. The last thing I see is the vision of a smile quirking the corners of Gustav's mouth. He's one of the best hunters in the East. He knows the woods and fields as well as I do. He wasn't among the bodies, and my heart tells me he's alive. Maybe he's taken cover in the woods. We used to keep lodging there when we hunted.

I stand as hope spirals like a gust of wind through my lungs.

"Maybe Gus is still alive," I say.

"Everyone here is dead," Frederick shouts. "The place has been wiped clean of anything living."

I run into the old communal area where the Rainbow People used to sit.

"Where are you going?" He follows me into the dust and smoke. There are mounds of black human bones around us. "Come back."

"My home has been destroyed. The people I grew up with are all dead."

"It must have been the creatures from the Forbidden Areas."

"No, I believe that Nourusa is behind all this. He has the largest army in the Triangle. The East was an easy target. There are no weapons here. People live in peace." Tears stream down my hot cheeks. Frederick takes me into his arms, but I push him away. I run as fast as I can. I don't look back. I will have my revenge. I swear it.

At nightfall, Frederick finds me sitting and staring into the Forbidden Areas. I lean against an old tree trunk taming my wild thoughts. Everything I knew is gone. There's nothing left. No hope, no place to call home. If I let Yggdrasil wither, I will be digging my own grave too.

I push my chin skywards to meet Frederick's eyes.

"Nourusa did this because he knew I would hesitate to open the gate. With the East in smoldered ashes and the West blown

241

up he knows he has weakened me. He knows there is little left of the North, barely enough to keep the people that live there. He thinks he has broken me. But he has not."

Frederick sits down facing me. "You feel him, don't you?"

"Like a sting in my heart."

"All this must be overwhelming. Too much to take in, but we cannot slow down. We have to search for the others. They can't be far from the beach where we came from."

"They'll arrive at the harbor north of this border," I say.

"Are you suggesting we cross this forest to get there? It's not such a great idea to wade through the woods. We're in danger already just by being here."

I look around. "Where's the car?"

"It was stolen."

"STOLEN?"

"Trolls took it. I saw their mud tracks."

I sigh. My head drops between my knees. "No, no, no!"

"The weapons?" I say. "They're our only hope if we want to survive."

"I knew you'd say that." Frederick pulls out his sack. I steal a glimpse at the sword. I long to hold it in my hand and to cut off Nourusa's head. "But we can't use them."

"To Helheim we can." I say and get up. I draw the sword, and swing it in the air. It makes a scraping sound when I brush its blade against the leaves.

"Nora, please," Frederick pleads. "I can't live to see you turn into what your ancestors were. You will be no different from Nourusa."

"Do you think he wants peace?" I say.

"If we get Magnus on our side, and I speak to my father, we'll stand stronger. Don't forget what you did for the Garms. They have their land back, and swore to help us. Enough blood has been splattered."

I pin the sword to the ground, and walk briskly into the Forbidden Areas. Frederick pulls it out and follows me angrily into the woods. I hear his heavy breathing. He has caged his rage and is struggling to keep it in control. He catches up with me. His ears are sharp as an elf's, and he also hears the strange sounds and mysterious whispers. But when I look around nothing comes into sight except Frederick's beautiful face.

"We need to get out of here fast," he whispers. "I have a bad feeling about this place."

"You also sense it?"

The ground underneath us trembles. We run following the winding trail. I stagger and fall to the ground. My head hits a tree trunk. Frederick is right across from me. A giant snake swirls from underneath the soil. It hisses at me, flicking its tongue, tasting the thick air. With red bloodshot eyes bloodshot it glares at me. It's a Jormungand—a great serpent that escaped Midgard before the Viking doom. The snake hurls its silver body slithering its way to me, its scaly skin shimmering in the darkness. The tail of the serpent twists around me. I can't move or breathe.

"Help, Frederick," I mutter. The blood drains from my body. I turn numb. I can't breathe. My head is heavy, and my eyes see only darkness. I fall to the ground, coughing out pockets of air, as if it was trapped between my airways.

A heavy thump shakes the earth. The Jormungand's body falls into two parts, and its head rolls into the forest like a big boulder. It smashes against a tree. A thick green slime oozes from its face. The serpent's long black tongue hangs limply from its mouth. I stare at it in disbelief. It was alive just a second ago.

Catching his breath, Frederick's hand reaches for me. I take it, and he pulls me in close. I feel safe.

"I thought I lost you." His chest is moving rapidly. Beads of sweat coat his face. I press my lips against his and kiss him gently. He responds with a tender kiss back, soft and velvety. For a brief minute I hold back and gaze into his deep blue eyes.

"I love you, Frederick."

"And I love you, Nora."

We kiss again, the warmth of his body pressed against mine. A thunderous sound makes the ground shiver. Hisses and snarls surround us. Eyes darting at us from the shadows. Red, dangerous eyes. I look down as thousands of black snakes rise from beneath us. Frederick takes out the shield. The sword still sits firmly in his grip coated in the Jormungand's blood. I shut my eyes for a moment. The image of the gateway hovers behind my lids. I see the door; I know where it is now.

"Nora!" he shouts. The earth splits and pulls me away.

A snake closes in on me. It's getting bigger and keeps rising to the sky. The snake jerks his head back and snaps just inches from my face

Get down!" familiar voices shout. I squat keeping my head low. The snakes just missed a taste of my flesh. Guns are shooting in our direction. Thousands of tails of snakes swirl away some die from the bullets hitting them, between the eyes, in the head.

I peek up. I can now only see smoke. The crack in the ground begins to close sweeping me closer to the shadows coming out of the mist.

"Hello again, Nora. I thought I might find you here." It's Niels. He stretches out his hand. But I don't take it. I pull myself up pushing my palms into the dirt. I stand tall, peering over his shoulder.

"Bring her to the gathering. We have very little time left," says Magnus. I barely see him as he marches out of the woods. The tone is his voice is sharp like daggers. This will not be a pleasant gathering. He's clearly vexed at me.

"What just happened?" says Frederick. He glares at Niels. Who begins to follow Magnus's trail.

"They've come for us," I say.

You know where the gate to the tree is, don't you? Frederick says in my mind.

I say nothing. I smile, and toss my arms behind my back. My right hand grabs hold of my left wrist. A warm glow prickles my palms. I'm ready to show the world what is has been waiting for. It's time to meet the Nine Worlds of the Vikings.

24

The Nine Worlds

AT THE GATHERING, every member of Jarl and Orkeney is there. My eyes find Helena among the familiar looking faces. She appears different. The bridge of her nose no longer wears the red framed specs. Her hair is tightly braided into a crown. In her hand she holds a map. She looks in my direction, determined, strong. She cannot speak to me, I understand that now. How I long to talk to her. But I can't. She follows orders from Magnus, and she has brought him here with the rest of her crew.

Standing next to Helena, is Tanya. I did not expect her to be involved, and wonder how long she knew about me before recruiting me as a raider. The older members of the council that Karen led nod their heads when they see me. Behind the crowd, a tall frame with wide shoulders comes through. It's Magnus. He has not changed much. Still, he carries an air of dominance. With dark smooth hair, icy gray eyes, and lips pursed he glares right into my mind. I feel Frederick's breathing grow heavy. There's tension in each inhale and exhale. He never liked Magnus. I don't know how to feel about my betrayal when I stare back at him.

Guilty? Responsible? Or just free?

"This is the last place I want to be right now," says Magnus keeping his eyes firmly locked into mine. "It's dangerous, and the only village here has been burned to the ground. We are not safe. Not here or anywhere."

"Then why are we *here*?" I say. "Surely not to mourn the people of Blossom Heights." I feel an energy running through the forest, a faint whisper in Norse. It's calling to me. The time has come for my decision.

"We are here because of your stupidity," he answers coldly.

"No, you are here because you are too cowardly to stop Nourusa," I say. "It appears the only one that will prevent him from destroying us is me."

"We would have defended ourselves, if we had the weapons," says Magnus. "Those you were tasked to bring back."

"You know damn well what the weapons are," says Frederick. "They spread evil and carry only the desire to kill. Is that a curse you're willing to carry?"

"That shouldn't prevent us or anyone else from using them to protect ourselves or those we care about." His eyes shift between Frederick and me like an angry bull. Frederick roars. His hand reveals the shield, the sword, the spear and the hammer. He tosses everything at Magnus's feet.

I give Frederick a look of annoyance. "What in the name of—"

"There," says Frederick cutting me off. "You carry the weapons and use them to finish off Nourusa. One swing of the sword is enough to finish him"

"I have a Viking assassin to do that," says Magnus. He peers back at Helena and Tanya who both seem to agree with him.

Niels looks amused.

"Does it really matter who it is?" says Niels. "Someone needs to get rid of the enemy." He stares at me expectantly.

"We'll forgive that you failed your duties as assassin, Nora," says Tanya. "But we will not forget. We still need your help defeating Nourusa. The weapons are for you to use, and the door is for you to open."

"That's just perfect," I say. "If everyone else is a coward—" I glance at Helena. She's out of words, and says nothing. I gather the weapons and put the sword into its sheath. "I'll use them. They were forged by my ancestors; they are my burden."

"Nora, don't you think it's time you set yourself free from this burden?" There's a faint hope in Helena's eyes. "If you betray the trust of your dynasty again there will be no hope left—"

"What?" I stagger backwards. She's meant to be my friend. Even Helena has turned against me. "How dare you tell me what to do?"

"Wait!" says Magnus. "First you need to ensure the safety of the people you have sworn to protect. *Your* people."

"My people are dead," I say. "What I am about to do, is not because it is my duty. I am doing it to save innocent lives."

Frederick grabs my wrist. "What do you think you are doing?"

"Setting her free and putting an end to this madness. What else?"

"And the gate?"

"I've seen it. I know where it is." I say.

I march ahead like an army sergeant. The image of the road burns behind my eyelids. I should have known she would lead me back to the East, to the one place I call home. What a fool

I have been. My vision shows me the road. All I have to do is follow it.

"Where are you going?" Magnus catches up with me. "Stop!"

I continue to walk into the dark forest. "We have little time left," I say. "If you want me to unlock the door to the Nine Worlds I need to do it now, before the tree withers."

I can hear Yggdrasil whispers in Norse getting louder as she continues to call for me.

"We still work as one, even though I find you difficult, stubborn, and untrustworthy." I ignore the truth that pours from Magnus's lips. "I trusted you, made you the leader of our band. If you had been back with the weapons on time all this could have been avoided. We could have stopped Nourusa. Because of you Tove and Tene, my sisters are dead."

"What?" I stop. "Magus I am—"

He waves me off and walks ahead of me. "I have no family left. I am alone."

"I'm sorry for your loss." I say. But he's not listening to me. He walks in the wrong direction, trailing off the path. I flash my torch at his feet. He stops.

"Save your words."

"Please. I'm giving you what you want. Isn't that why you're here? Your gathering seeks refuge in the Nine Worlds. I hold the keys in my palms and the door is close."

"You have duties, Nora Hunt. Just like the rest of us. We may not always like what we're tasked with, or how the world around us circles, but that doesn't mean we should make decisions that risk the lives of others. Now you tell me that you're ready for what you were tasked with your entire life. Now you show me the way. Well it's thousands of lives too late."

"It's never too late Magnus."

"Why didn't you come to me?" he says. "When did you stop trusting me?"

"When you sent me the message that I should kill my father."

"I did what?"

"When I was in the City of Vikings, don't you remember?"

"You've lost your mind. Why would I do that?"

"Then who did?"

Thunder strikes suddenly. I push my chin up and feel the first drops of rain wet my face. My eyes close and I realize that Robert did this. He must have used a spell to transmit a fake message. He wanted me to kill him and to become a traitor to my dynasty just like he was.

Lightning sparks in the darkness. Magnus's face illuminates for a brief second. He is closer to me than my own thoughts. I feel his soft breath against my face. I wonder if he still has feelings for me. Or has he replaced them with hate and loathing.

"Hurry," I say. "We need to follow this trail till the end. I look back. The voices of the others are getting closer. We huddle together. Niels gets one step ahead of me.

"Where is this gate," he says. "Are you sure it even exists? There's nothing but darkness and danger ahead of us."

"What do you mean? Of course it—"

"Have you drawn a map?" says Helena. She wipes the rain dripping from her face.

"I don't have to," I say. "It's in my mind. I know these woods inside out."

"You could lead us into our deaths. Who knows what's lurking in the shadows." Helen's voice is clipped. She doesn't move when I walk past her. So much for our friendship.

"If you want to live you have to follow me." I say.

The rain gets heavier, and I know it is Yggdrasil's doing. She is urging me to my calling. The others follow me. We wade with our torches through the thick forest. This part should be safer, with little risk from being attacked by the creatures that live here. But after what happened in Blossom Heights, I am not sure we are safe anywhere.

"Where is this path, Nora?" says Tanya. "How long are we trailing for?"

"We're on it and just need to keep moving."

"Are you sure? And what about—"

"Stop questioning me. I'm sure, okay?"

I hurry ahead, when yellow light flashes into my eyes.

"Nora!"

"Frederick," I crane my neck. "The trolls are back."

The car drives full speed in our direction. It misses, and crashes into a tree. Between the flashes of lightning I see elves, fairies, dwarfs, and other mystical creatures.

"Did you forget," says Tanya. "The Nine Worlds also belong to the fairies, trolls, giants, elves, dwarfs, wizards and witches and several other mystical creatures and dark forces lost in the Forbidden Areas."

"Is that supposed to scare me?" I say. "I've seen the Nine Worlds. Yggdrasil showed me the different mystical creatures living in them. The worlds that were, and the worlds that will become. They all belong in it, and are not here to fight, but to join me."

What about the trolls of Norumb," says Magnus. "Or the elf queen?"

"How do you know about them?" He shows me Odin's eye. "You used it to spy on me?"

"I used it to make sure you were okay," he says. "We don't have an alliance with the trolls or elves. It's been broken for centuries. The trolls can be bought with gold, and the elves with wisdom, but we do not have the time to make offerings. We need to get to that gate."

The troll that was driving the car gets out. He grunts loudly and grinds his teeth so my ears ache. He walks past me and blocks the path that would lead us to our destiny.

"You killed all the trolls of Norumb. You stole the key to the City of Vikings." The troll pulls a face. "And Sumras, our leader. You also killed him. You think we don't know. Trolls see and hear everything." He glares into my eyes.

"I'm sorry for what we did," I say. "Now is not the time to get your revenge—"

"You also entered the forbidden kingdom of the elves," says a small voice in the darkness. "You cut off the head of our elf queen."

My patience is running out, and I feel tired, dizzy, and hungry. The way the troll and fairy speak makes me feel itchy. I draw out my sword and point the tip down, spinning it around. Something tells me I should not underestimate the creatures accusing me for my doings. They may be small, but they all carry the strength I need to defeat Nourusa.

I stop the spinning and place the sword back into the sheath.

"I need your alliance, and in return you will get your worlds back from Yggdrasil. You will no longer dawdle in these cursed woods. You will have a place of your own. A place you can call home." I feel Frederick's hand fall heavy on my shoulders.

"Do you give us your word?" says the troll.

"You have my word," I say. "In the presence of the tree and in the spirit of the gods."

I catch a glimpse of lightning in the sky.

"You are a Viking assassin. Blood is written in your fate. The weapons you carry are a testament of your calling. How can you make a promise you have no control over?" says the elf. Her large green eyes consume me. The fairies also make themselves visible. Their feathery wings flap gently against the dark night.

"All I wish for is to set the Nine Worlds free. I had my doubts at first. I will not lie to you. This journey has not been easy. I left the East one year ago and have returned to find everything destroyed. I did not know that I was meant to become a Viking assassin. Neither did I know much about the tattoo on my back or what these weapons from the City of Assassins carry. I know now. I wish for us to live in peace. Nourusa is a threat to us all. If we don't stand up against him together, all the worlds will fall into eternal darkness."

The lightning in the sky disappears and the rain stops. Rays of bright light illuminate the path like a golden line leading straight to heaven. Frederick pulls at my arm.

"Come on. It's time," he says. "We're with you."

I look around the familiar faces. Helena, Magnus, Tanya, the members of the council. Then I look at all the creatures joining in with us. Finally, I look at Frederick. His eyes sparkle with joy.

I turn around and look over my shoulder. The dark forest is changing. I see green fields emerge faster than the storm cloud. Everything is transforming into beautiful, blooming things. The flowers and tall swaying trees spread their colors like eagle wings. The grounds beneath us moves like a soft blanket. I move my feet through soft brown soil.

Ahead of me the path that leads to the gate draws up like a

thirsty river. I follow it like a moth to a flame. A cool breeze flaps in my direction. Finally, it's in sight. The door through the tree that leads to the Nine Worlds. I look at my palm. The nine encrypted runes glow gloriously. My hand inches from touching the door.

"Stop it right there." It's a dark heavy voice. Whispers in Norse crowd my ears. *Kill him, kill him. Use the strength of those with you to kill him.* The sword shines from its sheath—a clear blue glow. I use my heightened senses to listen to the sound from beyond the woods. Screams of terror strike as an army of Nourusa's men approach the East. They ride the sea horses across the ocean. Soon they will be here.

Swiftly I turn. My hand moves away from the door and pulls out the sword. I swing it against the darkness, and blood splatters across my face. A heavy body thumps to the ground and lands between my feet. The shadow shrinks, screeching evil spells in Norse before turning into dust. I lick the air with my tongue as heat rises to my face. I've done it. I've killed Nourusa with the sword. In doing so, I have saved the Nine Worlds, but I have engaged with evil. His spirit enters my body. I feel my blood boil, my soul turn black. I scream in agony.

"What have you done?" I hear Frederick's voice become distant. The wind sweeps in from the sea—violent and angry. Nourusa's army is crushed under the waves, their shrieks muffled by the water. Their lungs filled with pain.

Magnus rushes to my side and places the palm of my hand against the door. The runes lock into the gate and opens. A gale blows our way and sweeps us in. Screeches, laughter, and cries. The ground beneath me moves and is no longer earthly. It is heavenly. I land on straws of green soft grass. Next to me I see Frederick. His body is sprawled against the field. He stretches his hand out to feel mine.

"We are here Nora! We've made it."

I stand. The sky shows her branches, and in them she holds the worlds dangling like sea pearls. I've never seen anything so beautiful. Frederick takes my hand and we walk toward the light and laughter. The still lake underneath the bridge shows the face that I wear—a face that belongs to me now. I gaze into Frederick's deep blue eyes. It is going to be a wonderful day in Midgard.

City of Assassins

I hope you enjoyed City of Assassins, book three in The Viking Assassin Series.

If you liked this book then share your experience with your friends and other readers; review the book on Goodreads and Amazon.com and talk about it in your favourite forums.

Sign up for the weekly newsletter or connect with me on Social Media to receive the latest info about the next book in the series.

Facebook (Farah Cook - Author)
  Instagram (@Farah.Cook)
  Twitter (@Author.Farah)
  Bookbub (Farah Cook)
  Amazon (Farah Cook)

Newsletter:
  Sign up (http://www.shadowislands.com/newsletter)

Website: www.farahcook.com
  Email: info@farahcook.com